Choosing

A Novel for Teenage Girls

Linda Ward

M.A. , MFCC

Plain View Press
P.O. 33311
Austin, TX 78764

512-441-2452
sbpvp@eden.com
http://www.eden.com/~sbpvp

Isbn: 0-911051-92-9
Library of Congress Number: 96-070924
Copyright Linda Ward, 1997.
All rights reserved

Cover photo by Daryl Bright Andrews. Young people pictured are not
necessarily engaged in making decisions that reflect the content of the book.

Acknowledgments

Many wonderful people helped me finally give birth to "Choosing." Special
thanks to my dear friends Lyla and Asher for their feedback and financial
support; to Chris for her special inspiration and guidance; our women's group of
over 25 years—Jann, Suzi, Sandi, Judy, Chris and myself; To Commonwoman's
Health Project; Kristine Henry, F.N.P.; Judith Searle, a fine and encouraging
editor; Susan Bright, who could see the merit of Publishing "Choosing;" my
mother, Eve Janney, for her support and faith in me; my many students and
daughters' friends who gave me their enthusiasm and insight; Arrigone's Deli-
Cafe for providing a much-needed writing space; and especially to my daughters
Kristy and Julie who gave me their honesty and so much encouragement;
"Choosing" is for you and young women everywhere.

Dedication

There are many paths in life, many choosing points and each colors our present and our future. Some are more painful, some less encumbered, but none of them has to destroy the individual or her spirit. With the help of loved ones and a compassionate and educated society, each young woman can determine the right course for her own self and not merely do what is expected of her. *"Choosing, A Novel for Teenage Girls"* is the result of a fervent desire to educate and to validate the awesome challenge and responsibility of being female.

This book is written from the context of my life which is anglo and for the most part middle class. We all write best from what we know. I want to say, however, that the issues Lisa and Jeff have to face and the choices they make should be familiar to people in all facets of American culture. I invite everyone, for the moment, to imagine their lives in the context, not of cultural identity alone, but also in terms of the choices young adults and their parents make about their lives. It is my hope that this book will be helpful to young women and men, and to parents everywhere.

Choosing

His blue sweater was the first thing Lisa noticed. Purple-blue, not pale or dark. He was sitting by the window talking to a boy wearing a black Falcon's hat. The boy in the sweater glanced toward the door and his eyes focused on Lisa for an instant. She suddenly felt as though she was the only person walking into class, the only one standing up, the only one clutching books and wearing clothes. She glanced down quickly and headed toward the back of the class, hoping to find an empty seat near some girl.

Lisa had moved to San Benito only two months ago, early in July. Too new and too late to land a summer job, she'd spent the rest of the summer helping her mother unpack, hanging out with her younger sister, Stephanie, and sometimes going to the mall. Bored and missing her friends from her hometown, she was glad when school started—glad and nervous.

The school seemed okay. It was spread out, the way so many California schools are, with open-to-the air corridors, everything on one level, lockers outdoors. She hadn't met many kids yet, but there hadn't been any bad incidents either. Having checked out what the kids were wearing when she was at the mall and around town, she wore sandals, a short skirt and a long Guess shirt. Not hippie, not punk. She let her long sand-colored hair hang down straight so that she was constantly scooping it up and pushing it back to keep it out of her eyes; it always fell right back two seconds later, which gave her something to do.

She found a seat next to a girl with lots of blond hair and eye makeup who was leaning forward to talk to the boy in front of her. When Lisa sat down, the girl gave a brief smile. Lisa searched in her purse for a pen, not looking at the boy in the purple-blue sweater. She found a ball-point pen and put her purse on the floor. In her spiral notebook she wrote English II. She looked around for the teacher but didn't see an adult in the class. Her new student schedule was behind the cover of her notebook. She certainly didn't want to be identified as a new student, something any returning student would know anyway, but she glanced down and read the name of a teacher, Mr. Thomas.

A dark haired man wearing glasses, a pink long-sleeved shirt and a black print tie came into the room carrying a bunch of papers under his arm and a coffee mug. She liked his looks. He put the papers and mug down and glanced around at the class. He nodded to a couple of students and said, " Hi, how're you doing?"

"Okay," came the reply.

The bell rang.

"Welcome to Junior English," Mr. Thomas said, "or English II as the computer says. I hope you're all ready to write your butts off. I'm known as a real work horse and I can promise you you'll learn how to write in this class, and when it's over you'll be able to carry on a literate conversation with anyone. Now I need to know who your English teacher was last year, so raise your hand when I come to his or her name: Mr. Wilde?" A dozen or so students raised their hands.

"Mrs. Stengel?" Fourteen hands went up. "How about Mrs. Gomes?" This time six hands were raised. "Well, that leaves two people who didn't raise their hands. Would the mystery people please identify themselves."

Lisa felt the heat in her face. God, the last thing she wanted was the whole class looking at her. She raised her hand, looked around to see who the other person was and saw a dark skinned girl with long black shiny hair put up her hand.

"Who was your teacher last year?"

"Mr. Peters," the girl said. "I was living in Modesto."

Mr. Thomas smiled. "Well, welcome to Galt High School." He said to Lisa, "And how about you?"

Her voice sounded funny, but she managed to say, " Mrs. Fulbright."

"And where was that?"

"In Eugene, Oregon."

"Well, good. We don't have many people moving south to California these days. Most everyone seems to be going north. Okay, now I need to read the roll."

It was going to be all right. Lisa exhaled and realized she had been holding her breath. She glanced around and saw the boy in the purple-blue sweater raise his hand; she hadn't heard his name. She did hear the name "Carol Darwin," and saw the girl next to her raise her hand. She wasn't able to follow much else but raised her own hand when she heard "Lisa Howard."

"We're starting off the year with a play," Mr. Thomas said.

He handed out a paper back, *Our Town*, by Thornton Wilder. A few groans went up, and Lisa heard someone mutter, "I hate plays," but she also heard several kids say, " Good."

"This is an unusual play in that not much really happens. It's just about life. Boring old life. And it's about life before there was any T.V., crack dealers, or car insurance payments. It's about people being born, growing up, and dying. But don't be fooled by the play's slow pace. There's a lot more going on than you'd think. Anyway, for tonight, I'd like you to read the first twenty pages." There was the same shuffling feet and papers. "In addition, you are each to write a minimum of three paragraphs about what you feel life is really about and what is most important to you." This time there were a lot of groans.

"Okay. Get to work. I suggest you use your time now," Mr. Thomas said.

Most of the kids opened their books and wrote their name in the inside cover. Some started reading. The girl next to Lisa, Carol, began writing what looked like a note. The boy in the purple-blue sweater glanced around the room and whispered something to the boy in front of him; they both laughed. Lisa opened her book to the first page and started reading.

○

That night she sat at her desk and thought about her English assignment. It was tough. She didn't know what life was really about. Did anybody her age know the answer to that one? What was important? Well, her family of course. That was probably important to everybody. After all, she wouldn't be who she was without them, with a different mother and father. It was hard to think of—not being herself. Hard to grasp that she could be someone else, only she wouldn't even know she was someone else; she'd just be that person.

What else was important? Friends, for sure. That's what she was missing most. She wished the phone would ring. It had been a long time. No one here even knew who she was yet. Her friends back in Eugene started school today too. They'd be calling each other, making plans, talking about who did what over the summer. Gwen had written that she missed Lisa. Lisa knew it was true, but there was no way Gwen could be missing her as much as she missed Gwen. It was so hard feeling left out. She was far away, and they were all together. Besides, Gwen had Todd now. They'd been going together all summer, and in Gwen's last letter she'd written that she and Todd had already had sex. "I can't describe it," she wrote. "It was only the most wonderful feeling I've ever had. I wish you were here so I could tell you all about it."

That was another thing that was probably important in life. Sex. But how would she know? She'd had several boyfriends and kissed and made out with more than one of them. But she hadn't even come close to having sex. Better to save that for when she was really in love, probably when she was married. At least that was what she thought she wanted. Lisa and Gwen had talked for hours and hours about whether it was okay to have sex before marriage; they'd started talking about it when they were twelve and changed their minds back and forth maybe six times. Now Gwen had gone and done it, and Lisa was far away and couldn't even be a small part of it all.

Well anyway, sex was important, but even more important was loving someone and having that person love you back. And something else that was important was making the world a better place. There was so much that needed fixing: the environment, the homeless, all the crack babies born, and all the violence. This was getting to be too much.

She put her head down on her desk and breathed in the smell of the wood and heard sounds from the TV in the family room.

The next thing she knew there was a knock on her door and her mother was saying, "Lisa." She jerked her head up and looked sleepily at her mother's concerned face with that crease between her eyebrows.

Her mother had that look a lot lately. Lisa knew she was worried about money and about her new job. The move had been tough on her too. She had left a lot friends in Eugene; she hadn't wanted to come to California; everything was too expensive and she'd been happy where she was. But Lisa's dad had been transferred and there wasn't much they could do about it.

"Are you okay, honey?" her mother asked.

"Yeah, I'm fine. Just sleepy. But I've got to finish this English assignment before I go to bed."

"How does the work seem?"

"I don't know yet. I can't tell. But so far it seems all right."

" Have you met any kids ?"

"Mom, it's only been one day!" Her mother was always worried about her; well, at least since they'd moved. But she meant well. That was better than having a mother who didn't care at all.

"You're right," her mother said. "It was kind of a silly question." She stood in the doorway and they were both silent. "Well, I'll let you get back too work. Try not to stay up too late."

"Okay, Mom. G'night."

Lisa's mind drifted back to her English class and to the play *Our Town*. So far nothing much had happened, just as the teacher had said. But there was a romance that was just starting. It was between George and Emily, two teenagers who had grown up next door to each other. Lisa liked the town and the times when they lived; it was a long time back; the people walked everywhere and had their milk delivered at home by a milkman; everyone knew everybody. Things seemed to happen slowly and the same people lived in the same town all their life. Nobody moved away or had to start all over. Maybe it got boring sometimes, but it all seemed safe and kind of happy.

She thought about the boy in the purple-blue sweater. He was cute. She liked the way he sat at his desk, sideways, his back against the wall, looking out at the class. It seemed like he kept his eye on everything. He was about six feet tall and had dark blond hair. She didn't know the color of his eyes, but they might be green or blue. He had a nice smile, a big smile, and from the little bit she had seen him, he smiled often. This was stupid. She didn't even know his name and surely he hadn't even noticed her. Get a grip!, she thought and went back to writing her paper.

The next thing she knew it was 11:30 and she'd finally finished five paragraphs. Falling into bed, she was so tired she didn't even think about Eugene, Oregon or the boy in the purple-blue sweater.

○

The next day in English class Mr. Thomas collected their papers and asked the class their impressions of the play so far. Lisa looked around when nobody raised their hand. She wanted to say that she liked the play but she felt too hesitant. Finally, one girl raised her hand and said she thought it was boring. "I mean, nothing happens. These people just have lives where nothing goes on."

"What would you have happen instead?" Mr. Thomas said.

"I dunno. But at least they could have a few problems or get into some kind of trouble."

10

Lisa looked at the girl. She wore what was obviously a cheerleader's sweater with a big "G" on the front. Her hair was pulled back into a pony tail. She seemed confident and Lisa liked the way she wasn't afraid to speak out. She used to speak out in class too. At least when she was in her old school.

"Well," Mr. Thomas said, "do any of these people have problems? What are the issues they wrestle with? Do they just float through life?"

Someone from the back of the class called out, "Maybe they're just all in denial," and everybody laughed.

"Ah yes, the famous *denial*," Mr. Thomas said. "That's the catch word these days. Guess what? I've got an assignment for you."

"I knew it," someone called out.

"I'm going to put you in small groups and you're to discuss some questions. You need to come to some kind of a group consensus. Select one person to write up your group opinion." He proceeded to read off names and locations for the groups in the classroom.

Lisa found herself headed to the front of the class near the windows. She stood for a few seconds, unsure what to do next. Two boys came over and one of them was the boy who had been wearing the purple-blue sweater. Today he was wearing a tee-shirt that said " Go Climb a Rock." Lisa sat down and he sat next to her. She noticed she was holding her breath and consciously made herself exhale. Mr. Thomas came around and gave them a sheet of paper with five questions on it. He handed it to a boy who was wearing a red 49er shirt.

The boy asked the girl next to Lisa whether she had seen Brian that morning and she said, "Yeah, he gave me a ride to school."

"Did he tell you he got tickets for Pearl Jam?"

"Yeah," she answered. "That is so cool."

Lisa thought it was cool too, but she didn't say anything. That was one thing that might be positive about moving to California—getting to go to some concerts. They didn't get too many big name groups in Eugene. Lisa sat back and listened while the kids talked about all the concerts they'd been to.

"So, do you like Pearl Jam?" she heard someone say. She looked up and the boy next to her was looking right at her, the boy in the "Go Climb a Rock" tee shirt.

"Who, me?" she asked. "Yeah, I do. A lot."

"Me too," he said. "But I also like reggae. You like reggae?"

She felt herself blushing. "I. . . I don't know much about it. I mean it wasn't so big where I was living before."

"Whaa?" He stared at her. " You don't know what you're missing! You gotta know reggae, girl!" He looked around the group. " Don't you think this girl's gotta know reggae?" They all smiled and nodded. Lisa felt a rush of feelings. She was happy to be noticed, to have him pay attention to her, but this was too much all at once.

"Okay, Jeff," the girl next to her said. " Let's move on. We've got these questions to answer."

Lisa's mind latched onto the name "Jeff." So that was it. That was his name. For the next few minutes she barely heard the rest of the talk.

"We need someone to write down our group opinion," the girl said. "Who wants to?" No one said anything. "Well, hey, I'm not going to," she said. "Come on, Heather, you're good at it."

"No way," Heather said. " I always get stuck with that job. Besides, it doesn't have to be a girl."

"Oh yes it does," the boys said in unison. "Girls are always the secretaries and boys are policemen."

"Shut up!" Heather said, but they were all laughing.

" Okay. Okay. I'll take notes," Jeff said. "What's the first question?"

The boy in the red 49er shirt looked over the sheet of paper and said, "We're supposed to decide if the people in *Our Town* led meaningful lives. We're supposed to figure out what their values are."

"Say whaaat?" said the boy wearing a baseball cap. "What is all this *meaningful* crap! God, in English we always have to talk about what's *meaningful*. And what does this *mean* and that *mean*. Why do things always have to *mean* something?"

"Shut up, Stewart. What's *meaningful* to you? A little Friday night joint? A touchdown?"

"Get off it, Heather. You don't know me. So what's *meaningful* to you? Birth control pills?"

"You dumb fuck," Heather answered back with a sullen look on her face.

"Hey. Hey," Jeff said. "Let's not get nasty. We all know you two have history together."

The group grew quiet. Everyone waited. Jeff turned to the Chicano kid next to him.

"So Sal, my man. What's meaningful to you? Come on. Enlighten us."

Sal was darkly handsome with almost Indian features. He was liked by all the kids because he was a star soccer goalie who could play the position with a style most good goalies didn't achieve until their 20's. And he didn't forsake his Chicano friends to hang out with the whities. He was one of those rare kids who could straddle two groups and come out on top.

Sal gave a slow smile. "Okay, now don't laugh. I think sports and my family, that's what's important."

"Yeah. Yeah. And what about Martine?" Heather said.

"Well, her too." He smiled.

"Okay, fine, but what's this got to do with *Our Town*?" someone asked. "I mean first we have to agree on what's meaningful and then we have to look at the play—right?"

Lisa drew in her breath and ventured, "Yeah, but what's meaningful to us may not be meaningful to someone else. I mean everybody's different."

Jeff turned and looked directly at her. "Right. Good point," he said. "Well, how 'bout if everyone says one or two things that are meaningful to them and we'll make a list. Come on, we've only got 15 minutes." He glanced around the room. The four other groups were talking and occasionally laughing.

"Okay. I'll start," Heather said. "I say *friends*."

They went around the group.

Family. Sports. Love. Music. Church. Sex (everybody laughed). *Friends.* (Getting high.)

"Okay. We've got eight items here and *friends* is mentioned twice. So, anyone want to add anything?" No one said a word. "Well, how 'bout *family*? Do the people in the play value *family*?"

Everyone nodded. "That's all this play is about really—two families."

"What about *sports*?"

"Only a little. Just that one boy when he's young."

"Okay. Scratch *sports* .

"What about *love*?"

"Oh yeah. *Love* is very big in *Our Town*. Everybody does it. Everybody has kids."

"Not sex, Duane. Love. L-O-V-E. There's a difference," said a girl wearing overalls and a tank top.

"Yeah, Duane," the boys said. "Get your head out from between your legs." Duane pulled his hat down over his eyes.

"So, what about *love*?" Jeff said.

Everybody said "yes."

"What about *music*?"

"It's no big deal. Just music in the church choirs. They didn't have MTV or tapes or anything."

"What about *church*?"

"Yeah, *church* seems big in their lives. Most people go to church whether they want to or not."

"Sounds like my family. How many people here go to church?"

"I go to temple sometimes," said a kid wearing a tee shirt that said 'Just Do It.'"

Sal said, "I go a lot."

One other girl said, "I go all the time."

"That's 'cause you're reborn," said Jeff.

"Well, it wouldn't hurt you," she shot back.

"Ahh. You got me on that one." Jeff smiled at her.

"What about *sex*?"

"I think it is," Heather said.

"Is what?"

"You know, important. That girl and boy fall in love and get married and have kids. I think that's one of their values."

"Yeah but I don't think *sex* is a very big deal for them. They've got their minds on other stuff. They're pretty up-tight."

"I don't think they're up-tight," said the girl in overalls. "I think it's nice, the way they live." About four people groaned. "Well, I do," she said. Lisa silently agreed with her.

"Let's vote." Only two people thought *sex* was important.

"How 'bout *friends?*" Everyone agreed.

They started gathering up their books. The bell was about to ring. Mr. T called out, "Okay I need you to hand in your groups' written conclusions."

"Wait. We've got one more—*getting high.* How many of you think *getting high* was a meaningful part of these people's lives?"

"Only the old town drunk," said Duane. "These people don't do anything for fun. They think *getting high* means going up on a ladder."

"Whoa. Good one, Duane."

"So, how do you vote?"

Everyone said no.

"Okay. So did the people in *Our Town* lead *meaningful* lives? They valued *family, love, church and friends.* Everyone vote."

The bell rang. Everyone got up saying, "Yeah, they did." "Yeah." "Yeah, but it was boring."

Jeff scribbled their vote on the paper and handed it to Mr. T. "Where do you get these ideas Mr. T? You need to lighten up!"

The teacher laughed, took the paper and looked it over. Lisa took her time leaving the class and walked out the door with Jeff.

" So, do you want to go hear some reggae sometime?" he asked.

"That'd be great," Lisa said, trying to act casual.

"Okay, I'll call you. What's your number?"

Lisa had to think. She'd hardly said her new phone number out loud to anyone. Finally it came to her. "Uh, 845-0631. Listen, is this the way to Mr. Spence's class?" she asked, pointing off to the left.

Jeff paused. "Yep. That's right." He headed in the opposite direction. "I'll see you tomorrow."

Lisa's head felt like it was going to blow right off. God, she couldn't believe it!

That night for the first time in months Lisa didn't think about her old friends back in Eugene.

◯

It took three or four days, but Jeff finally called and they made a date to go hear a reggae band playing in San Francisco. A group of kids was going together in someone's van. Lisa's folks didn't feel at all good about the hour's trip on the freeway and they wanted her back by 1 a.m. On the phone that night Lisa told Jeff about her curfew.

He was quiet for a moment, then said, "Listen, the concert isn't even over until 1 a.m. Can't you talk to them?"

Lisa said she would try. "Oh hey, the other thing I'm supposed to ask who's driving. You guys don't drink and drive, do you?"

Jeff laughed. "What's wrong with that?" There was a silence. "Come on. We know one or two things down here in California. Of course not."

Lisa felt embarrassed but relieved. She'd asked everything she was supposed to. "Okay. I'm going to go talk to my mom. Could you call me back in an hour?"

"No, you call me this time."

"Okay. Talk to you soon."

She put the phone down and went to find her mother, who was paying bills in the dining room. "Mom, you know this concert I'm going to Saturday night?"

"Yes." Her mother scrutinized the utilities bill. "Boy, the water bill is so high down here. We never had rates like this in Oregon."

"Mom, I know you want me home by 1 a.m., but the concert doesn't even end until then. Even if we leave right away, I can't possibly get home till 2 at the earliest."

Her mother frowned. She looked at Lisa. "I know you really want this to happen, but I don't feel good about your being out driving on the freeway at that time of night. There are all kinds of crazy drivers then. And who's driving? Is he responsible? Is there going to be drinking? I don't even know these kids."

"It's not a *he*. It's a *she*—Sally, Sally something. Jeff said she's real dependable."

"Well, when are we going to meet Jeff?"

"Saturday."

"And what about the drinking?"

"Mom, don't worry about that. I don't think there'll be any and you know I won't."

Lisa had tried drinking a couple of times but the last time was a disaster and her parents had found out. She'd been with her friends in Eugene on a summer night. They'd gone to the local park to meet, and listen to some tapes on a portable stereo, and someone had shown up with beer and wine coolers. Actually, she knew who it was—a guy a couple of years older who had a job, a car, and some extra money. Everyone had tried one of the drinks or both.

Lisa had had mixed feelings. Part of her didn't even want to try the stuff. She kind of prided herself on not drinking, though she'd never talked about it. But it had been a warm summer night and they were all having so much fun. So, Lisa sipped a beer, then had a strawberry wine cooler. Before she knew it, they were singing and dancing in the park, the boom box turned up. Then the police arrived and broke up the party. The kids protested and the cops packed several of them into their squad cars and took them down to police headquarters. The next thing she knew, her parents were in the waiting room picking her up to take her home. There had been no charges, just warnings. Her parents drove her home in angry silence and she was grounded for the next month. Since then, she hadn't touched anything alcoholic.

Her mother sighed. "Okay. Just be careful."

The trip down in the van was wild. Everyone was telling jokes, cutting each other down, singing to tapes, beating time to the music on anything they could find. Some of the girls braided their hair in corn rows with beads; some wore jeans, some long skirts. The boys looked basically the same. Every now and then one would roll down the window and yell, "We're goin' to rage!" followed by many whoops and shouts.

Sally drove within the speed limit and was pretty quiet. Lisa sat next to Jeff. He had his arm along the back of her seat and occasionally said something to her. Mostly he talked to the kids around him. Lisa was happy — happy to be there with Jeff, happy to be going to a concert, happy to be with other kids.

They approached the Golden Gate Bridge. It was a clear night. San Francisco and the East Bay sparkled. "Hey, look at the city!" someone called out.

"Oh wow! That is so cool." Lisa had been across the Golden Gate only a few times; it was a great moment.

They maneuvered through San Francisco and twice had to stop to ask for directions. By the time they parked, everyone was overloaded with energy. They jumped from the van. Someone had a nerf football and they threw it around for awhile. A couple of the boys stayed in the van and Lisa was aware of the toasty, pungent smell of marijuana coming through the open window.

"Come on, you guys. Finish that joint. Let's go!" someone called out.

The boys left the van, silly grins on their faces. "You can't do reggae without weed!" one of them said.

They approached the concert hall. The sidewalk was jammed with all kinds of people: young and old hippies; blacks with dreadlocks; white men and women. "My man! My man!" "Dude, how're you doin?" "I be fine."

They finally got through the doors. It was dark and warm inside and the smell of pot engulfed her; Lisa moved closer to Jeff. He put his arm around her. "All right! We're here!" he called out to no one in particular. A warm-up band was playing and people were moving to the beat, greeting each other.

Lisa felt self-conscious. She looked at Jeff, who was kind of stiffly shuffling his feet.

"Come on, girl," he said. "Let's dance!"

She kept her head down at first, then began glancing around her. Everywhere she looked she saw long hair, earrings, people moving their whole bodies, arms, legs. She loosened up, looked at Jeff. He was smiling a big goofy grin. It felt fine!

The music stopped and they wandered over to their friends. Jeff held her hand. One of the girls from the van, Kathy, turned to Lisa and said, "So, what do you think? Isn't it cool!"

Lisa nodded and smiled.

"Want to go to the bathroom with me?"

"Yeah," Lisa answered. She turned to Jeff. "I'll be right back."

They pushed their way through the crowd and found the women's room, a dingy two-stalled hole in the wall. A bunch of girls were crowded around a mirror. Someone was smoking weed. Some girls were drinking what looked like tequila from a bottle stashed in a purse.

"Boy! Some smell!" Kathy said. "You could get high just standing here."

"Whew. It's pretty strong. Kids just don't smoke it that much where I'm from. I've tried it though."

"Oh, I've smoked it a couple of times too, but I don't, you know, use it. Most of us don't, but a few kids, like Steve and Craig, they do. So how do you like Jeff?"

"He's nice," Lisa said.

"He's a very cool guy. We've been friends for years, ever since 6th grade. That's when I moved up from L.A. It's not easy being new, huh? But you'll see; it'll get better."

"It is already."

"You know, Jeff used to go out with my best friend, Molly. They went together for over a year."

"I guess I don't know who she is," Lisa said.

"Oh, she moved to Sacramento. It was awful. I miss her but we still write and call each other. When I get my license, I'm going to drive up there as often as I can."

Lisa was dying to know more about Jeff, but Kathy didn't volunteer any further information. They took their turn in the toilets and shook out their hair in front of the mirror. Kathy's hair was long, dark, and curly.

"God. You have great hair," Lisa said.

"Thanks. I like it now, but it was a real pain when I was little."

They went back to the dance floor and looked for their friends. The main band was ready to begin and everyone was jumping around.

"Come on," Jeff said, grabbing Lisa's hand. "Let's get down close."

When the band began, the lights came up and flashed all around the hall and everyone started screaming. The music was loud and the reggae beat overpowering. All the musicians, even the white ones, had dreadlocks. They were decked out in brightly colored shirts and flashy vests. The temperature rose in the room with everyone moving, bobbing their heads and rubber-like bodies. It was such happy music that Lisa just couldn't feel self-conscious anymore. Her body jerked and swayed; she laughed with Jeff and her head felt as though it was floating in the flashing lights and smoke and the electric feeling in the air. She hadn't felt so good—ever!

On the way home everyone was much more subdued, exhausted. Lisa leaned against Jeff and dozed off. She could vaguely hear him talking now and then but mostly she felt safe and content. A couple of times when he kissed her temples she felt warm and slushy inside. She woke up when they pulled off the freeway and looked up at him.

"Thanks," she whispered. "It was great."

He leaned down and kissed her full on the mouth. It was a soft kiss and Lisa freely returned it. She never even asked herself if she was kissing him too soon, too early on. It felt too right.

○

She slept in late the next morning and woke up feeling life couldn't get any better. She lay in bed and went over and over the details of last night: the music, the dancing, the kissing. She remembered Jeff's smell, some cologne mingled with sweat and the leather smell of his jacket. She felt his damp, blond hair and the roughness of his sweater.

Over and over during the day she saw his face as it had looked in the passing headlights on the freeway — the outline of his lips, his nose, his eyes in shadows. Then, by the end of the day, she couldn't recall his face any longer, and that distressed her. She tried repeatedly to see it but the memory had faded. She thought about calling him and almost did about four times but then couldn't get up her nerve, fearing his voice might not be so caring the day after.

That night he called and they talked for an hour. They agreed to meet at school the next day and Lisa felt excited and secure at the same time.

○

From that point on they were a couple and were together at school, a night or two during the week, and at least once on the weekend. Jeff came over a lot and they spent hours studying or half studying. They lay on the couch together in the family room and watched T.V., Jeff's head in Lisa's lap or his arms around her. Her parents liked Jeff and often invited him along when the family went out.

One night Lisa was home more or less "baby-sitting" Stephanie, who was watching a favorite television show. Jeff had come over and they wound up in her bedroom with the door closed. It was a rule that her door was to be left open if a boy was over, but this time they were breaking the rule.

Lisa's mother had talked with her many times about being "careful." She had talked about AIDS, about Lisa's waiting until she was older and in love before having sex. They discussed the pill and condoms. Each time Lisa felt uncomfortable talking, but she knew her mom meant well. She'd never before quite understood how a girl could be so stupid as to get pregnant unless she wanted to.

But now, lying with Jeff on her bed, their bodies pressed closer to each other, the farthest thought from her mind was getting pregnant. She wasn't thinking at all.

She was caught up in their kissing, in his touching her. She returned his kisses and leaned against him. She felt him harden through his sweat pants. She loved feeling his hands move under her bra and she heard him say her name. His voice sounded fuzzy to her ears and a brief thought danced through her head: We should talk about this.

He asked her, "Are you okay?"

Now was the time she should stop him, they should talk but she waited for him. She felt herself sinking down as though some large presence was taking her over. Her body pressed close to him, her mind dimly tried to communicate a thought.

O

Do you want Lisa and Jeff to stop and talk about whether or not to have sex? If so, turn to **TALK** printed on tan paper.

Should Jeff and Lisa continue on without talking? If so, turn to **SEX** printed on cream colored paper.

These stickers are brought to you by an old friend—human error. May error always lead to wisdom and the power of transformation.

TALK

She felt so pulled in different directions. Finally, one voice made its way to the surface.

"I don't want to have a baby, not now," Lisa heard herself saying. "Jeff, wait. We have to talk." She could feel him grow still and she hoped he wasn't going to get angry. They were quiet for a minute, listening to their own breathing. Well, even if he was angry, he'd just have to understand.

"Jeff, I don't want to get pregnant. I couldn't handle that now. Besides, it's too soon."

He looked at her and his eyes widened. "What do you mean? I asked you if you were okay. I mean, you're using something, aren't you?"

"Using something? You mean taking the pill?"

"Yeah, the pill."

"No, I'm not on the pill. Jeff, I've never even had sex before."

They were both sitting up now, rearranging their clothes. "My god," he said, "I'm sorry. I thought you were. . . on the pill. I guess we should have talked about it. I just got carried away."

She loved his honesty and reached out and took his hand. He hugged her close.

"I love you," he said. She moved her head to kiss him.

"I love you too. I don't want to be stupid, Jeff. I want to be smart. I just don't think I'm ready."

"Ready for what? Sex or the pill?" he said teasingly.

She laughed a little and poked him in the ribs. "God, I don't know, neither one right now. What should we do? I mean, are you ready?"

"For what? Sex or the pill?"

"Oh, shut up. You know what I mean."

"Well, I'm ready for sex—or least I was a few minutes ago" he said with a smile. "But I'm sure not ready to be a father. And I don't want to deal with abortion."

"Abortion? God, that's such an ugly word," Lisa said, looking down at the rumpled bedspread. "Have you ever had sex before?" she asked shyly.

Jeff looked away. "Well, yeah. . . kind of. . . yeah."

"What do you mean—kind of?"

"There was this girl last summer. She was a couple of years older than me. I didn't care about her, but we did it a couple of times."

"What was her name? What was it like?"

"Her name was Melanie and—God, Lisa, it's hard to talk about it."

"Yeah, but if it's hard to talk about, why are we even thinking about doing it? It's crazy."

Jeff was quiet for a moment. "You're right," he said. "Well, it felt great. She knew what she was doing."

Lisa felt a mixture of intrigue and disappointment. She also felt left out and didn't like the idea of Jeff having been with another girl.

"Well, I don't know what I'm doing," she said. "Besides, how do you know she didn't give you AIDS, and then you could have passed it on to me?"

"AIDS? Are you kidding? What do you think we were doing? Shooting up with infected needles?"

"Jeff, don't be stupid. You can get AIDS other ways. She might have gotten AIDS from a blood transfusion. Or maybe she'd had sex with someone else and he gave it to her, only they didn't know about it."

"Lisa, I'm sure! She didn't have AIDS. She wasn't that kind of girl."

"Give me a break! Jeff, you don't have to be a hooker to have AIDS. Don't you know anything about it? Don't they teach you anything in California schools? Didn't you take health?"

Jeff grabbed her and pushed her down on the bed. "I've had about enough out of you," he said laughing. "Just shut up." And he began kissing her.

Lisa kissed him back. She felt closer to him now; he was more wonderful than she had thought. Some guys would have gotten angry.

"Jeff, let's make a deal. I'll tell you when I'm ready and you tell me."

"Lisa, I'm ready now. "

"You're not ready!" Lisa said. "You don't even have a condom!"

"Okay. Okay. But I'm ready in other ways. And I want to be careful and I want you to feel good about everything."

"And what if I'm not ready for six months, or a year, or five years?"

"Five years! You're kidding, I know. A year or six months? We'll just have to see what happens."

"You mean we'll split up if we don't have sex?" Lisa asked.

"I didn't say that. Boy, this is complicated, " Jeff said. "You know as well as I do that we don't know what's going to happen in life. You can't plan ahead like that."

Lisa knew he was right but she didn't want to hear it. "Well, at least let's plan to be smart if we decide to do it. Let's get birth control, use something. Is that a deal?"

"Okay. That's a deal," Jeff said.

"Let's promise," Lisa said twisting his arm in mock anger.

"Okay. Okay, I promise."

"I do too."

They leaned over and kissed each other. Just then Lisa heard the sound of her parent's car. "Oh my god. Come on. My parents are home."

They jumped off the bed and Lisa tried to smooth it out. "Come on, get out of here," she said, switching on the light. They raced to the kitchen and Lisa grabbed some cookies.

"Hi Steph," she said to her sister.

Stephanie muttered "Oh, hi."

Her mom came in first and gave Lisa a sharp look. "Hi." She turned to Stephanie. "Are you still up? It's 10:30. Come on. Get to bed. Lisa, I told you she was supposed to be in bed by 10:00."

"I know, I just forgot. But she's old enough to deal with that herself; she's not clueless."

"Hello Jeff," her mother said.

"Hi, Mrs. Howard."

Her dad came in next. "Jeff, how are you?"

"Fine." Jeff looked uneasy. "Well, I gotta be going." He looked over at Lisa and grinned. "I'll see you tomorrow."

"Wait, I'll go out with you," Lisa said.

"Whew! That was close," Jeff said when they were outside.

" Oh my god. What if they had come home ten minutes earlier?"

"We were lucky," he said.

"Yeah. But we were also smart." Lisa kissed him. "I'll see you tomorrow.

"Night," he said and gave her a big, wet kiss.

"Yuck! Get out of here!" Lisa waved as he drove off.

When she came back in the house, the lights were out in the kitchen, and she went back to her bedroom, closed her door, and flopped on the bed. There was a lot to think about.

She heard a knock. "Lisa?" Her mother opened her door.

"Hi."

"Lisa, I need to talk to you."

Lisa felt her heart contract. *Shit.*

Sitting on the bed, her mother continued. "I thought we had an understanding about being in your room with a boy, with Jeff. You know you're to keep the door open. In fact, I don't even want you in your bedroom with him when we're not home."

"Mom! We weren't doing anything! What am I, a child?"

"Lisa, I saw the light go on and I know you two were in here. I want to be able to trust you. I think you're seeing too much of Jeff. You know we like him, but it's just not good to be together so much."

"Mom, what are you afraid of? What do you think we were doing?"

"I wasn't born yesterday," her mother said. "I just don't want you to get hurt."

"How am I going to get hurt? What's really worrying you? Say it."

"Well," her mother paused, "I don't want you getting in trouble, pregnant. And, there's so much going around these days—AIDS, STDs."

"Mom, we didn't do anything. God! Why can't you trust me? Besides, I'm not dumb."

"Lisa, you know I trust you most of the time. It's just that feelings sometimes are bigger than we're ready to handle. I told you, when the time comes that you're ready to be sexually active, I'll help you. But I hope you'll wait until you're older."

"Mom, I'm 16!"

"In my day 16 was not considered old."

Part of Lisa wanted to talk with her mother, but another part wanted to keep things just between her and Jeff. She wanted to handle this on her own; if she had to go to her mother, how could she possibly be ready to have sex?

Her mother looked expectant, as though she was waiting for Lisa to say something. She had that worried look across her eyes and forehead.

"Is there anything you want to talk about?" her mother said, shifting her position on the bed.

Lisa knew her mother wanted her to open up, talk about sex, ask questions. She just couldn't bring herself to do it. "No, I'm okay . . . How're you doing? How's your job?"

Her mother's face relaxed. "It's all right at least for the present. I wouldn't want to do it forever but it fits my needs now. . . Well, I guess you have things to do."

She leaned over and kissed Lisa on the forehead, something she rarely did these days. "And remember, not quite so much time with Jeff."

Lisa didn't respond but turned off the light and lay quietly on her bed after her mother left. She thought about Jeff, about how they had both been lying here together just a half hour ago. She felt that warm feeling in her crotch and turned over onto her stomach holding her pillow. It had felt so good lying next to him. She pressed her body into the bed and slowly moved back and forth. She put her fingers against her clitoris, gently moving them. Sometimes this helped her relax, but tonight her head just wouldn't stop chattering.

Jeff was so sweet and he had been understanding. He had said he was ready for sex but not to be a father. When would she be ready? The idea of having sex was confusing. She wanted to, but she couldn't imagine it. He'd see her naked, see her breasts, her pubic hair. She'd see his . . . penis. And what if she smelled funny and what if it was all messy? What if she didn't do it right? What if he didn't like it? How would she feel afterward? And then, she wouldn't be a virgin any longer. Did she want to still be a virgin? Didn't she want to save sex for the first time with the man she was going to marry? Would she marry Jeff? Wasn't she too young?

She threw her pillow across the room. This was stupid. For a brief moment her brain was still. Then she thought of Gwen. That was it! She would call Gwen. Gwen would help her out. She glanced at the clock—11 p.m.. She hoped she wasn't too late.

Hearing her mother moving about, Lisa got up and went out into the kitchen and asked if she could make the call. "To Gwen?" her mother said. "In Oregon?"

"Well, sure."

Her mother looked a little hurt but said, "I guess. Just don't make it too long. It's long distance, you know."

"Yes Mom, I know that. That's why I asked," Lisa said with an edge to her voice.

She went back to her room, picked up the phone and dialed Gwen's number from memory. She was in luck! Gwen answered on the second ring. She sounded excited to hear from Lisa, and they talked about old friends and school. Then Lisa asked how Todd was. There was a short silence.

"He's okay," Gwen answered. "I guess. We're not together anymore."

Lisa was stunned. "Are you all right?"

"Yeah. I miss him sometimes, but he was also a jerk. I'm going out with Theo James now."

"Theo? You're kidding! I thought he was with Sara," Lisa said.

Gwen laughed. "They split up two months ago. I guess I forgot to tell you."

"Well, what happened to you and Todd?"

"I don't know. It just got too intense. It was great for a while and we were real happy. Then things changed, and it didn't seem so special any more. I think it got kind of boring. Then he didn't want to be together so much. And I got all wrapped up in school and I was playing soccer. We started being apart more, and then we both got jealous and got in fights. It was hard."

"But. . . but," Lisa said, "you had sex together. I mean, you were so close. Are you sorry now, do you wish you hadn't? I mean, I really have to know. I'm going out with this wonderful guy and we, we're. . . ."

"My god! How great!" Gwen cut in. "Tell me about him."

"Well, he's really sweet. He's cute. He plays basketball. We have a good time together. I'm really happy."

"Wow. I am so glad for you. So have you done it yet? Tell me the truth."

"No. No, we came close, but we stopped. I'm so confused. I don't know if I'm ready or not. The whole thing kind of scares me. That's why I wanted to call you. What do you think? Are you sorry now that you and Todd had sex?"

Gwen was quiet for a moment. "I'm not sure. I've thought a lot about it. He was so cool in the beginning, but now when I see him, he acts so stupid and immature. And I feel so awkward; I'm always afraid he's going to tell someone about us. He probably already has, even though we promised each other we wouldn't. I know that I'm sorry that my first time is over. You know how we always said that we wanted to wait till we were absolutely with the right guy—you know, to get married and everything? And now I don't have that to look forward to anymore. It's funny, I feel like I opened a door and now I can't go back to the other side. Theo and I haven't done anything yet, but I sure want to sometimes. We're trying to take it slow. One thing I will say though—be careful. Don't take any chances. Todd and I did it once without using anything, and I thought for a whole month I was pregnant. It was hell. I was scared, and Todd and I got in fights. We couldn't get along. We almost broke up then, but I was lucky and finally I got my period. God, what a relief!"

"So, what did you do then?"

"We used condoms for a while, but I got nervous about those. So I went and got the pill and that worked. It made my face break out at first, but then it cleared up. And then I was worrying about AIDS which Todd said was silly. I was always asking questions like, 'When you had sex before, how do you know the girl didn't have AIDS?' And he was in the hospital one time when he was little and had a blood transfusion. I mean, how do you know? God, it was all so complicated. I'm glad I don't have to think about that stuff now. Except sometimes I wonder—what if I have AIDS and I don't know it?"

Lisa was quiet for a few seconds. "Gwen, this is all so heavy. I'm tired just thinking about it. I wish I'd been there for you. Why didn't you call me?"

"I almost did. A hundred times. I dunno. It just felt too much to explain. I wish we could see each other. Could you come up some time? Or maybe I could come down over vacation?"

"Oh, that would be so great! I'll talk to my parents. You talk to yours, okay?"

"Yes! Great! Listen, I gotta go.'

"Me too. We'll talk next week. You call me this time."

"Cool. See ya. Bye."

"Bye."

Lisa hung up the phone, lay back on her bed, and let out a long sigh. Her head felt like it was twisting and turning inside, and no matter which direction she looked, she felt cornered, blocked.

There was a knock on her door. "Lisa?" It was Stephanie.

Her sister opened the door and stood uncertainly in the doorway.

"What's up, Steph? What are you doing? It's late."

"I dunno. I couldn't sleep. I could hear you talking on the phone. Was that Gwen?"

Lisa nodded. She looked at her sister. Her long hair was tangled and she had on a Chicago Bulls tee shirt and flannel shorts. She had grown. She looked so much taller, and Lisa could tell she was developing breasts. She also realized that she really hadn't looked at her sister for a long time. She suddenly felt guilty. She'd been so wrapped up in her own life that she had forgotten all about Stephanie.

"I wish we'd never moved," Stephanie said. "Sometimes I hate it here. I wish I was back at my old school with Shannon and Mike and Joey, with all the kids in the neighborhood., And I liked Mr. Greer, my teacher. My teacher here isn't nearly so nice."

Lisa sighed again. "I know," she said. "Everything seemed easier in Eugene. I know what you mean." She wanted to cheer up her sister, but she didn't have the energy. "Still, you seem happy here. You already have friends and you're playing soccer."

"Sometimes it's okay," she said sitting on Lisa's bed. "But it's all so different. And you're gone and Mom's gone a lot and Dad's never here and everything has changed so much."

Lisa felt a flood of love for her sister. To Lisa, Stephanie's life seemed pure and simple and fun. But she could tell that it wasn't so. And Lisa knew that in just a couple of years, life would become much more complicated for Stephanie. She wished there were some way she could protect her.

"Stephanie, remember when we were little how we used to play in the woods near our house? Let's go for a hike in the hills this weekend. We'll take a lunch."

Stephanie's face brightened. "That would be great!" she said. "But I've got soccer Saturday. How 'bout Sunday?"

She'd hoped to see Jeff on Sunday, but right now this seemed more important. Besides, a hike would be good for her. "Okay, we'll do it Sunday."

"You won't change your mind?"

"No way," Lisa said.

"Okay. Deal. Well, I've got to get to bed. Night, Lisa."

"G'night, poopy pants," Lisa said, remembering an old nickname.

"G'night, fart head," Stephanie said with a giggle.

○

The following Monday at school Lisa felt better than she had in a long time. It had been a good weekend: she'd actually done all her homework, and she and Jeff had gone to a movie and then hung out with their friends Saturday night. They had felt close, been able to laugh, and the subject of sex never came up. On Sunday she and Stephanie had gone for a great hike. The weather had been cold and the big park almost deserted except for a few runners. The two of them had been silly, walking and talking for nearly six miles. When they returned, they were tired but happy. And their parents had been thrilled that the two had finally spent some time together.

Lisa felt full of energy. She and Kathy had become good friends, always met at their lockers, and walked to first period together. They talked about the weekend, their friends and Jeff. Lisa hadn't mentioned anything about the issue of sex, but she wanted to. One of these days—soon.

"You know what I'm doing today?" Kathy asked. "After school I'm trying out for the play, the one coming up in a couple of months."

"Really? Which one?"

"Uh, it's called *Revenge*. I was in one last year. God! It was so much fun. Come with me. Try out."

Lisa shuddered. "No way. I've never been in a play. I couldn't do it. But I'll come with you. It'd be fun to see."

"Cool. It's at 3:15 in the auditorium," Kathy said going into class. "I'll see you there."

After the final bell, Lisa walked into the darkened auditorium and looked for Kathy. There were about 20 kids sitting around, talking and looking at papers. She sat down behind Kathy, who had her head down, studying something.

"Hi. What's that?" Lisa asked.

"It's the part we're supposed to read for tryouts. This one is the part for a grandmother. I'm trying out for that. Here, want to look? There are lots of smaller parts too."

Lisa took the paper and read it over.

"Come on," Kathy said. "Give it a try. The worst that can happen is you won't make it. But then lots of other people won't make it either. But it's still all fun. You wouldn't believe how close everyone gets by the end of the production. It's so cool. You'd only have to read for three minutes or so. Try out for the aunt and the daughter."

Lisa's heart was pounding. She wanted to, but she was also scared to death. Ordinarily she wouldn't think of trying out for a play, but today she felt brave and upbeat, and Kathy's energy was contagious. Surprisingly, she heard herself say, "Okay."

Kathy's reading had gone very well; Lisa was sure she would get the part. When it was her turn, her knees felt light and wiggly and her palms were sweaty. She felt like she was far away and could barely hear the director when he said, "Speak up." The three minutes flew by, and before she knew it she was sitting back in her seat watching the others. The parts would be announced the next day.

At dinner that night she told her family about the try outs. "Course, I probably won't get anything, but it was fun just to do it." Both her parents smiled. She knew they were happy about it.

That night she was baby-sitting at a neighbor's, and she called Jeff and told him what she had done. He was surprised.

"That's great!" he said. "Just don't fall in love with the leading man."

"Oh right! Jeff, I probably won't even get a part."

She felt pleased by what he had said. They talked about his basketball and the coming vacation. Jeff was going to be gone part of the time with his family down in southern California. Lisa mentioned she hoped to go up to Eugene to visit her old friends. They finally hung up after agreeing to see each other at break the next day.

The cast for the play was posted on the wall. Lisa waited for a long time before she approached the bulletin board and was glad there weren't too many other kids around. She read over the list and didn't see her name. She felt a great sinking inside and forced herself to look over the paper again. Then she saw it— *Lisa Howard*. She let out a big sigh. Her name was next to the part of Aunt Claire—a small part, but a part just the same. She couldn't believe it! Then she saw Kathy's name next to the part of the grandmother and suddenly she heard her name, and Kathy came racing down the hall. The two of them hugged and jumped around.

"This is so wonderful!" Kathy said. "I am so glad for both of us," and they laughed and kept hugging. "Come on. Let's go to the drama room. You've got to get to know everyone!"

The drama room was different from any other room Lisa had seen at the school. There was a small stage, lots of chairs and papers scattered around. There

28

were some old props: a milk bottle, an ironing board, a tall lamp and a torn picture of Ronald Reagan with a mustache drawn on it. There were also two photographs tacked up showing past productions. The place was noisy with laughter and exaggerated-style talk. Most of the kids wore some form of black clothing—a turtleneck, jeans or black leggings, hats, lacy skirts. Lisa saw lots of earrings on both boys and girls and a few nose rings. There were all styles of haircuts, from long and curly to shaved heads. Where had all these kids been? How come she hadn't seen them before? Her eyes searched the room for the few straight looking kids, and she was grateful that Kathy was there.

Kathy poked her in the side. "Kinda different, huh? But you'll see. After a while, you'll get along great with them. Hey, Zeke!" she called out to a boy with a bi-level haircut, part of it colored orange.

"Hey, Kathy," he answered back with a smile. "How ya been?"

"Great," Kathy answered. "Zeke, this is Lisa. She's going to be Aunt Claire in the play. She's new here."

"How ya doin?" he said to Lisa. Zeke was wearing an earring in one ear and had nice green eyes; they looked directly at Lisa.

"Hi," she answered back.

"So, where have you been?" he asked Kathy. "At all the football games?"

"Well, sure. You know me—Miss Straight, All-American Girl! So what are you up to? Where are you living now?"

"I'm back with my dad. My mom split again. We haven't heard from her since September. You know Mom; she just can't stay around too long." He had a small tight smile on his face.

"Yeah. I remember. But she was always so nice to me. She used to feed me granola every time I came over. And she was fun," Kathy said.

"Well, she has that side too. I just wish she'd figure out what she wants. Anyway, we've got a new play, and I think it will be a good one."

The director was calling everyone together so they all moved closer and sat down in chairs or on the stage.

"All right, everyone! Let me have your attention! Let me hear a big howl and I mean big!"

The whole group whooped at the top of their lungs, and Lisa felt herself jump. God. What had she gotten herself into?

Everyone laughed after the howling had stopped.

"Remember," the director said, "we are going to be loose, let it all hang out. No more tight bodies and tight throats. You're going to have to slip out of your skin and into the skin of your character. After two months you will *be* that character: you'll eat, sleep, move, think and feel like that character. Got it?"

Everyone answered, "Yeah."

"What? I didn't hear that."

"Yeah."

"What?"

"YEAH!" came a booming reply.

He smiled. "That's more like it. Okay, here are copies of the script. Rehearsal will be after school Monday through Thursday. You guys are flakes on Fridays. Three to five o'clock. Bring your script every day, and by tomorrow I want you to be able to describe your character to the whole group. Remember, this is your new family, and we all have to get to know each other. Okay, see you tomorrow at three p.m. sharp!"

Lisa and Kathy walked out the door together. "Wow! This is different than I thought it was going to be," Lisa said.

"I know, it's another world. I like it. It's different from the rest of the places we hang out."

Lisa liked how Kathy said "we hang out." It felt like she really belonged. "So, what's with Zeke?" she asked.

"Zeke and I go back to sixth grade," Kathy said. "We've been friends all that time except for a while in junior high when he got real extreme and was in a lot of trouble. Then we just couldn't talk. He's gone through lots of changes. He used to be real straight. That's when he was a jock and into soccer and baseball. After that, he hung out with a punk group and he got in trouble for stealing. Later, in high school, he was kind of a loner and we met up again in drama last year. He was my boyfriend in sixth grade. He was so sweet. We used to go to the movies, hold hands and kiss. His parents are cool, but they have lots of problems and they split up when he was in junior high. He first lived with his dad, then his mom, and now he's back with his dad. His mom is really a neat lady, but she goes on binges sometimes and uses drugs and alcohol and just checks out for a while. He's got a little sister who has gone back and forth too. I guess she must be in seventh grade by now. I baby-sat for her a few times." Kathy sighed. "He has a lot to deal with. He's good in drama—you'll see."

Lisa listened quietly. She had lots of pictures in her head about the kind of life Zeke had led and none of them matched her own life. It was a lot to take in.

"Well, listen, do you want a ride? I've got the car today?"

"No, thanks. I'm going over to Paul's house. I'll see you tomorrow."

"Kathy," Lisa said, "thanks for getting me to try out. I am so glad I made it."

"Me too," Kathy said. "I'll see you tomorrow."

That night Lisa talked with Jeff on the phone and told him about the play. "I like it," she said. "Those kids kind of live in a different world."

"Boy, you can say that again," Jeff said. "Just don't forget your first boyfriend over here. . . Is everything okay?"

Lisa knew he was talking not just in general but about their love life as well. "Everything is good," she said.

"So, what do you want to do after the basketball game Friday?" he asked.

"I dunno. Let's just go somewhere and eat."

"Sounds good," he said.

They lost the basketball game that night and Jeff was in a bad mood. He gave Lisa a half-hearted hug and then lapsed into silence as he sat behind the steering wheel. " What do you want to do?" he asked.

"How 'bout if we just go get a coke," Lisa said, sensing he wasn't much in the mood for anything else. Jeff started the car and, looking over his shoulder, pulled out on the road.

They drove several blocks from the school, pulled up to a 7-11 and got out. Standing at the counter, Lisa tried putting her arm through Jeff's, but he acted indifferent, so she just stood there. When they got back in the car they were silent, and it wasn't until he pulled the car over on a quiet street and parked that she dared to say anything.

"What's wrong? Is it 'cause we lost the game?" she asked. He slumped down in his seat and took a long swallow of Coke. "I guess," he said. "I just feel like crap. Before I left the house tonight my dad and I got in a big argument. I'm getting sick of it. He's always on my case lately. My life sucks right now."

"At least you played well tonight."

"Lisa, give me a break. I didn't play well. I missed those two free throws and a bunch of other shots. We all just played shitty."

Lisa sat silently. She knew that no matter what she said it wouldn't be right. She leaned over next to him and kissed him. He sat there unmoving, but slowly he loosened up and then returned her kisses. He drew her to him and let out a big sigh.

"I've missed you," he said, nuzzling her neck.

She kissed him back passionately, warmed by the fact that she could help him feel better.

"You smell good," he said, holding her tightly.

Pressed against him, she felt herself grow tingly and excited. Her hand accidentally brushed his crotch and she felt how hard he was. She felt a kind of power knowing she was the cause of this. His knee was between her legs and she felt a little dizzy.

"Jeff, Jeff," she said, barely able to get the words out. "I. . . I. . . wait, wait a minute."

He stopped kissing and stroking her and suddenly there seemed to be a great distance between them where, just seconds ago, they had been like one person.

"I'm sorry. I'm sorry," she said. "Remember, we had a deal. I want to be ready but I'm just not. I'm scared."

He sat there looking straight ahead. Suddenly he smacked the steering wheel and said, "Shit! You're always scared." He got out and slammed the car door.

"Where are you going?"

He didn't answer and walked around to the back of the car and stood there a long time.

She watched him. How did things get screwed up so fast? Maybe she was doing the wrong thing. Maybe she was just a prick teaser. . . . If she really loved him, she wouldn't be making him so unhappy; she wouldn't be making such a big deal out of sex. Looking out the back window she could see his breath in the cold night air. Finally he came around the car and got in.

"Sorry," he said. "I had to cool off. You're right, I know. I just forget sometimes. I guess I'm still pissed about the game." He gave her hand a squeeze.

"I'm sorry," she said kissing him on the cheek.

"Don't be. You were right. Let's go over to Dillon's. Okay?"

"Yeah. I think it's a good idea now."

O

Dillon's house was packed with kids and loud music. Beer was everywhere and the sweet smell of marijuana drifted about the house.

"Wow! This place is jumping," Jeff said.

Lisa held tightly to his hand. She knew most of the kids, but there were others here she'd never seen. "Who are all these people?" she asked.

"Looks like some kids from Ridgview and Lake City." Jeff's eyes searched the room for Dillon.

"Hey Jeff, have a beer! Too bad about the game," Brad said, handing him a brown bottle.

"Hey man. No thanks, not tonight." They moved on and spotted Dillon in the kitchen.

"You need help?"

"Maybe later, man. Stick around will ya? It's getting pretty wild. Hey Lisa! How ya doing?" Dillon asked as he moved off.

It was amazing to Lisa how Dillon could manage to have these parties. His folks were gone a lot and there had never been any trouble, so maybe they didn't know. Or maybe they didn't care. She liked Dillon. He was always friendly and fun to be around. He and Jeff had been friends for years.

They drifted into the back part of the house. The bathroom door was open and Lisa saw a couple of girls in the mirror. They were holding something up to their nose. She grabbed Jeff's arm and nodded her head in their direction. "Jesus," he said. "That's Tiffany and Sherri. They're doing coke. They'll be wired in a couple of minutes."

"But where'd they get it?"

"Aw, it's everywhere. We'll probably see lots of it tonight. It isn't hard to get. Pool your money and you can get enough."

"Have you ever tried it?" Lisa asked.

"Coke? Yeah. Once. Boy, I didn't slow down till 5 a.m. It was fun, but I was so wiped out later I couldn't function. And I didn't like that. Besides, it messes you up for sports. Come on. Let's go back to the living room."

Things had quieted down some and Jeff looked around for Dillon. He saw a bunch of kids outside and then noticed a lot of headlights.

"What's going on?" he asked.

"These guys showed up from Lake City. Say they want to kick Dillon's ass. Come on," said one of Jeff's friends. "It's getting hot."

Dillon was outside with his friends. He was trying to talk but wasn't getting anywhere. Jeff was afraid he would blow, and Dillon had a real bad temper if he was pushed. There were about 10 guys from Lake City, and he spotted one kid he knew from basketball.

"How're you doin'?" he said.

They kid nodded back. "Hey Jeff," he said.

"Listen," Jeff said, "we don't want a fight and we don't want the cops. How 'bout you guys take off?"

The leader of the group said, "I got no problem with you. It's just Dillon. Come on man."

Looking over at Dillon Jeff said, "This isn't cool. Don't get into it here."

"This goes back a long time," Dillon said. "Look, Cal," he said turning to the group's leader, "I'll fight you but not here. We can settle it tomorrow. Just you and me."

Out of the corner of his eye Jeff saw one the guys from the back of the group move over toward them and suddenly grab Dillon, yelling, "Take your shot, Cal."

Cal stepped over and let fly a solid punch. Dillon was down before any of his friends knew what had happened. In a second everyone was punching everyone else. The air was wild with crazy energy as swinging arms and legs moved in and out of the shadows, the headlights, and the dust rising from their scuffling feet. You could hear punches being landed and "Fuck you," over and over again.

The girls watched, frozen and huddled together; a few were crying. Lisa tried to find Jeff but he was lost in the crowd of guys grabbing and slugging each other.

Suddenly the police siren was heard and someone yelled "Cops." Everything stopped as quickly as it had begun. The Lake City kids raced to their cars, backing up in a wild frenzy to get out fast. As they took off, several kids yelled "Fuck you Dillon. Fuck Galt," and they raced down the road, away from the sirens.

The Galt kids tried to pull themselves together and into the house. A few of them had blood on their faces and made their way to the bathroom. The girls ran around picking up beer and wine bottles. Dillon's eye and nose were smeared with blood; he threw some water on his face.

"Shit," he said. "Oh shit! My ass is cooked."

Jeff wiped some blood from his hand and straightened his jacket. Lisa came over and grabbed a hold of him. She was crying.

"Jeff, my god, that was awful. What are we going to do?" Thoughts raced through her head about being arrested and her folks coming down to the police station. Jeff held onto her but looked grim.

The police came up to the open door and walked in. "What's going on here?

Whose house is this?"

Dillon stepped forward. "It's mine," he said.

"Name? Age? Where are your folks?"

"Dillon Marway. 17. They're gone to Los Angeles." Dillon hardly looked at them. He was staring at the floor.

"What happened?"

"Me and my friends were here having a party and these kids from Lake City showed up and wanted to fight."

"What was the problem?"

"I dunno. They were pissed at me about some girl, I think. But we were just here, not doing anything."

"Did they look like they were gang members?"

"Naw. This didn't have anything to do with gangs."

"Well," the policeman went on, "it's a good thing someone called the police. This could have turned into a real brawl and your home might have ended up trashed. That would have been pretty hard to explain to your folks when they got home."

"Who called the police?" Dillon asked.

"A neighbor. You kids go to Galt?"

"Yeah," a bunch of them answered. Except for a few wasted kids in the back room everyone was standing around listening. They were very quiet.

"I went there myself," said a young officer. "Is Mr. Boon still there?"

"Yeah," several answered. "He's still around. He's pretty old, but he still kicks butt."

The policeman chuckled. Dillon was starting to feel a little easier, and then the policeman turned and looked right at him. "Listen. It's stupid to do this. To have a party. You were damned lucky. You know, you have a party and word gets around. You never know who's going to show up, and then things get out of hand. We could haul you and your friends in. We know there's been drinking and who knows what else. I'm not so old that I don't remember. We'll have to notify your parents. They have no business taking off and leaving you alone, unsupervised, and able to throw a party like this."

Dillon stood before them, his head down. Every once in a while he glanced at the officer. The rest of the kids just stood and listened.

"We're not going to arrest anyone but we may have to take a bunch or you down to the police station. When are your folks due home?" he said, addressing Dillon.

"Sunday night."

"What time?"

"About 10, I think."

"Okay. We'll have to find a place for you. Is there a neighbor you could stay with or a relative?"

Paula, a girl with long dark hair and a ring in her left nostril, spoke up. "He

34

could stay at my house. Our parents are good friends."

Dillon flashed her a grateful smile.

"All right, we'll look into it. Everyone line up and get ready to take a sobriety test. We're not letting anyone drive home who's been drinking."

The kids got in a line. A few muttered "Shit" and "Oh God, my parents are going to be so pissed."

Lisa held onto Jeff's arm, thankful that she and Jeff hadn't had anything to drink. They took their turn walking the line and answering questions, and the policeman said they were free to go. Jeff found Dillon in the kitchen talking to another policeman.

"Hey, Dillon. Excuse me. Could I just talk to my friend a second?" he asked. Hey man. I'm sorry. I'll come back tomorrow and help you clean up."

"You leaving?" Dillon said with a look of hurt on his face. He reached out and grabbed Jeff's arm. "Thanks man. This is really hard."

Lisa could see the tears in his eyes. "I'll come too," she said. She glanced back at the rest of the kids. Some were being let go, but most were getting into police cars to be taken downtown, where their parents would be called to come pick them up.

Driving back home, Jeff and Lisa were both quiet.

"What a fucked up night," Jeff finally said.

"Poor Dillon. School's going to be awful Monday."

"Life has sure gotten complicated. Sometimes I wish I was 10 years old again."

"I know." Lisa sighed. She leaned over against Jeff and put her hand on his thigh just as they pulled up to her house. "What time is it?"

"God. It's only midnight."

"Well, at least I'm home early. What are you going to tell your folks?"

"I'm not saying anything. But they'll find out. They've known Dillon's parents for ages. I'll wait and see. You know, we didn't do anything to get in trouble for. What are you going to tell yours?"

"Nothing. They probably won't find out. They don't really know anyone yet. I guess that's one advantage to being new."

Jeff leaned over and pulled Lisa to him. They sat together, neither saying anything. She reached up and kissed him.

"I better go in."

"Yeah. I know. G'night." He gave her a long deep kiss and reached under her sweater to her bare back. Lisa felt very warm and safe. It was hard to pull away.

"I'll see you tomorrow. Call me before you go up to Dillon's, okay?"

"Okay. Night, Lisa."

She got out of the car and shut the door. "Bye," she said reluctantly.

Lisa walked into the house and heard the T.V. Her mother was still up.

"Hi."

"Well hi. I'm glad you're home early. How was the game?"

"We lost. Jeff was in a bad mood. But he's okay now."

Her mother smiled. "Would you like something to eat?"

"No thanks. I'm tired. I'm going to bed. Oh Mom, I talked to Gwen the other night. We were wondering if there's any way I could go up and visit her over Christmas vacation. I sure would like to."

Her mother didn't say anything right away, but she had that look of concentration across her forehead. "It might work. Maybe you could take Stephanie."

Lisa frowned. "That's not exactly how I pictured it. . . She couldn't stay at Gwen's, you know."

"Oh, I know. Perhaps she could stay with her friend Carrie. I'll talk it over with your dad. It would be nice for everyone, especially since we'll both be working." Her mother's voice gathered more energy as she talked. Lisa could tell she was liking the idea.

"What about Jeff? Wouldn't you miss him?"

"Well, he's going to L.A. with his family."

"Oh." Her mother smiled again. "So that's part of it."

"Well, sure," Lisa said.

"You like him a lot, don't you"?" She paused. "Are you two having any problems? Anything you want to talk about?"

"No, everything's good, Mom." Lisa waited a moment. "Well, g'night," and she kissed her cheek.

"Night, dear. Sleep well," her mother said.

Lisa could hear a trace of disappointment in her voice.

○

The last two weeks before Christmas vacation whizzed by. There were final papers due, projects, basketball games and drama. In between it all, Jeff and Lisa had little time together except at school. Jeff's parents had had a long talk with him, and even though they believed him when he said he'd done nothing wrong, they had grounded him for the week. It was just as well; both he and Lisa had caught up on a lot of work. Jeff was leaving with his family two days after school was out and wouldn't be back until January 2nd. It was going to be a long stretch without each other.

Christmas seemed to get lost in the pressure of school. With all the homework and activity, Lisa had hardly felt a moment of Christmas spirit. She'd barely done any shopping—only a present for Jeff. Her family's Christmas tree was up, and seeing all the old familiar ornaments brought back warm feelings, but it just wasn't like Christmas used to be. The weather was cold and sunny, but this new house simply didn't have the comforting ways of her old house in Eugene. Lisa felt a kind of vacant space in her life, and she was grateful that she was going to be able to spend time with Gwen and her old friends, after all.

Saturday night was the last time she and Jeff would be together until the New Year, and Lisa was excited. They were going out to dinner and exchanging presents. Lisa was wearing her black dress that was slit up the side. With Kathy's help, she'd fixed her hair in a French braid with a few loose curls at the side. When Jeff saw her that night, he didn't hide his pleasure.

"Wow! You look great," he said, giving her a gentle squeeze about the waist.

That night they talked about school and Christmas. It felt very special to be out alone in a nice place, eating fine food. The waiter took their plates away and brought over a dessert tray filled with chocolate cakes, mousses, and dishes of whipped cream and berries.

"We also have ice cream if you'd like," he said.

Lisa looked at Jeff and a big smile spread across her face. He winked at her.

"Go on, pick one. I'll have a bite."

She selected one called "chocolate supreme," a dark cake with raspberries and whipped cream. They looked at each other and laughed and Lisa felt a warm flush of pleasure.

"You know, I'm glad we moved to California after all."

"Me too," he answered and squeezed her hand.

After dinner they drove back to his house to watch a movie. Since Dillon's party, neither one of them had felt much like socializing with a lot of other kids. Tonight was the first night they'd been out, and they felt like being alone.

The house was quiet, and they both kicked off their shoes and flopped on the couch to watch a Spike Lee movie. It was good, but half way through they found themselves entangled with each other, oblivious to the film. The night had been so special that Lisa felt close to forgetting all her wise decisions about sex and birth control. Kissing Jeff, feeling his hands caressing her breasts, the hardness of his crotch lying against hers, she felt incapable of controlling her feelings.

"Jeff. . . Jeff. . . don't," was all she could barely murmur.

Slowly, Jeff stopped moving his hands and paused to breathe. "God. This is getting too difficult," he said, pulling away and straightening up.

They both sat quietly for a while just hearing their breathing and the voices from the movie.

Lisa leaned over and kissed him quickly on the cheek. "Thanks," she said getting up. "Hey, I've got something for you. Just a minute." Pausing to pull down and straighten her dress and hair, she glanced at her reflection in the mirror on the wall. "Whew! It looks like I've been in a tornado." She noticed the pillow over his lap to cover his erection; this was tough—for both of them.

"Now, close your eyes and hold out your hand. You don't need two hands. It's not that big!"

He opened his eyes, looked at the small box wrapped in sparkling red paper and smiled up at her.

"Come on. Open it!"

He took off the ribbon and paper and lifted the lid off the box. Inside was a gold chain with a small disc in the center. He looked at it closely. On one side it had the initials "J.B." and, turning it over, he read "L.H."

"Lisa, this is so cool. Thank you," he said reaching up and taking her hand, pulling her down on the couch next to him. He gave her a long warm kiss and whispered, "I really like it."

Lisa felt so pleased. It had been a good choice.

"Now your turn. Wait here." Jeff got up and left the room.

Lisa sat quietly looking at the chain she had given him. She'd never given anything like that to a boy—or to anyone—before. It felt like a commitment, something lasting. She took a deep breath and closed her eyes. How could she be here now, in Jeff's living room when four months ago she didn't even know him? Five months ago she wasn't even living in California. Life was strange, more strange than she ever realized.

He came back to the room saying, "Now you close your eyes. Put your hands out."

She put out her hands and felt a large box. It was heavy. "Jeff, what did you buy?"

"Just open it."

Slowly, she took off the ribbon and paper. She felt a strange mixture of excitement and nervousness. It was obviously something to wear. God, she hoped it wasn't a negligee or something, Lifting the lid, she saw a mound of white tissue paper. She ruffled through it and felt something soft. It was pink and turquoise with silver threads and made of wool—a gorgeous sweater with Indian-like designs.

"Jeff, I can't believe it, " she exclaimed holding it up to see its full size. In doing so, she heard a slight clink.

"Hey, you dropped something."

She glanced down and held up a shiny, silver chain. It was a bracelet. She looked at it closely. It was almost a braid of silver and as the light caught it, it turned bright and then dark and shadowy. Dangling from one small link was a silver 'L'.

"Jeff, it's so beautiful!"

"You really like it?"

"My god, I love it," she said. "It's the prettiest bracelet I've ever had. And the sweater. . . Jeff, you went crazy!" She turned and threw her arms about him, squeezing him tight. They kissed a passionate, happy kiss.

"Merry Christmas," Jeff said.

"I'll never forget this. Merry Christmas, Jeff."

Just then they heard a car drive up and a garage door open. Lisa felt her heart sink. She looked at Jeff and saw his face mirrored her feelings.

"Damn!" he whispered. "Why'd they come home so early?"

Lisa straightened her clothes again and managed a smile as Jeff's parents came into the room.

"Lisa! How are you? We haven't seen you for a while. Merry Christmas!" Jeff's mother was young looking for her 45 years. She had short blond hair and a good figure to go with her small frame. She always made Lisa feel welcome. "Oh, what's this?" she said looking at the sweater.

"Isn't it beautiful! And this too," Lisa said, holding up the bracelet.

"Jeff, they're lovely," she said, looking glowingly at her son. He was their youngest child, the older one gone from the house, and Lisa knew Jeff often got special treatment from his mom.

Jeff's father came into the room. "Lisa. Merry Christmas! How are things? Did you two have a good evening?"

"Just great," Lisa answered. Jeff's father was different from his mother, more formal and removed, but he was always nice to Lisa.

"How was your dinner?" he said turning to Jeff.

"Good, real good," Jeff answered.

"So, what are you watching?" he said, glancing at the crumpled tissue paper on the couch and the T.V.

"Ah, it's a Spike Lee film," Jeff said. They all looked over at the same time; there was a moment of silence as they watched Spike Lee cooling off his girlfriend with ice cubes.

"But we kind of lost track of it." Jeff looked around and his father frowned. An awkward moment encompassed them all.

Jeff's mother finally said, "Bob, it's a good movie. Remember, we saw it. The one about living in New York, all the problems, the different ethnic groups. Anyway, let's go to bed. I'm beat and I think I had a tad too much celebration. Go ahead you two, finish watching it."

"Naw. It's too late now. Lisa's got to get home."

"What are you doing over vacation, Lisa?"

"I'm going to Oregon for a while, to see some of my old friends."

"How great! Well, have a good time. Merry Christmas," she said going down the hall.

"Thanks. Merry Christmas," she called out to both of them.

Lisa and Jeff looked at each other. She felt such a mixture of feelings: excitement, nervousness, disappointment for the moment that had been lost between them.

"I don't really have to go home just yet," she said.

"I know. But I want to get out of here. Let's go."

Lisa carefully put her sweater back in the box. "Here, help me put this on, will you?" she said holding the bracelet. She held out her wrist and Jeff fastened the silver bracelet, fumbling a little with the clasp.

"Here, your turn," he said holding out the chain. He turned his back and squatted down so she could see what she was doing. "How's it look?" he said with a big smile.

"You look completely handsome!"

That night they sat for a long time in the car in front of her house. Their kissing was passionate and they held each other intensely knowing they wouldn't be together for a long time. Jeff's hands explored Lisa's breasts and moved down along her thighs. He reached up inside her dress and this time Lisa didn't stop him. He was stymied by the panty hose.

"God, these things are awful."

Lisa giggled. "They are, and they're hard to take off. Anyway, they protect me from beasts like you," she said, kissing him. She could feel his fingers move over her crotch, touch the hair growing there; she felt herself growing wet. "Jeff, I want to, but not like this. Not here, not yet."

"Lisa, I'm going crazy," he said. He reached over and took her hand, putting it on his crotch. "Feel this," he whispered. "Touch it."

She felt his penis. It seemed about to burst through his pants. He unzipped himself and took it out. In the pale light from the distant street lamp, it looked so large and white. Lisa felt it tentatively, then placed her whole hand around it. Jeff groaned.

"God that feels good," he said.

Under the soft skin Lisa felt what seemed like long cords.

"Move your hand," Jeff said. She did and his penis grew larger, standing upright. She felt a few drops of something and the next thing she knew Jeff was moaning and clenching his teeth and all this white stuff was spouting down on Lisa's hand. She gasped. It was amazing to see that happen. Lisa forgot about her own excitement; she was transfixed by Jeff's.

"Lisa. Wow, that was so great. Thanks," he said, kissing her. "Whew! What an explosion. What a mess!" He looked around for Kleenex but couldn't find any.

"Wait a minute," she said reaching for her sweater box.

"Lisa, don't use your sweater!"

"You dork!" she said grabbing the tissue paper from inside and wiping off her hand. He took some too and wiped off his pants.

He looked at her and gave her a slight smile. "Are you okay? I hope that wasn't too gross."

"No, I'm fine. It was all pretty amazing."

A pungent smell pervaded the car, and Jeff rolled down the windows, taking a deep breath.

"I have a lot to learn," Lisa said.

"You're doing great, Lisa," Jeff said and held her close. "I'm going to miss you. I won't see you till next year." They kissed a deliciously warm kiss.

"Thank you for my presents, Jeff."

"Me too," he replied. "Especially that last one."

"I love you," she whispered getting out of the car.

"Don't forget me in Oregon," he said.

○

A couple of weeks later, she cried while leaving Eugene, but she also felt a kind of relief when she got on the train with her sister. For at least two hours Stephanie talked off and on about how much fun she'd had. Lisa enjoyed her sister's enthusiasm and her simple view of things. After a while they both slept, then alternately read and looked out the window. Lisa was glad to have the time to think; she had a lot to sort out.

Their parents met them in Oakland and Lisa sensed that they had changed while she had been gone. They seemed more relaxed, especially her dad. She watched him while he drove. He was a nice looking man with a long straight nose, dark eyes and hair that was beginning to gray a bit. His formerly straight and firm jaw had softened due to some weight he had gained. It showed in the stomach he had acquired too. He was getting older and Lisa suddenly felt sad. The truth was she really had spent almost no time with him since they'd moved to California. How could that be? Her mind wandered back to that play they had read in English class—*Our Town*. The girl, Emily, had been right; humans really don't appreciate life while they're living it.

"So, what have you been up to, Dad?" she asked.

He gave her what felt like a grateful smile; Lisa knew he often felt left out by the three women in his life.

"Oh, just the same old things—work, work, and work. But I am resolving to go on a diet," he said.

Her mother turned around from the front seat, and the three of them burst into laughter; her dad's losing weight had become an old joke.

It felt good riding home in the car. The long train trip had lessened the pain of leaving Oregon, and the closer Lisa got to home, the less she thought about Gwen, Sam and all the kids, and the more she thought of Jeff and her California school. As they crossed the Richmond Bridge, Lisa glanced over toward San Francisco. There was no fog, only a slight wind and sailboats everywhere; the bay sparkled. It was a gorgeous place to live.

○

After winter vacation, school started up with intensity and pressure. The teachers wanted to crowd all the material they hadn't covered into the last two weeks before finals, and Lisa was inundated with studying and papers to write plus drama rehearsal. Jeff was in the same situation with school and basketball.

Finally, Saturday came, and while getting ready to go out with Jeff that night, Lisa realized she was feeling a lot of excitement and hesitancy. They went to a movie, which made the night special because they seldom ever had twelve dollars to spend, but it was also special because it was their first real "date" since before Christmas. It was wonderful to sit next to Jeff, hold his hand and occasionally lean over and kiss him.

The movie was a love story about a woman who was happily married to her husband but then the first real love of her life suddenly showed up. She thought he had died in the Viet Nam War, but he had been found in a POW camp and returned home four years later. When he called her on the phone, she went completely limp and from that point on she was totally confused and got herself into a lot of painful experiences. She wound up pregnant, never knowing who the father was. Eventually, she left both men and decided to dedicate her life to raising her daughter.

Lisa cried at the end and Jeff was irritated.

"That was so good," Lisa said, squeezing Jeff's hand as they walked to his car. He didn't say anything, and they sat quietly for a few moments in front seat. "Didn't you like it?" she asked.

"It was okay. The acting was good, but I don't like movies that make everything so complicated." He started the car and they drove off.

"But something like that could happen," Lisa said glancing out the window at the familiar shops and homes.

"Oh maybe, but I think you know when you really love someone." He pulled over onto a side street parking under a tall tree. He turned and looked at her. "C'mere," he said reaching over and drawing her close.

They kissed a long deep kiss and Lisa felt a deep fluttering inside. She moved closer to Jeff and his hands caressed her back and shoulders.

"Lisa, I missed you all vacation. I kept thinking about that last time we were together and I kept thinking about what it would be like if we — you know, did more."

Lisa was turned on, there was no doubt about that. Jeff's words jumped out at her. She too had thought about their last time together. Kissing and holding Jeff that night, she knew she loved him. She loved the soft way his eyes looked at her, his large hands with the dark hairs on the back, his wonderful smell—like a fresh shower and something of the woods. She sighed. With their bodies pressed together she knew Jeff was wanting her. It was all she could do not to give in to his wants. Her own body wanted him too. She felt all hot and moist, almost a throbbing.

Jeff was becoming aroused and Lisa confused. If she talked about how she felt, Jeff would become upset, but if she didn't say anything, she felt like she would be lying and she knew she wouldn't feel comfortable.

"Jeff," she ventured. "Don't you think it's important to be honest with each other?"

"Sure I do," he said nuzzling her with a kiss behind her ear. "Shh, let's talk later."

Lisa was squirming. "Jeff, you know I care about you, but we can't go any further now. We're not safe."

"I've got something," he said, patting his pocket. She could hear the crackle sound of a wrapped condom.

Oh god. He was ready.

"Jeff. Jeff," she said taking a big breath, "wait just a little longer. . . " Lisa knew she was at a crossroads; she had to make a decision.

O

If you want Lisa to say no to having sex, turn to **ABSTAIN** printed on green paper.

If you want Lisa to go ahead and have safer sex with Jeff, turn to **SAFER SEX** printed on blue paper.

SEX

But the thought was lost in being with Jeff, in his kisses and warmth. His knee came up between her legs and she moved back and forth, her crotch becoming moist. He moved to pull down her pants and she helped. In the next moment, she felt his penis hard and long, pushing its way between her legs, pushing its way into her vagina. It hurt. She felt a sharp pain and she wanted to stop; it felt so strange and large. But she felt Jeff's urgency and so opened her legs wider, and then he was inside her and moving and the brief thought said, *so this is it; I love him.* And then it felt like he exploded, and he clutched her and she was bewildered and worried as he collapsed on top of her, breathing heavily and kissing her. She looked up at him. "Jeff?" she said.

"Wow. My god."

"I love you."

"I love you too," he said, and they both lay quietly

Then Lisa felt a wetness between her legs. She saw her bedroom walls and then thought of her parents and her sister. "Oh my god, Jeff," she said. "Come on. Get up." She hurriedly pulled up her pants. She was embarrassed and awkward. This was her bedroom, her bed. She saw her stuffed animals, the bear she'd had since she was three. She felt scared and started to cry. Jeff reached up.

"Hey, Lisa. Come here. I'm sorry it happened so fast. It'll be okay."

She loved feeling his arms around her, but she also felt torn, nervous. She smiled at him. "I know. It's just not . . . I dunno. I'll be all right."

Feeling like she had to check on her other life, she opened the door and went down the hall to the family room. "Hi, Steph," she said.

Stephanie didn't even look up from watching "Full House." "Hi," she answered.

Lisa wondered if Stephanie could tell what had just happened to her. "You hungry?" Lisa asked.

"No."

Lisa got a glass of water and went back to her room, leaving the door open. Jeff was standing up, looking at something on her desk. He smiled when she came in and he put his arms around her. "You okay?" he asked.

She nodded her head and held onto him. She looked at the bed. It was all rumpled and there was a dark stain on the spread. She glanced at the clock. Her folks would he home in about 10 minutes.

"Listen, you better go," she said. "My folks will be home really soon."

"Okay." He held her and kissed her sweetly on the temples. "I love you," he whispered. Her heart felt warm and very full.

She stayed in her room and heard him say, "G'bye Steph," as he left. Then she grabbed her bed spread, gathered up some laundry and started the washing machine. In the bathroom, she turned on the shower and stood under the warm water. She felt confused. Was that it? Did that mean she was no longer a virgin? She guessed so. She had to call Gwen! She was going to be so surprised!

O

During the next few weeks it felt as though a new bond connected them. English class was the best; they usually managed to sit next to each other and endured the jokes from their friends. Even Mr. T. would sometimes make reference to "young love" and look their way. So far, however, no one had said anything that indicated they knew that Jeff and Lisa were "going together" in every sense of the word.

Kathy walked to 6th period with her saying, "Boy, Jeff has really fallen for you. I can't believe it!"

Lisa smiled and said, "He's a great guy. Thank goodness we ended up in the same English class! And went out that night with you guys!"

Kathy had become a real friend and had even convinced Lisa to try out for the school play. Unbelievably, Lisa had gotten a part. Life was looking great! She wanted to say more, to be able to talk to Kathy, tell her everything, ask her questions about Jeff's past. But the experience with Jeff was still too new, and she just couldn't put it into words yet. She wondered if Jeff had. She'd have to ask him but they hadn't even talked about it to each other yet.

Several nights later, he came over, and they sat for a while in the family room and tried to be alone, but her sister and parents kept walking through, making small talk. Finally, Jeff had to leave and she walked with him outside. The air was cold and clear with a million stars shining overhead. Jeff pulled her close and they kissed a long, slow, deep kiss. She could feel her own body grow warm and knew Jeff was feeling the same.

"God, I can't wait to be with you again," he said. "Are you okay?"

She kissed him and pressed against him. "Yes, really. Listen, have you told anyone yet . . . about . . . about us?"

"No, have you?"

"Just Gwen, in Oregon. I had to tell her, but no one else. Let's not say anything, okay? I want it to be just for us."

"Okay. You know, I'd like to stay but I've got to get home. There's a party Friday night at Dillon's. Want to go?"

"If you do, but I'd rather just be with you."

He kissed her once more. "Maybe we can do both. I'll see you tomorrow."

That night as she lay in bed she listened to Whitney Houston and slowly went over every detail of the time she and Jeff had spent in her room. What if she was pregnant? The idea cast a dark shadow on her memory. God, they had to talk about it because it could happen again. She thought it had been too close to her period. Even so. . . .it was possible. Lisa knew they had to be smart!

O

The party at Dillon's started off wild right from the beginning. His parents were gone and lots of kids showed up with beer, wine coolers, and marijuana. Lisa drank coke and talked to Kathy and some of the other girls. She was starting to feel really

46

comfortable with them, almost like she belonged. They slept over at each other's houses and exchanged clothes and C.D.s. Jeff had made all the difference in her life. School was going good too, and her parents had relaxed a little.

Someone offered her a wine cooler and, for a change, she took it. It tasted sweet and cold; the air was stuffy in the house. There were so many bodies packed in, and kids were in every room, laughing and dancing. They all felt so free, with Christmas vacation just a couple of weeks away. Jeff came up, kissed her and whispered, "I vant to be alone with you so I can bite you on the neck!" She laughed and pushed him away, but felt a lovely, warm feeling all over. Jeff was a little high, she could tell. He was just a bit louder, his movements a bit larger. She'd never seen him high and it was funny; she wanted to join him and grabbed another wine cooler, and they danced and shared it together.

She felt like her eyes were glowing so brightly that they were spotlights. She hugged Jeff, "We've got to talk, Jeffie," she said laughing.

"Okay, Lissie, let's talk. Not here though; let's go outside."

It was freezing out in the backyard, and Lisa saw Kathy and Paul over by the corner of the house. They were so close their bodies made only one shadow. She smiled and squeezed Jeff's hand.

The wine coolers helped the words tumble out. "Jeff, listen, we've got to be smart."

"We are smart," he said kissing her neck and around her ears. "We picked each other. What if you had never moved here? What if we hadn't had English together? I'd still be hanging around doing dumb things." He kissed her again, and this time their tongues explored each other's mouths and Lisa felt his hands move under her sweater.

"Jeff," she said pulling away. "Listen, we've got to use something."

"Huh? Use what? What are you talking about?" he said kissing her again.

"Jeff, you know. We've got to use condoms or something."

"Condoms? I thought you said you were okay!"

"Okay? What do you mean *okay?*"

"I meant were you taking the pill?"

"The pill? How would I get the pill? I mean, I've never done that. I don't know anything about it."

"Oh god," he said. "Well, do you think you're okay?"

"You mean *pregnant?*"

"Yeah."

"No, I don't think so."

"God, Lisa, I hope not," he said, sighing and holding her. "I'd feel so bad." They stood very close together, holding each other.

"We've got to be smart."

"I know. I just thought you were taking care of it."

She was silent. *Should I have 'taken care of it'? Should I have known?* She wasn't thinking too clearly, but somehow she knew she should have. *But he should have too.*

"Jeff? Was I your first?" she said reaching for his hand.

He was quiet. "You were—really—but once, last summer, I met this girl I didn't care about and we just did it. It wasn't so great. She was two years older and knew what she was doing, but I didn't care about her. It wasn't anything like with you. How 'bout you? Am I your first?"

"You know you are," she said, putting her arms around his waist and her head on his shoulder. "What are we going to do? I mean, what's next, and what about AIDS?"

"God, Lisa. I don't have AIDS and neither do you. We'll go to a clinic and get the pill, if you're okay with that. Or I'll use a condom if I have to."

"But how you do know you don't have AIDS? Maybe that girl had AIDS. How do you know?"

"I just know. Come on now, lay off."

Even in her somewhat fuzzy state, Lisa knew you couldn't 'just tell,' but she decided not to say anything else. "I wonder if I should tell my mother?" she said.

"Why would you tell your mother? God, I'd be so embarrassed if you did that. How could I show my face at your house if you did? Come on, let's go back inside. Enough of this heavy shit."

They went back in the warm house and were quiet for a while, then began dancing, and soon they were laughing.

○

Lisa made an appointment at the women's clinic in the neighboring town, but couldn't get in until Thursday; Jeff said he would drive her. When Thursday came, she waited for him after school. He had tryouts for basketball and was anxious and excited. "I should be done by 4:30, so just wait," he'd said. She did some homework in the library and talked to a couple of kids, then wandered over by the gym. It was 4:15 and the boys were still shooting balls and playing 15-minute games. She grew nervous and chewed the inside of her lip. She stood in the doorway and watched, hoping to catch Jeff's eye. He signaled to her, raising his five fingers for five more minutes. He was sweaty, his hair plastered on his forehead, and he watched the ball with an intensity she'd never seen in him before. He was fast on the court and good at maneuvering the ball in to the guy under the basket. It looked to Lisa as though he got more rebounds than anyone else. She glanced at her watch—4:25.

Finally the coach blew the whistle, and it was 4:30. Jeff came over saying, "I'll grab my stuff and be right there."

"Don't bother," she said. "It's too late." She turned away, feeling thoroughly pissed.

Jeff stood still, breathing heavily. "Are you sure? Maybe you could still get in."

"No, I couldn't. They told me to be on time. You are such an ass!"

"Wait! I'll give you ride," he said, turning and hurrying toward the locker room.

She could hear the guys yelling from inside. How could he have screwed this up? How could basketball be more important than birth control?

He came out of the gym, his hair newly wet. "Fastest shower in the west!" he said.

Lisa was silent.

"Lisa, I'm sorry. I didn't know tryouts would take so long." He put his arm around her. "Well, say something."

"I just don't get it! This is so important. How could you screw up like this?"

"I didn't do it on purpose, you know! Come on. It'll work out."

They drove to her house in silence and kissed goodbye. "I'll call you. Lisa, make another appointment. Okay?"

She went inside and heard her sister in the kitchen but went straight to her room and slammed her door. She threw her books and her jacket on the floor. She flopped on the bed, and the tears came pouring out. The next thing she knew, her mother was knocking on her door and coming in.

"Lisa? Honey, are you okay?"

She looked up at her mother, who was still dressed for work. She looked good with her hair pulled back in a clip and gold hoop earrings. Some gray was showing by her temples and her face now showed new lines, especially around her dark brown eyes.

"What is it? Is it Jeff?"

Lisa wanted to talk, but the words wouldn't come. She nodded her head.

"Did you have a fight?"

"Sort of," Lisa said.

"Well, you've been spending a lot of time together. Maybe you need a break from each other. . . I hope you come talk to me if you have any questions."

Lisa thought the last thing she needed was to be away from Jeff, even if he was a total jerk. She wanted to be with him. All the time. And she wanted to talk with her mother about missing the appointment and about sex and birth control, but she didn't feel ready to include her—not right this minute.

"It'll be okay," she said hearing Jeff's words in her head.

○

The next day she called the clinic from school and made an appointment, but couldn't get in until Wednesday of the following week. Jeff promised he would be free to go with her.

"So, do you feel better now?" he asked, standing by the telephone.

She turned, looked at him, and smiled. "Yes I do, much better." She put her arms about his waist as they walked to English class. They agreed to stay home and study Friday night and go out Saturday.

○

Saturday there was another party, this time at Brad's house, but Lisa and Jeff only stayed a couple of hours and left early because they weren't in a party mood. They went to Lyon's and had a coke, talking about the kids, school and basketball. Lisa looked at Jeff. He had on that same beautiful blue sweater.

"I remember that sweater," she said. "You wore it the first day of school."

"I did?"

"Yeah, and I was dying to know your name."

"You noticed me right away?"

She nodded and sipped her coke. "Did you notice me?"

"Yeah, but I don't remember what you were wearing. You were the new girl and I liked your hair."

"You did?" she said, laughing.

A couple of kids came in and joined them, and they all joked around for a while. Jeff reached under the table and put his hand on Lisa's knee. He stroked it a few times and leaned against her. "Well guys, it's time to go. Lisa's gotta be home early. See ya," he said, getting up.

"Jeff, I don't have to be home till one," she said when they were outside.

"I know," he answered, hugging her close. "Come on, let's go to my house. My folks are gone."

She'd been in Jeff's house several times. It was closer to the school and much larger than Lisa's. His family had lived in town a long time and had been able to buy when prices were cheaper. They went to the kitchen and Jeff found some crackers to munch on.

"You want something?"

"Do you have any hot chocolate?"

He rummaged around in a cupboard and came up with a packet. "Here, how's this?"

"Great," she said, putting some water on to boil. "Would your parents be mad if they knew we were here alone?"

"Oh, they'd probably be okay with it. Not thrilled, but okay."

"It's nice to be alone," she said. They moved closer to each other and pressed the full length of their bodies together. Their kissing was long and passionate. Then the tea kettle whistled and they moved apart, laughing self-consciously. "I'm saved by the whistle," she said, pouring the water into her cup. Jeff took her hand and they made their way to his room.

There was a jumble of clothes on the floor, books and papers strewn around. He put on a Marvin Gaye tape. Lisa smiled at him. They sat on his bed, each feeling a level of tension and excitement. Lisa sipped her hot chocolate. She wanted to say something but was unsure exactly what. She put her cup down and they began kissing. The music "Let's Get It On, " enveloped them, and they lay down on his bed. Lisa could feel Jeff's hard-on, and his knee slowly came up between her legs. She felt a kind of hot ache and kissed him deeply. His hands moved under her shirt and to her breasts. He kissed her neck and moved his head down to her chest.

"Jeff, Jeff, we can't. It's not safe."

"Shhh," he said. "It's okay. I've got something." He turned aside and fumbled in his bedside table drawer.

She heard the crackle sound of foil and knew he had a condom. Jeff's back was to her and he had pulled off his sweat pants. She suddenly didn't feel so excited any more.

"Boy, this isn't easy," Jeff mumbled. Then he turned toward her and held Lisa close to him, kissing her again. She could feel the tension between them, but kissing helped it diminish and soon she was feeling very intense again, thinking of Jeff, wanting to please him. He tugged at her pants, and she helped pull them down. Soon he was lying on top of her, and she could feel the hardness of his penis as it pushed its way between her legs and into her vagina. She had a brief thought that she didn't feel the condom and then he was moving rapidly inside of her and they were kissing, and then Jeff's whole body jerked and he let out a great sigh and collapsed on top of her. Lisa felt a kind of heady confusion, excitement, disbelief, love. She hugged Jeff tightly and kissed his face

Jeff moved and kissed her back, "Oh Lisa," he said rolling over on his side. Then she heard him say "Oh no," and she felt a wetness all over her legs.

"Jeff, what is it? What's wrong?"

"Oh god, it broke or it came off."

She felt herself grow tight, and a fear flooded her mind. "Jeff, do you think? I mean . . ."

"I don't know," he said. "God, I'm so sorry. I thought it was on okay. I didn't want anything to happen." He pulled off the soggy condom that was leaking semen.

Lisa felt angry and scared, but Jeff's being upset was bothering her more. "Jeff, maybe it'll be okay," she said as she moved off the bed and pulled up her pants, feeling the stickiness between her legs.

The tape had come to an end and started on the second side. Jeff moved, pulled up his pants, and stood up. They put their arms around each other.

"Keep your fingers crossed," he said.

○

Lisa woke the next morning feeling ugly. She tried to recapture the warm, loving feeling that she usually had when she thought of Jeff, but it was tarnished and cold. She felt something wonderful had left her life. How could she have done that last night? How could Jeff have screwed up like that?

She went out to the kitchen, where her mom and dad were reading the paper. "Morning, kiddo," her dad said. He looked tired, the lines on his face were deeper, his hair rumpled. She saw so little of him lately. Her mother looked washed out too, and her bathrobe was worn and old; still, they both seemed in pretty good spirits.

"Hi," she answered without any feeling; the last thing Lisa wanted was to talk but, of course, the inevitable question came.

"Did you have fun last night? What did you do?"

"We went to a party. I was home by one."

" I know. I heard you. I tried to stay up but I was so tired. Come in and wake me next time, will you?"

"Lisa, your mom and I have been talking about Christmas vacation. We'd like to go to the snow, but we both have to work. We were thinking maybe you and Stephanie might like to go up and visit your old friends in Eugene. What do you think?"

Lisa suddenly brightened. "Oh, I would love to!" She could see Gwen, and all her friends. Then she thought of Jeff. How could she be gone from him a week or more? "That would be so great! I just wish there was some way Jeff could come too. I'd love to have him meet everyone up there."

Her mother and father looked at each other with a slight frown. "Well, I don't think that would work out too well. Maybe it would be good to have a little break from each other," her mother said. "You two certainly have been together a lot."

Lisa felt the edge, the criticism, in her mother's voice. "Oh come on, Mom. We're not together so much. You should see some of the kids. They're together all the time. Besides, Jeff has basketball now. He's not going to be around like he has been."

"Oh?" her father said. "I didn't know he played basketball. We'll have to go to a game sometime. I used to play myself."

Lisa mumbled, "Yeah, okay," and went off to her room. "Can I call Gwen and tell her?"

"Tell her what?" said Stephanie, dragging into the kitchen. She had on her old pajama bottoms and a Trail Blazers tee shirt. Her hair was all tangled.

"God, comb your hair, Stephanie," Lisa said. "You're a mess! We might get to go up to Eugene to visit everyone over Christmas."

"Really? All of us?"

"Just you amd me," Lisa said in a whisper to Stephanie. "And, you have me to thank."

"How do you figure that?" Stephanie asked.

"Cause, Mom and Dad are trying to get me away from Jeff. If it weren't for me, we wouldn't be going!"

Lisa grabbed the portable phone and quickly closed her bedroom door. It felt so good to have something to look forward to. She thought of calling Jeff but wasn't ready to, not after last night. That was not going to happen again. She dialed Gwen's number.

○

On Wednesday after school Jeff was ready to take Lisa to the clinic to get birth control. On the way, they were both nervous and made small talk about other kids, classes, and basketball. Jeff parked the car, and as he turned off the engine, he looked at Lisa and said, "I'm glad we're doing this. And I'm sorry about the other night. That'll never happen again." He leaned over and kissed her on the forehead.

She felt a surge of quiet warmth and looked into his eyes. "It's okay."

○

Lisa waited well over a week for her period to begin so she could start taking her birth control pills. What was wrong? It was weird. She felt nervous, jumpy, and longed to talk to someone other than Jeff. The whole subject of birth control had become awkward. The truth was, they were both sick of it.

She managed to get out of drama rehearsal fifteen minutes early and went to a pay phone at the deli across the street from the school. She dialed the number of the birth control clinic, all the time glancing around to see if there was anyone around who could overhear her.

"Could I speak to a doctor, please?"

"Our doctors are all busy now. Could I help you? Is there a problem?" said a pleasant voice. Lisa wondered if it was the same woman who had talked to her in the office.

"Well," Lisa stammered. "Ah. . . ah, I came a while back to get the pill, and I've been waiting to get my period so I could start taking it, but I haven't started yet and I'm wondering if maybe I should just go ahead and take it anyway."

"How late are you?"

"A little over two weeks."

"Is that usual for you?"

"No, I'm really not ever late."

"Have you had sexual intercourse? Is there a chance you could be pregnant?"

Lisa felt herself go white-hot all over. Her heart was pounding. "I. . . I don't think so. Well, maybe." *My god, could that be the reason? Pregnant—just when I went to the clinic and got the pill? When I was doing the right thing?* She felt shaky all over, and her throat was dry. She knew if she talked, she would cry. There was a silence on the phone.

"Perhaps you'd like to come in for a pregnancy test and talk to someone," the lady said.

"Maybe. I'll call back," she said, barely able to get the words out before she hung up the phone. She leaned her head against the glass wall and stood perfectly still for what must have been minutes. *I have to get control of myself. What should I do? What is next?*

She walked away trying to pull her thoughts together. When could she get to the clinic? How much would it cost? What should she tell Jeff? She walked on. She could get one of those home tests. Then she'd know if she was or not. Maybe she wasn't. She shouldn't get all worked up about this. Were those tests accurate?

She turned and retraced her steps; it was two blocks to the nearest drug store.

Searching the pharmaceutical department, Lisa finally found the pregnancy test kits. She tried to appear casual and glanced at the opposite shelves that displayed feminine hygiene products. She looked around —no one else was on the aisle. Her eyes swept over the different boxes, and she grabbed one with pink and blue colors. It was $15.95! It would take most of the money she had put aside for her haircut! Well shit, what was more important here? She also took a box of Tampax, just in case.

She avoided the long lines at the front of the store and bought the kit at the drug counter. She was grateful no one else was around and breathed a sigh of relief as the clerk slipped her purchases into a plastic bag. Leaving, she saw a couple of kids she knew from school, but they were clear at the other end of the store.

O

"Hi, Steph," she said coming in the front door. Stephanie was at the kitchen table eating cookies and an ice cream sandwich.

"Hi," she mumbled.

Lisa hurried back to her bedroom and put the bag on the floor by the end of her bed. She glanced in her mirror on the way out the door; she looked awful.

"So, what's doing?" she said coming back into the kitchen.

"I'm just trying to do this stupid homework. I hate it. Miss Holtz is so stupid. We have to look up 40 words by tomorrow. She thinks we don't ever have anything else to do. And she's so dumb."

The phone rang and Stephanie went to answer it. Lisa could tell it wasn't for her. She took a cookie and idly looked at Stephanie's word list "irrevocable. . . abolish . . . declaration." She read the words, but none of them registered in her brain. She felt strangely removed from everything.

"That was Jessica. We're going to share the words. Want to help me?" Stephanie said. "What's 'abolish' mean?"

"Ah. . . .to do away with."

"What about 'irrevocable'?"

"Listen, Steph, I just can't think right now. Maybe later, okay?" *Yeah, later, when I find out if my life is over, if my situation is irrevocable.*

She took the box out of the bag and went in the bathroom, locking the door. Reading the instructions, she felt her underarms and hands grow sweaty. She whispered aloud the steps to follow: "1) Place a small amount of your urine in the shallow indentation. 2) Add two drops of the solution from the bottle provided. 3) Watch to see if the solution turns pink; if it does, pregnancy is indicated."

Lisa held her breath as she watched the yellow urine turn pink. *Oh my god.*

No. No. She tightly closed her eyes, feeling the stinging tears. *Oh my god.* She opened them, praying she had seen the wrong color. But there it was—clearly pink. A sob burst from her lips. She turned on the water faucet full force and cried a long, long time.

◯

Later, after she had carefully wrapped up the pregnancy kit box in a paper bag and stashed it in the back of her closet, Lisa lay on her bed and thought. She should tell Jeff. She should talk to her mother. She should do her English homework. How far along was she? She counted back—it must be about a month, maybe six weeks. She had trouble focusing. There had been two times : that one time in her bedroom, the first, and the other time when the condom came off. But she'd had a period in between the two, hadn't she? She was sure she had. So, it must have been the second time and that was just over two weeks ago. Was the test really accurate? Even if you were just two weeks pregnant? Then she remembered the words "Accurate even in the first month of pregnancy." Maybe it was wrong. Did that mean during the first weeks? She needed to get another test at the clinic. But she didn't have any more money. Jeff would help. He had to. And then what? *If I'm pregnant, what will I do?*

She'd have to tell her mother. The thought of the conversation made her shudder as she imagined her mother freaking out. The last thing she wanted to do was hurt her parents. This year had been so hard. She had really screwed things up. The tears rolled down Lisa's cheeks. She could never go back to being the same girl in her family—not if she told them. And if she didn't tell them. . . she couldn't bear the weight of such a secret—being pregnant and trying to hide it or having an abortion and hiding that. Oh god, she was ahead of herself. Slow down. First she had to tell Jeff, and then she'd have go to the clinic.

That night Lisa managed to see Jeff. He came over around 10 o'clock after Lisa's father told her he wasn't happy with such a late hour. Oh Dad, if you only knew, she thought. Jeff plopped on the couch next to her. They were alone, since everyone else had gone to bed. Lisa felt awkward. For one thing, they hadn't been together for nearly five days, and that fact, coupled with Lisa's new knowledge, made for a lot of tension.

"Hey, what's wrong?" Jeff said as he pulled Lisa close to him. "C'mere, Lis."

Lisa let herself be hugged but she also felt stiff. "We've got to talk, Jeff." There was a silence. "Jeff." She looked right in his eyes and then glanced down. "Jeff—I think I'm pregnant."

She felt his arm tighten before the words were even all said. "Oh no," he said. "Oh god, are you sure?"

"Pretty sure," she said wiping her eyes. "I took one of those home pregnancy tests and it turned pink. That means you're pregnant." She looked up at Jeff, who had taken his arm away and was covering his face with his hands.

"Shit! I am so sorry," he said. "We tried to be careful Lisa, I just can't believe it!"

Lisa felt all jumbled inside. She was sad for Jeff, sad and afraid for herself. She was scared they'd split up. She was angry. It wasn't fair. They hadn't been stupid. . . well, maybe just a little bit and a "little bit" was all it took.

Jeff reached over and took her hand. "How are you feeling? Are you sick or anything?"

"No, I feel great . . . .I just keep hoping I'm wrong. I think I should go back to the clinic and get an official test—just to be sure."

"That's a good idea," he said quietly. "Maybe it'll turn out that you're not."

"Can you pay for it? I'm broke. Will you take me?"

"Sure. Don't worry. Well, if you are—you know, pregnant, what are you going to do?"

"You mean what are _we_ going to do?"

"Yeah. Come on, you know I mean 'we'."

"I dunno. Let's wait and see."

"Have you told your mom?"

"Not yet. I'm scared to. I thought I'd wait till I've been to the clinic again. Jeff. . . this is all so awful. This isn't what I wanted." Lisa began crying, and Jeff put his arm around her. Their heads were touching, but each was filled with private fears.

Jeff felt dazed. He loved Lisa, but he certainly knew he wasn't ready to be a father, to give up school, get a job, live on . . . live on what? He couldn't make more than $6.00 an hour right now. And Lisa—she was just a kid. So was he. He couldn't imagine her being pregnant with a huge belly or taking care of a baby. He let out a big sigh. He knew he had to act strong, but inside he felt weak and dizzy.

"We'll figure something out," he said, not believing it himself.

○

The next day they cut school at lunch time and went to the clinic. Three other people were there ahead of them, so they had to wait 45 minutes before their turn. Jeff kept glancing at his watch and fiddling with his hat. Lisa kept looking out the window and picking at her fingernails. Finally, the receptionist called out, "Lisa." Jeff quickly touched her arm and she glanced at him, managing a shaky smile before she went inside.

"How may I help you?" the receptionist asked.

Lisa wondered if the woman remembered her from the last time. She hesitated and she felt her face grow red. "I'm here for a pregnancy test."

"Okay. Have we seen you before?"

"Yes."

"That will be $10.00. Let me get your file. Oh yes, I remember," she said. "You were here for birth control pills."

Lisa searched in her purse for the money so she wouldn't have to look at the woman's face. She was afraid of seeing judgment in her eyes, but when she looked up, she saw none. She handed her the money.

"Well, let's check things out first," the woman said in an easy way opening the door for her. "Just take this cup in the bathroom. Sit over the toilet and pee into the cup and when you're done, leave the cup here on this shelf and have a seat over by my desk. We'll have the results in a couple of minutes."

"That fast?"

"Yes. It's very quick and simple."

After the door closed, Lisa sat on the toilet and inhaled deeply. She kept her fingers crossed as the cup filled with the warm urine. She placed the cup on the shelf and went back into the office. The next two minutes became five minutes as Lisa sat near the desk. The receptionist answered the phone several times and Lisa caught a peek of Jeff in the waiting room reading a magazine. Finally, a young woman dressed in jeans and a tee shirt came up to the desk and handed a slip of paper to the receptionist who glanced at it and turned to Lisa.

"The result is positive," she said.

Lisa couldn't bear to look at her. She kept her eyes on her shoes. "That means I'm pregnant?"

"Well, a positive result usually indicates pregnancy, but that really is up to a doctor to diagnose."

The phone rang. Lisa stood up to go. She heard the woman saying, "Will you please hold?" and then she said to Lisa. "Listen, if you're confused about what to do we have some fine counselors who could talk to you. They won't put any pressure on you, just help you to see what your options are. Would you like to make an appointment?"

Lisa stammered. "Yes, I guess so." She felt the tears sting her eyes. She desperately wanted to get out the door, and she couldn't trust her voice to talk.

"Here, look over this brochure and call back as soon as you can. We have lots of times available and there's no cost for the initial visit."

"Okay," Lisa mumbled and she took the paper. She was already out into the parking lot before Jeff could even get to his feet. She burst into tears and Jeff put his arms around her and held her close.

"What are we going to do?" she sobbed.

After several minutes had passed, Lisa told Jeff about the counseling available. "I think it's a good idea," she said. "I'm so confused. Will you come with me?"

Jeff gulped. "You mean for counseling, therapy?"

"Not therapy—counseling, just to help us make up our minds."

"Well, yeah, if you want. What do you do?"

"Talk about what choices I—we—have, I guess. But I don't feel like I have any choice at all," she said in a shaky voice. "I just can't believe it. I mean, I knew better and so did you."

Jeff was quiet. "Well, what choices are there? I guess you stay pregnant or you don't."

Lisa felt like Jeff was putting the whole thing on her. "But if I stay pregnant, that means I'll be a mother or else give it up for adoption. I can't do either of those." The tears rolled down her cheeks. In spite of Jeff's closeness and his arms about her, she felt so alone. Alone and lost.

○

Lisa stayed home from school the next three days. It was true that she didn't feel well, but she really could have gone if she'd wanted to. She told her mother she had a sore throat and headache. She had thrown up only once but it didn't seem like that awful morning sickness she'd heard about. She missed two tests and rehearsals, and her school work was piling up. At this point though, nothing much mattered.

At noon time on the third day her mother unexpectedly came home. Lisa thought she'd heard her car drive up but had ignored the sounds and drifted back to sleep. The next thing she knew, her mother was gently nudging her shoulder.

"Lisa, Lisa honey, wake up. How are you feeling?"

Lisa struggled to open her eyes. "Hi, Mom. What are you doing home?"

"I was worried about you. Here, I brought you some juice."

Lisa looked at the orange juice and felt her stomach grow queasy. "Maybe later," she said.

"How 'bout some tea then?"

"Yeah, okay, that'd be good. "

"I'll be right back," her mother said, leaving the room.

Lisa sat up. She could feel a 'talk' coming, and her heart was thumping loudly under her tee shirt. She wanted desperately to talk to her mother, and she wanted desperately not to hurt her.

Her mother came back with spearmint tea. "Here, try this," she said putting the mug in Lisa's hands and sitting on the edge of the bed. Lisa bowed her head over the mug and felt her mother's eyes boring into her. She avoided looking at her and concentrated on her tea.

"Lisa, I'm worried about you. It's not the fact that you're home sick from school. It's more that I feel I've lost touch with you. I suppose it's my fault. I've been so busy with my job and the move and all."

Lisa could hear the uncertainty in her mother's voice. "Mom, it's not you. . . "

"No, let me go on. I know that a certain amount of distance between a mother and daughter is natural at your age, but I just have to tell you that I'd like things to be different. I'd like the two of us to make it a point to do something together once in a while. I miss you. . . You know, my own mother died when I was fifteen, and I never had a chance to be close to her. I don't want to lose a good opportunity with you. Besides, I hardly know what's going on with you any more, and you seem to be so quiet lately and I'm. . . I'm just worried."

There was silence. Her mother continued, "Is there anything bothering you?"

Lisa looked up at her mother's soft face, her moist eyes. A huge lump filled her throat, and she lowered her own eyes to the faded balloons on the tea mug.

She took a deep breath. "Mom, I. . . .I don't know how to say this. . . "

Her mother waited.

"I'm in trouble. I'm pregnant."

"Oh Lisa," her mother managed to say. "Oh Lisa, no."

The words were out and Lisa was sobbing. She felt her mother take the mug out of her hands and put her arms around her. She buried her face in her mother's shoulder and wished she was five or six again and could just stay there and hide away forever.

"Mom, I didn't mean to hurt you. Dad's going to be so mad. Everything's so awful. I don't know what to do. I'm so scared."

"Lisa, oh my God." Her mother wiped the tears from her own eyes. "It's not the way it should be. Not now. Not like this. How far along are you? How pregnant?"

"I guess it's about two and a half weeks; I missed my last period."

"And what about Jeff? What does he say? How could he have done this?"

"He's upset. He doesn't know what to do. We've hardly talked about it."

"Well," her mother said, taking a shaky breath, "I'm glad you told me. I need time, at least a little time, to get used to the idea. You do have choices. We need to tell your dad."

"Mom, no!"

Her mother was firm. "Yes, we do. This is a terribly difficult time for you. You need all the support and help you can get. Besides, he's your father; he has a right to know."

"But Dad will be furious. I can't face him."

"You'll have to. But don't forget that he loves you very much. We'll try to talk tonight. I'm sorry, I've got to get back to work. I'm late. Try to sleep, okay? I love you."

"Thanks, Mom, but I still don't know what to do."

"Shh—we'll talk later. You don't have to decide that right now. You still have some time. Don't forget, you're not the first girl who's ever found herself in this situation."

Lisa heard the door close and then the water running in her mother's bathroom. She knew her mother was crying. *God, what have I done?*

○

Several hours later Lisa heard a lot of yelling coming from the kitchen. She heard her father shout, "God damnit!" and the front door slam. She grabbed her pillow and bit her lip.

That night about 10 p.m. there was a knock on her door and she heard her father's voice.

"Lisa, can I come in?"

She wanted to pull the covers over her head.

"Yeah," she answered.

His face looked awful. His eyes were all puffy and his skin blotchy.

"Hi," he said.

"Hi Dad," she said and, before she knew it, the tears were pouring out. "Dad, Dad I'm so sorry.".

He reached over and took her hand and looked into her eyes. "We'll figure something out. It's just all so hard to believe," and he grew silent. "I'd like to speak to Jeff," he went on and Lisa heard the anger in his voice. "What a stupid ass thing to let happen. Lisa, you're so young; I just never thought. . . ."

"It wasn't just Jeff, Dad. It was me too."

Her father turned his head away. "I know," he mumbled. "Well, it's late now. I'm exhausted. Your mother and I want to talk with you about this tomorrow. Jeff should probably be here too."

"Not yet, Dad. Just the three of us first, please."

"Okay, okay. . . You're still my girl, you know," he said and his eyes were glistening with tears barely held back. "I guess you're just not so little any more," and he kissed her on the top of her head.

"Thanks, Dad," she said. "Nite."

○

She waited a few minutes numbly staring at her blanket and the walls of her room. Sighing, she reached for the phone, and thankfully Jeff, and not his parents, answered the phone.

"Lisa, hi. How are you feeling? How's everything?"

"It's awful. Both my parents know, and I feel so bad. But they've been really great about it."

"You told them? Both of them?"

"Yeah."

"God, I don't know how I'll ever come over there again."

"Well, you'll have to because my dad wants to talk to you."

Jeff was silent.

"Mom and Dad and I are going to talk tomorrow. He wanted you to be there too, but I managed to put him off for a little while. I didn't think you'd want to."

"I guess I should, though.

"Yeah."

"Were they furious?"

"No. It was worse. They were sad. Jeff, I feel like I ruined everybody's life."

○

The next night, while Stephanie was gone to a friend's house, Lisa and her parents sat at the kitchen table. She noticed that her mother had a book called *When Your Daughter Is Pregnant.*

"Lisa," her father began, "Your mother and I have already talked about this, and we've agreed we don't want to get into blaming or accusing either you or Jeff. It's not that we're not angry; we are. But we feel it's more important to help you out now. You've got some big decisions to make."

Lisa was listening and feeling an intense pressure in her chest. She was thinking how weird and formal this all seemed, but then she realized that it was fitting to be so serious. She wished they were talking about allowances, using the car, or even an accident—anything other than this.

"So, all this is your decision—well, yours and Jeff's— but we want to be here for you. What do you think your choices are?"

Lisa looked at them with tears in her eyes. "Well, I guess it all comes down to whether or not I stay pregnant. The thing is, I can't see myself doing any of this: I can't see myself being pregnant and going to school and walking around with this huge stomach. I sure can't see myself as a mother. I'm not ready for that. But I also can't see myself having a baby and then giving it up for adoption. And then there's abortion. It's awful. All of it. No matter what, there's no way to win; I lose any way I choose."

They were all silent for a few minutes.

"You said it far better than I could have," her dad said, and he squeezed her hand. "One thing I can tell you is that Mom and I want you to know that we simply don't want to raise another child; we feel we just can't do it. And that's a hard decision for us too."

"In some ways, I'd really like to make this decision for you, Lisa," her mother said with tears in her eyes. "I'd like to just step in and take your life in hand. I know now I should have been more directive with you. I should have watched you more closely."

"Mom, this isn't your fault . . . What would you do if you were me?"

"Oh honey, I don't know. I'm your mother, not you. I want to influence you and I don't want to influence you. . . It's sad to say, but this decision puts you into the whole arena of being an adult; it's really *your* decision."

"The clinic said I could go in for counseling. I think I will. Maybe it would help me figure out what I want to do. . . except I don't *want* to do any of it."

"That's a good idea," her mother said. "Maybe you can go in tomorrow. I'll go with you if you like. But you do need to think about being back in school too. You can't go on just being absent and not doing your work."

"It just seems so stupid to think about school right now."

"Lisa, you can't hide out from things. This is a crisis, yes. But the rest of your life doesn't just stop."

"Just let me stay out of school for the rest of the week. Then I'll go back, and after that will be Christmas vacation."

Her mom and dad looked at each other. "Okay."

"I guess this means the trip to Oregon is off," Lisa said.

"Well, it seems that way. First things first."

"Stephanie will be so disappointed."

Just then the front door closed, and Stephanie came bounding into the kitchen. "Hi! What's going on? What are you guys doing?"

"Just having a talk," her dad said. Stephanie put her arms around her dad's neck. She didn't hug him very often any more, but she seemed to sense something unusual.

Lisa was struck by her sister's youth and spirit. With her long shiny hair and open face, she looked like she didn't have a worry in the world.

Lisa felt very old.

○

If you decide Lisa should consider abortion, turn to *ABORTION* printed on yellow paper.

If you decide Lisa should consider adoption, turn to *ADOPTION* printed on pink paper.

If you decide Lisa should consider keeping the baby, turn to *TEEN PARENT* printed on gold paper.

ABSTAIN

Lisa's mind was reacting and her heart was racing. The first time she had sex in her life, she wanted to feel total love for the man she was with, the kind of love where she never even thought about anyone else, where she wasn't confused.

○

Her confusion caused her to remember her Christmas visit to Gwen's house in Eugene. Once she'd arrived, it felt like she'd never been gone. Gwen's bedroom was the same as before, but pictures of Tom Cruise were replaced with pictures of River Phoenix and Denzel Washington. Her bookcase still held the same clutter of trophies from junior high days, books, and a few dance pictures. The first night she and Gwen stayed up till 3 a.m. talking and laughing. The next day Lisa slept in till noon, and when she came downstairs she could smell the scent of French toast.

"Hi," Gwen said. "We left some for you in the oven."

"I can't believe it's noon. I'm still exhausted. That was so much fun last night. So, what's up for today?" she said sitting down at the table with her plate.

"A bunch of us girls are going over to Kim's house, and then there's a party tonight. It's going to be so cool. Everyone can't wait to see you."

It felt good to be getting so much attention. And it felt right to be back in Eugene. Life in California seemed very far away right now—even Jeff; Lisa was immediately overcome with guilt.

"Thinking about Jeff?" Gwen asked.

"Yeah."

"I guess you miss him."

"I do. He's the most wonderful guy, Gwen. But right now, I'm just so glad to be here, to be back."

"Is California awful?"

"Oh no, I like the town and the school. The kids have been really neat but, you know, I've lived here all my life and it's just hard being in a whole new place. Still, you've got to meet Jeff. Maybe you could come down next summer."

"I'd love it. You know I would. So, how are you two? I mean how close are you?"

"You mean, am I still a virgin?" Lisa asked. "Yes, but probably not for long."

"Oooh, how exciting!"

"How 'bout you? Well, I know you're not a virgin, but what about you and Theo?"

"We're still going out. He's a great guy. He really wants to have sex, but he's giving me some space. I want to and then I get scared. Then I think, well I did it with Todd, so I should do it with Theo. Then I think, that's a totally stupid way to think. . . Sometimes I'm sorry I ever had sex with Todd. I mean, it didn't last between us. I actually thought we might get married some day. And now I'll never again be able to look forward to that 'first time' in my life. I dunno, life doesn't seem so easy any more. There's so many things to consider, like STDs and AIDS. I think about my mom's life when girls just had to worry about getting pregnant. You know what a nurse told me? She said, 'Getting pregnant is not the end of the world but getting AIDS is.' And then there's abortions and abortion clinics. Can you believe a doctor was killed just because he performed abortions!"

"I know, but I'd hate to go to an abortion clinic. It sounds so awful. I don't know what I'd do if I were pregnant."

"Remember Chelsea? Chelsea Cummings? She had an abortion this fall."

"You're kidding? Chelsea? Who was the guy?"

" Dan Gould."

"My god—Dan—that's hard to believe. How's she doing?"

"She's okay. She won't talk about it. I think she's seeing a counselor. She's pretty much her old self, but she's different too. She's quieter, not as outgoing. And she didn't play volleyball this year."

Lisa was quiet. She and Chelsea had been in class together for years. They were never really close but had always been friends.

"Does everybody know? And what about Dan?"

"Most kids know, but no one says anything about it to either of them. It's gotta be hard, though. This is a small town. Dan just acts the same. He doesn't seem different at all. I see him talking to Chelsea sometimes, but they don't go out. I don't think she goes out with anyone."

"It's so weird—how one little event can change your whole life. I guess I can see why parents flip out about sex, but sometimes they act like we don't have a brain in our heads, like we don't know about condoms and things."

"Yeah, Yeah . . . ," Gwen said pulling her long auburn hair back and twisting it into a knot, " I told you didn't I? One time Todd and I did it without using anything. Boy, that was so stupid. I'm still surprised it happened. Looking back on it I knew what I should have done, but at the time. . . "

"I know. I know. It's easy to forget all that 'smart information,' but what about Todd? What about Dan? What about the guys? How come they don't take care of it? Why do girls have to always be the ones?"

"I guess it's 'cause they don't end up pregnant and we do. My Aunt Ginny says all their brains are in their penis." They both laughed.

"Still," Lisa said, "the set-up sucks. If I ever have a son, I'm going to raise him to be smart and careful and not to leave everything up to his girlfriend."

"Yeah. And I'm going to keep mine on a leash."

The party that night was jammed with kids, music, beer and wine coolers. Lisa saw so many old friends she felt high just from all the attention. Everyone wanted to hear about California and Jeff. A sense of security and happiness filled her with warmth, and she realized how held-in she'd been the last five months. She talked, laughed, and danced with everyone, and finally an old boy friend, Sam, came up to her.

"Sam, how are you?" she said, giving him a big hug.

"Lisa! You look great!" The music was an old rock and roll song by Chuck Berry from the 50's. The two of them danced, sweated, and bumped into everyone else. When it ended, they were gasping for breath.

"Boy, I need a break," Sam said, taking her hand. He grabbed a beer and they went out into the garage. The door was open and the rain falling steadily.

"God, it smells so good! I love this rain!"

"Maybe we could send some of it down to California," Sam said.

Lisa looked at him. How he had changed! He was over 6 feet now and played football. He'd let his hair grow. They'd been friends since grade school, and Sam had been her first boyfriend when she went to junior high. She let out a soft laugh.

"What's funny?"

"Oh, I was remembering that party we went to in eighth grade."

"What party?"

"Janine Goldberg's. Don't you remember? Come on, Sam. We made out like crazy. You were the second boy I'd ever kissed. The first one really doesn't count 'cause I was only in third grade."

"Oh yeah, I remember." Sam took a sip of beer and stood next to Lisa and they both watched the rain making puddles on the driveway.

Sam was very close and Lisa could feel his presence, hear his breathing. She turned and looked up at him. He put his arm out and drew her close.

"Welcome back," he said, and she suddenly felt excited to be with Sam. She wondered what it would be like to kiss him again after so many years. She glanced up, and at the same time Sam leaned down and sought her lips. It was a very sweet kiss and Lisa felt herself drawn to him.

"You're a much better kisser now," Sam said.

"You are too." She laughed and pulled away at the same time. What was she doing? What was she doing kissing Sam when she was in love with Jeff?

"Take it easy. I know you've got a boyfriend. We're just two old friends who are glad to see each other," he said, hugging her.

"Yeah. You're right." She squeezed him back, took his beer and drank a long sip. "Come on. Let's go back and dance some more."

It was 2 a.m., and Gwen and Lisa were still sleepily talking about the party and the kids. "Did you talk to Jennifer? She has changed so much," Gwen said. "She's just all of a sudden become Miss Priss and she bad-mouths anyone who takes a drink or a toke."

"I thought I saw her give me funny look. I guess she smelled beer on me."

"I saw you come out of the garage with old Sam! Were you being a good girl, Lisa?"

"What do you think Gwen? Give me a break. We're just old friends. You know Sam."

Nevertheless, as she was sinking into sleep, she felt confused. How could she possibly have enjoyed kissing Sam when she was in love with Jeff? The question turned over and over in her mind until all thinking stopped and she drifted off.

O

The next few days flew by. There was always something to do, lots of kids to see, and she and Sam frequently found themselves together. It was fun being around him; he had an easy, relaxed way and the two of them laughed a lot. Two days before she was to leave for California, the kids had a party at a cabin on a nearby lake. It was cold but sunny, and happily there was no rain in sight. After unpacking all the food and sleeping bags, ten of them took off for the top of a low mountain peak about four miles away. There was so much underbrush to wade through that it wasn't easy going, but after about two miles, pines and evergreens took over the landscape, and the hiking got easier, though steeper.

The air smelled crystal fresh, a mixture of damp pine needles and untouched woods. Lisa felt so strong and vibrant. Her legs moved steadily, each foot planted firmly, and her breathing, though rapid, was not shallow. They were all alternately talking, laughing and being quiet. Occasionally one of them would start singing and the rest would join in.

"You know," Gwen said, "this whole thing looks really hokey. I mean, we are the original happy campers! The church youth group! But it sure is fun!" and everyone joined in with a big "Yahoo!"

They paused to rest, pass the water bottles, and look out over a vast plain leading to the lake below; it shimmered blue-silver in the sunlight. Someone passed a joint, but only a couple of kids took a hit.

"This is too cool, just the way it is," someone said.

Lisa passed the water to Sam, who took a long swig.

"So, do you have this in California?" he asked.

"Oh yeah. I think so. Maybe not so green, but there are some killer places there. At least, that's what I've heard." She thought about Jeff and touched her bracelet. He would love this. All the time she'd been in California she hadn't done anything like this. First of all, she hadn't known where to go or anyone to go with. And then she'd been too busy with school. Lisa let out a big sigh.

"Come on Lisa. Let's go," said Sam as he pulled her to her feet. "Only another mile straight up!"

From the top of the low mountain you could see all around for miles. In the far distance were snow covered peaks; the rest was greenery. Most of the kids were quiet, just looking and hearing the sound of their own breathing. Finally someone started singing, "Oh beautiful for spacious skies." That was the cue for everyone else to start yelling and punching, making a great heap of jacket-clad bodies in a mock wrestling match.

Soon they were all lying on the ground laughing and calling out wisecracks. Lisa was entangled with two other kids and she smiled. She looked up at the sky, so blue and clear like a mountain lake turned upside down; life was good.

Later that night they all stuffed themselves on pasta and garlic bread. There was a big fire, and most everyone sat around talking while a few kids were giving each other back rubs. There was a soft and mellow light in the warm room and a feeling of drowsiness. A couple of joints were passed around and soon someone got the munchies. Several boxes of cookies appeared and were devoured in minutes. Another kid started talking about the universe and the big bang theory; it was at that point that the jokes began, and in a matter of minutes several kids were laughing so hard they were crying. Every one had his own theory about the origin of life, but they all agreed that it was up to Mr. Spock and Captain Kirk to preserve life for the planet. Someone turned on a tape and a few kids danced.

Lisa found herself once again next to Sam. She was leaning against him, sitting between his legs. She could feel his chest move in and out and feel the rumble of his laughter inside. He was playing with her hair, trying his hand at braiding.

"It's no use. I'm no good at braiding. I'll never make it as a hairdresser. Oh damn!" he said in a high-pitched voice.

Lisa reached up and grabbed his hand. It was large and rough. "Don't worry. You'll find another profession for yourself," she said and kissed his hand. She could feel Sam stiffen and his face drew very near to hers. He was nuzzling her hair. She turned slightly and found his lips. They dissolved in a long and passionate kiss. Their lips and tongues were moist and sweet, and Lisa felt as though she was sinking down, melting like warm ice cream. Her head was foggy. Was it the pot? Was this all right to be doing? What about Jeff? Sam felt so strong and familiar, yet strange too. He had changed since grade school; both of them had.

The room was dark and quiet. Sam and Lisa lay together, their bodies fully clothed in jeans and sweatshirts. Along with everyone else, they had fallen asleep. Sam reached over and pulled Lisa next to him. She felt confused. Her body wanted to be close to Sam, but her mind told her no and chattered about Jeff. She pulled away.

"Sam, I can't do this."

"Hey. We're not doing anything wrong. I just want to be close to you. You'll be gone tomorrow. I'll miss you."

In a way, Lisa thought, Sam's words could be interpreted as just a line of sweet talk, a way for him to get closer to her body. She looked at him, the young face becoming manly, the ease of his smile. "Me too," she said and snuggled up. She wasn't doing anything wrong, was she? Just a kiss with an old friend, a good friend. Then why did she feel like she was betraying Jeff? What was she doing? She closed her eyes and drifted back to sleep.

Back in the car with Jeff, Lisa's mind was reacting and her mind was racing. The first time she had sex in her life, she wanted to feel total love for the man she was with, the kind of love where she never even thought about anyone else, where she was very clear and not confused at all.

"Jeff, I can't. I'm just not ready."

Jeff stopped kissing her. "God, you are making such a big deal out of this!" he said, taking his arms away from her and staring out the window. There was steam forming on the windshield, and the shadows from tree branches made strange designs of crisscrossing lines.

"Well, it is a big deal, Jeff."

"Yeah, but I thought you cared about me. . . Lisa, we'll use condoms and we'll get birth control pills. We'll be careful. It'll be okay. People, our friends, do this all the time, and some of them aren't even careful. What more do you want?"

How could she tell him that she loved him but she wasn't ready to lose her virginity? How could she tell him that just over a week ago she had been lying on the floor of a mountain cabin with Sam and feeling very close and happy? She couldn't. She couldn't tell him that.

"I want to be older, more ready. I don't want things to be complicated. Besides, even if we were careful, I could still get pregnant. And then what would we do? There's no guarantees. Mistakes can happen. . . And I don't care if all the other kids do it. It almost seems like once they start having sex, that's all they do. Besides, I just want everything to be perfect." She paused, her heart beating rapidly. "Just give me a little more time. We haven't really seen each other in a while. Please, don't pressure me," she said, taking his hand.

He pulled his hand away and sat rigidly, looking straight ahead. He was silent for a long time before he spoke. "Okay," he said sighing. "You're one tough lady, Lisa," and he started up the car.

"Are we going home already?"

"Look, let's just cool off."

She could feel the distance between them now, and she suddenly felt she'd done a terrible thing.

"Jeff, I'm sorry. I guess I sound really stupid or mean."

"No, no you're right. You know, when you said the word 'pressure,' I remembered one thing my mom told me once," he said, slowing down to check the rear view mirror. "She said sometimes girls have sex just because they're pressured to, not because they want to. I wouldn't want that. Besides, I do know it's a different thing for girls."

Instantly, her heart warmed. He did understand. "Jeff, thank you," she said putting her hand on his knee.

"But you've got to understand me too," he said moving her hand. "It's just too difficult for me to be close to you now. And the truth is, I'm starting to feel a little crazy."

What a mess she'd made of everything! Before Christmas, Jeff was the only guy she'd thought about. She was totally in love. How much did she care about Sam anyway? Really, how much? He wasn't even in her life, and he certainly wasn't worth losing Jeff over . . . God, she sounded like such a bitch. . . What was wrong with her?

Jeff dropped her off and drove off with squealing tires. Opening the back door, Lisa felt engulfed in a black heaviness.

"Lisa? You're back early," her mother called out from the living room.

"Yeah," she said, reaching in the refrigerator for a can of already opened Coke. Reluctantly, she went into the living room.

"Was that Jeff driving off like that?"

"Uh huh."

Her mother was quiet for a short time, as though waiting for an explanation, then she said, "What movie did you see?"

"Broken Promises."

"Was it good?"

The air felt so tight and stiff. "I liked it a lot, but Jeff didn't." Lisa stood in the doorway to the hall, not knowing whether to sit down or go to her room.

"Why not?"

"Why not what?"

"Why didn't Jeff like it?"

"Oh, he said something like it made life too complicated. . . " Lisa moved over to the couch and said, "Things are all screwed up. Everything was easier before."

"I'm sorry. I know you were so anxious to see him." Her mother waited for Lisa to say something

"I was and I am, but I guess Jeff just wants to move a little faster than I do." She drank her Coke waiting for her mother to ask the big questions.

Instead, her mother sighed and said, "It's so hard in relationships. Two people are seldom ready for the same things at the same time."

Lisa was surprised by her mother's words. It almost seemed like she was talking about herself instead of Lisa. For a moment she wanted to ask all kinds of things : *Were you a virgin when you married Dad? When did you lose your virginity? Have you ever loved someone and hurt him at the same time? Does it mean you're cold if you don't want to have sex? Does it mean that there's something wrong with you? What's the right age to have sex? Is sixteen too old to be a virgin? Am I making too much out of this sex thing?*

But Lisa also felt a wave of fatigue. In truth, she just wanted to go to bed, sleep for about two days, then wake up with a clear head and conscience, and ready to be with Jeff.

"Well, I'm going to go to bed." Lisa finished her drink. "Were you waiting up for me?"

"In a way. I was also just enjoying the peace and quiet."

"So, how's your job going?" Lisa asked in a polite way, realizing she really didn't know much about her mom's life anymore. At the same time, she hoped it wouldn't turn into a long conversation.

"It's getting better. Here, you might want to read this. I found it while I was reading a story in this magazine."

Lisa glanced at the title of the article, "Teens Ask Questions," and inwardly she groaned. "Thanks, Mom. G'night." She kissed her mother on the cheek.

"Night, honey. Sleep well."

Lisa closed her bedroom door, and tossed the magazine on her pillow. She took off her clothes and dropped them on the floor, pulled on an extra large tee shirt, and flopped on the bed. She let out a big sigh and lay there for a few minutes in quiet, then turned on the radio. She was about to turn off the light when the words "your virginity" caught her eye.

The article was written by a counselor who worked with adolescent girls and wrote, "Many girls wonder when is the right age to lose their virginity. Of course this is an issue for them. Losing your virginity is one of the absolute landmarks in a girl's life. It signals her transition from girlhood to womanhood. While menstruation also is indicative of this change, sexual intercourse involves another person; it is not a solitary change but one that goes beyond the girl herself."

Lisa thought this sounded pretty intellectual, but she read on: "In many societies the loss of a girl's virginity was celebrated with ritual and fanfare, and the bloody sheets from the night's passion with her new husband were displayed for all to view." Great! She could just imagine hanging her sheets out the bedroom window for all the neighbors to come and examine and cheer about.

"This is one of the main reasons behind the elaborate festivities of our weddings, why the girl wears white and is given over from one man, her father, to another. What is unfortunate is that a woman's virginity came to be seen as a prize and something awarded to men; thus, a man became the possessor of women and the more virgin conquests he could claim as his own, the 'greater' the man."

Jeff wasn't after her virginity, but he was wanting to have sex. Was her virginity a 'prize'? She didn't think so, but she'd heard boys boasting about 'scoring' and talking about how much pussy they'd gotten, like a competition.

She read on. "In our society, we seem to have gone to an opposite extreme, and many young girls indiscriminately give away their virginity to their boyfriends; often, it is not seen as a positive to be a virgin, but as a negative. Therefore, a girl may actually want to 'get rid' of it. Girls as young as eleven and twelve talk boastfully about not being virgins and often put each other down if they still are."

Twelve—my god, that was Stephanie's age. It was unthinkable when it came to Stephanie, but she'd sure heard stories of girls in junior high school having sex with lots of different boys.

The article continued: "One of the sad things for people today is that the greater meaning of losing one's virginity or becoming a woman is entirely lost. What we don't seem to grasp is that this enormous step is a transition from the

70

child's place in the world to the adult's. It means that we are finally ready and able to see beyond our own individual needs to the needs of another, and this means so much more than just sexual needs.

"When sex occurs in a mature and committed relationship, it means that the other person's wants, hopes and feelings are on a par with our own. We are involved with the total person, not just the sexual person. We step beyond the self-centered world of the child to the world of the adult where another person becomes equally and sometimes even more important than our own self. That, of course, is love. And if you wait until it really is the right time and the right person, it is more likely to be a meaningful and lasting experience.

"If a young woman is in touch with herself as a person, if she values who she is, she will know when she is ready to open the door to the larger world of deeply caring for another, and then losing her virginity will be a part of this total commitment."

Lisa lay on the bed and stared straight ahead, the words of the article echoing in her brain. She felt a little awestruck; this article wasn't really about sex but about something much bigger; it almost felt spiritual. One thing she did know was that, even though she loved Jeff, she wasn't ready to commit to him, not in the way the article talked about. In that way she wasn't ready for sex. Her body might be ready but not the rest of her. She had been right when she'd said she needed a little more time.

And what if she lost Jeff because she wasn't willing to have sex? She took a deep breath and very clearly heard the words that came from within: *then he doesn't love me enough and, in the long run, it won't matter. When you love someone, you wouldn't want that person to do something that they really don't want to do.*

Her body relaxed, and she rolled over and stared at the ceiling, letting this new-found calm flow through her whole being. And then she let out a laugh. It was too much!—the timing of the incredible song that came on the radio—"I would do anything for love. . . but I won't do that!"

She listened to it all with a kind of wonder, almost as if she'd never heard the words before. Finally the song ended and Lisa wiped the tears from her eyes. She knew now she just couldn't go ahead and have sex with Jeff; she had to stay true to herself and how she felt. And it wouldn't matter if other kids thought it was stupid to wait. She had to do what was right for her. She hoped things would work out with Jeff . . . time would tell.

Lisa reached up to turn off to turn off the light and radio and pulled the covers up around her shoulders. Sighing deeply, she felt very much at peace with herself and easily fell asleep.

O

Almost two months had passed since that night of Lisa's decision. There had been a lot of rumors about her and Jeff, and most of their friends believed they'd had sex anyway. Lisa had to laugh; people believed what they wanted to. School had gone on, as had basketball and play rehearsal. There was a kind of routine to the weeks. Jeff and Lisa still went out, but their relationship was changing. The intensity between them had lessened, and Lisa spent most of her time in rehearsals, sometimes not getting home until 11 at night.

She and Kathy spent a lot of time together, and Zeke often joined them if they went out for coffee. The three of them talked about the play and the director. They also talked about school, about their lives and the future. Lisa liked listening to Zeke; his views on things were different from hers.

Whenever she and Kathy talked about college, Zeke would say something like, "But when are you two going to bust out of the mainstream? Come on, there's a world out there. Meet me in Paris or Nepal. Get a life!" It soon got to be a joke between them. "I'll see you at UCLA," Zeke said.

Lisa responded, "No, make that Moscow!" and Kathy would add something like "No, Tasmania!"

Sometimes when she was with Jeff, Lisa would spot Zeke, but they never really acknowledged each other except with "Hey," or "What's up?" Their friendship seemed to center around rehearsals.

The play ran for seven performances. Lisa's mom, dad, and Stephanie came twice and Jeff came opening night. Everyone complimented her on her performance and Lisa basked in all the attention. She wasn't the star by any means, but she carried her part well. More than anything, she loved the feeling of losing herself on stage. It felt like Lisa—the person—disappeared and Aunt Claire took over. And Kathy and Zeke were no longer themselves, either. The play was a success because the cast members were able to become the characters they portrayed. It always took a couple of hours after the play ended to come down to reality afterwards.

The night of the last performance there was an unofficial cast party that didn't even get going until 11 p.m. Everyone showed up: actors, crew and director. It began with a speech by the drama teacher praising the entire production, then the music was turned on and the food and soft drinks came out. The teacher left about 12:30, and then the beer and pot appeared. Not every one indulged, but most had at least a hit or a couple of sips. There was much dancing and several actual singing performances. It was a very exhibitionistic group.

Lisa found herself laughing and singing along with all the others. At some point she realized she was having more fun than she'd had in ages. She danced with a bunch of different guys and girls too. When the slow music finally came on about 2 a.m. only about fifteen kids were still there. She found herself dancing with Zeke.

They talked and told a few jokes, but mostly they were exhausted and just kind of hung on to one another.

"I don't 'spose I'll see much of you after this," said Zeke.

"Why not?"

"Well, we don't exactly hang out in the same circles, " he said.

"Zeke, I like you. Nothing's going to change that. I don't want to lose you as a friend. There's no reason why we still can't get together."

"What about Jeff?" They had never mentioned his name before and Lisa suddenly felt awkward.

"Well, that's not a problem. I'm entitled to my own friends." Was she? Even if they were boys?

"Good," Zeke said and he held her a little tighter. Lisa found herself nestling her head into his shoulder. He smelled like talcum powder and cold cream, the result of taking off his stage make up.

"It's been a good five months, hasn't it?" Lisa said. Life was funny. A year ago she was still living in Oregon. Now she had a whole new life. It was wonderful but also complicated.

"Tell you what," Zeke said. "Try out for the next play—*Our Town*."

"I love that play! But I don't know . . . I'm not sure. . . Being in a play takes a lot of time. Besides, I probably wouldn't get a part."

"You didn't think you'd get one this time either, did you?"

"No. I did surprise myself."

"Just think about it," Zeke said, squeezing her hand.

"Okay. All right. I'll think about it."

"Good. I'd like that."

○

Lisa kept to herself for the next few days, but finally she called Jeff on Wednesday and said she wanted to talk. He showed up at six that night.

"So, what's up?" he said as they sat in her backyard.

"I've been thinking a lot lately. . . "

"About?"

"About us." She cleared her throat and looked away. "Spring vacation starts next week."

"Lisa, get to the point."

"Well, my family and I are going to Disneyland for the first time. I'm probably the only sixteen-year-old in this whole town who hasn't been there." Jeff reached up and pulled some leaves off the bay tree. He waited. "Jeff, I don't know how to say this . . . "

"You want to break up, is that it?"

"Jeff, I don't really want to break up, but I'm so confused lately, and I know you're not that happy." She waited for him to say something, but he was silent. "I mean you've made this year so special . . . Oh, I dunno. I don't know what I mean."

"It's that Zeke guy, isn't it?"

"No, we're just friends. It's just that I don't think I'm ready to be with just one person. I mean it feels like too big a commitment. And I know that you. . . you want more from me than I'm ready for." She started talking very fast, afraid she couldn't get the words out in time. "There's just a lot I want to do, and I was thinking maybe we should just take a break from each other; you know, be free to see other people and stuff."

Jeff let out a big sigh and Lisa was afraid he was going to explode.

"Wow!" he said.

"What? What is it?"

He shrugged his shoulders and a half smile appeared. "This blows my mind."

"What does?"

"What are you—a mind reader?" He laughed and looked right at her. "I've been wanting to talk about this, but I didn't know how. I didn't want to hurt you."

"You mean *you* want to break up?"

"Oh, I don't know about 'break up,' but I know I want to be more free, just be able to fool around more. I don't mean with other girls, just be more free."

Lisa suddenly felt very close to him. God, what was she doing? He was such a neat guy. "I know. Do you want to end everything? Do you want your bracelet back?"

"Do you want to give it to me?"

"No way. I want to keep it forever. And I want you to keep the chain I gave you. I want you to keep it forever too." Her throat felt thick, and she thought she was going to cry. "Someday I'm going to have a daughter and she'll ask me where I got that bracelet and I'll tell her the whole story about you and me." She touched his arm.

He laughed and hugged her. "Lisa, you are such a romantic! There's only one thing. . ."

"What is it?"

"I didn't get to be your first one. That would have been pretty neat."

"It would have, but I don't think you'd be able to wait that long. I'm not going to be ready for a long time."

"Lisa, you are so serious; lighten up, girl. Who knows, maybe I'll be your first one yet?"

"Who knows? Anyway, we'll stay friends, right?"

"Right!" he said, extending his hand.

"Oh, stop," she said with a laugh. "Don't you know that friends hug each other? C'mere."

○

The prom was two weeks away, and tryouts for the next play were in three days. Together with Kathy and Zeke, Lisa decided to audition.

The fact that the director had selected *Our Town* as their spring play met with mixed reactions. Some thought it was too boring and been done too many times. Others thought it was neat because at least it was a play most everyone had read if they were a junior or older.

When the news came that Lisa had been selected, she was thrilled. But she was even happier that Kathy and Zeke had made it too. Kathy would play mother to Lisa as Emily, and Zeke would be George.

"You know, Lisa, in this play you and I are going to wind up falling in love and getting married," Zeke said, putting his arm around her while they looked at the posted list of cast members.

Lisa felt her face redden.

Leaving school that day, Lisa and Zeke talked about the play and how much rehearsal time it was going to involve. Then Lisa asked, "So, are you going?"

"To the prom? Do you really think if I had the money I would spend it on such a bourgeois event?"

"Zeke, it's not all totally plastic. It's fun too. I mean, don't you want to tell your children about all the dances you went to, the football games, the pep rallies?"

"Oh, right! I forgot. I have to have these all-American memories, all that 50s crap you see in the old movies: kids worrying about not getting asked to dances or not having the totally cool car."

Lisa was silent for a minute. "Zeke, it's not that I think a person has to have all that stuff, but what I don't get is why you're so negative, so sarcastic all the time."

"Lisa, it just seems that life is about a lot more than whether or not you go to the prom."

"But don't you wish you had someone special in your life—you know, like a girl friend?"

"Sometimes, but she'd have to be pretty unusual. I'm not so easy to put up with. And most girls I know are pretty selfish; make that most women are pretty selfish."

There was a long silence. "Are you talking about your mother?" Lisa asked quietly.

"What's she got to do with it?" he said, tossing his hair away from his eyes.

"Well, I heard she just took off . . . is that true?"

"I guess you could say that." Zeke kept outlining a figure eight over and over in the dirt with the toe of his shoe.

"What's that like?"

"What? To have your mother do her own thing?"

"Yeah. I mean it's great she wants to make her own life, but what's it like for you? Is it okay for you? What's your dad say?"

"My dad doesn't say anything. He's pretty caught up in his own life. He has a new girlfriend who's kind of a bitch. My mom's pretty weird. I mean, I like it when she's around, but she's always got these big ideas about what her life is going to be like, how she's going to be so successful. And then it doesn't work out and she comes back and gets all depressed. I wish she'd just settle on one thing. . . I wish she'd just be in one place and . . . you know, be available."

Lisa looked over at Zeke. There was a small twitch near the left side of his mouth, as though it was taking great effort to hold something back. She reached over and put her hand on his knee. He gave her a quick glance and for a second his eyes softened, then his mouth tightened.

"You can probably guess I don't like talking about it much."

"I didn't mean to make you uncomfortable. I'd just like to see you happier."

"Look. Being happy is only one aspect of living. There's also just surviving and figuring things out. In the long run, I think I'll be prepared for life because there's a lot I've had to do on my own. I've pulled myself out of a pretty heavy-duty drug habit; I've learned that if you want something in life, you have to create it; no one hands it to you, or—if they do—there are strings attached. And I've learned the only person you can count on is yourself."

Lisa sat and looked out at the newly green leaves sprouting from all the oak trees. She took a deep breath. "It sounds lonely, Zeke, but maybe that's just because your life is so different from mine. One thing I do know, though, I'm glad we're friends."

Zeke gently nudged her. "Friends last longer than lovers," he said. "I gotta go. You better start getting ready for the ball, Cinderella."

They stood up and smiled at each other. "See you. Don't forget to practice your lines!"

O

A week before opening night, Lisa and Zeke walked close together, their arms about each other's shoulders.

"Look up," Zeke said. "There's the Big Dipper." Lisa stopped and took in the enormous dark sky with its millions of small bright lights. Just then a shooting star cascaded over-head. "Look! It's good luck," Zeke turned to Lisa, whose face was lit up in a big smile. As she moved toward Zeke, he slipped his arms around her, and their lips met in a warm, gentle kiss. They both stepped back, staring at each other, then Zeke pulled Lisa close and kissed her again, and this time there was an excitement between them.

"Oh Zeke, "Lisa said, stepping away. "I don't know if this is such a good idea; I don't want to ruin a friendship."

"I don't know either, but it feels good," Zeke said. "Let's keep on."

Lisa laughed and they walked back to the drama building holding hands.

O

Weeks later, sitting in English class and anxious to finish the last final of her junior year, Lisa listened to Mr. T. She glanced around the room. Jeff was there, Kathy, and a whole bunch of her friends. She was no longer the new girl, and she looked forward to going back up to Oregon for the summer, where she had a six week job in a summer camp. She had been hired to do recreation and drama. Lisa liked the way her life was going.

Mr. T.'s voice broke into her thoughts. He was passing out a paper. "Keep this face down until I give the word. Before you begin this final, I want to say that this has been an extraordinarily good year. I think you all have grown, not only in your ability to express yourselves, but in your development as human beings. I like what I see and I feel better about the future of our world knowing that there are going to be adults like you out there. I want to wish you all good luck next year, and I hope the future will be kind. In the words of the famous *Desiderata*: "For all its sham, drudgery and broken dreams, it is still a beautiful world. Be careful. Strive to be happy."

There was a moment of silence and Lisa and Kathy glanced over at each other. Someone coughed, and Jeff turned around and winked at Lisa, who smiled back

"You have the full two hours to write your final essay. You will be graded on the content of your ideas, the organization and the presentation of those ideas, and, of course, the correctness of your grammar and punctuation. You may use a dictionary. Okay, begin."

There was a shuffling of paper as everyone turned the sheet of paper over and started reading. A few students sighed, one slammed down his pencil in disgust, and almost everyone shifted in their seats. Lisa read the final:

"Throughout the year, beginning with *Our Town*, we have discussed individual and cultural values as a yardstick for measuring the quality of life. It seems clear that without values, life loses its brilliancy and importance. As far as we know, our values separate us from other forms of living creatures.

"In a thoughtful and well organized essay discuss the values that you believe to be important in life and provide specific examples of these values as revealed in at least four of the literary works and presentations we have experienced this year; to refresh your memory, a list of these is posted on the board."

Lisa looked up and read the list:

The Scarlet Letter
Our Town
Huckleberry Finn
Walled
Poetry of Robert Frost, Maya Angelou, Langston Hughes, Gary Soto, Emily Dickinson, e.e. cummings
The Grapes of Wrath
The Declaration of Independence
Beloved
The Education of Little Tree
The Color Purple
Presentations from AIDS and Sexual Harassment Awareness Days

Lisa inhaled deeply. It would certainly take the full two hours to put all her ideas together. She jotted down several values she thought were important: Friendship, compassion for Others, Hard Work, Freedom, Family, God. Then she thought of all the literary works posted on the board and was sure she could easily include four of them. Thinking of Friendship, her mind drifted off to Gwen and Kathy and how important all her friends were. Then she pictured Sam's face, Jeff's, and Zeke's. The truth was, she had three wonderful guys in her life and she felt differently about each of them. She remembered the whole struggle about sex and finally deciding to abstain, to wait until she was older and truly ready.

How had she known to do that? For a long while she had been confused, but she tried to be honest with herself, to admit to all her feelings: wanting the first time in her life to be with someone she could hopefully spend her life with; feeling attracted to more than one guy; acknowledging she felt young; and, mostly, letting herself know that she just wasn't ready—and that was okay.

She knew she had missed out on something very important, but she also had that something to still look forward to in her life. She was glad she hadn't been careless and given herself away lightly. Even better, she hadn't had to worry about getting pregnant or getting AIDS. And she hadn't had to live with any guilt or hiding the truth from her parents. She knew she had avoided a whole lot of complication, pain, and disappointment.

After all, it seems we have only have one life to live and we can choose to live that life the best way possible, with the most care and the most awareness. She thought for a moment and began writing :

"America has always emphasized the freedom of the person to choose her own course in life. From *Huckleberry Finn* to the *The Color Purple*, the individual struggles with her conscience to be true to herself and to live life accordingly. In my own life, I have had to wrestle with confusion and listen to my own inner voice. Sometimes my values conflicted with one another and I became lost while trying to honor family, friendship, and myself. The unifying thread, however, was choosing what was right for me and trying to follow that course in my life. . . "

Lisa smiled. The essay was just flowing out of her. The present—and the future—looked very bright indeed.

O

Lisa Howard went on to college and several years later got her Masters degree in Political Science. She is now married and lives with her husband and their three-year-old daughter in Bangkok, Thailand.

Jeff Branley graduated from college and works for AT&T in Los Angeles. He is married and he and his wife hope to have several children.

Zeke is still single and has spent many years traveling in Europe and has appeared in five off-Broadway productions and three television shows.

SAFER SEX

"Oh, you devil!" she said hugging him hard. "Listen, condoms are great but I want to be completely safe." She paused and looked at him, her eyes twinkling. "Besides, I'm going to the clinic on Tuesday. I've made up my mind!"

He stopped hugging her and sat back. Through the faint light she could see the smile on his face. "You're getting on the pill?" He reached for her hand.

She nodded feeling she was about to do something very mature.

"Will you come with me?"

She heard Jeff inhale quickly. "You want me to go too?"

"Well, yeah. I mean this involves both of us. Why should I be the only one to go? Anyway, you should get tested for AIDS, don't you think?"

"AIDS? Why, for god's sake?"

Lisa felt his body stiffen and saw that his jaw was squarely set. "Jeff, come on. We've been over this before." She was starting to feel really annoyed. It seemed like Jeff's head was about two feet thick. "That girl you had sex with . . . had she ever had sex with anyone before you?"

"I. . . I don't know."

"Boy, you sure are discriminating in your sex partners." Jeff gave her a sharp look and Lisa felt she'd stepped over some line. She hurried to cover it up. "Well see. . . you never know. No matter how great a person may seem. I mean, they probably wouldn't even know themselves if they have AIDS." She looked at Jeff, but he wouldn't make eye contact with her.

"Look," she said, hearing the irritation in her voice, "I've never had sex before; I've never had a blood transfusion, and I don't do drugs with needles. I don't have AIDS. And you don't use needles, and you haven't had a transfusion, but you have had sex before. Did you use a condom?"

"No, but when did you get to be such an authority on sex?" Jeff was glaring at her.

"I'm not an authority, but I'm not dumb, and I just happen to care a lot about my life. I'd like to live long enough to see my grandchildren."

"Jesus, Lisa, you are so dramatic! You don't have to freak out."

Lisa held her breath and dug her fingernails into the palms of her hands. This issue was too big to let go of, but she didn't want to blow the whole thing either. She purposely lowered her voice. "Jeff, this means a lot to me. Will you go with me?"

Jeff shoved his hands into his pockets and leaned back against the seat. "Yeah. Okay. Only let's not go to the clinic here."

Lisa smiled. "I agree. I don't particularly want to see anyone I know, either." She reached over to hug him. "Thanks. I always knew you were a smart guy. So, we'll go on Tuesday."

"Lisa, you are one tough lady," he said kissing her temple. Lisa smiled and felt they had just cleared a big hurdle.

The next Tuesday Jeff was waiting to drive the two of them to the clinic after school. On the way they were both nervous and made small talk about other kids, classes, and basketball. Twenty minutes later they pulled into the parking lot and Jeff turned to Lisa.

"I'm glad we're doing this. I'm sorry I made it so hard for you to get me here." He leaned over and kissed her on the forehead. She felt a surge of quiet warmth and looked into his eyes.

"Thanks," she said.

They entered the waiting room self consciously, and Jeff sat down in the nearest chair while Lisa went to the reception window . There were five or six women and a couple. Each person was quietly looking at a magazine. Two or three of the people appeared to be teenagers, and Lisa gratefully didn't recognize anyone. She glanced over at Jeff but he had his head buried in a *Sports Illustrated*. She hoped the receptionist wouldn't say her name out loud.

The woman looked up and smiled at Lisa while she wrote down her name and told her to take a seat. "It will be just a few minutes," she said.

Lisa sat down next to Jeff, who barely looked over at her. Directly across from her was a wall rack with 10 to 15 brochures: "Teenagers and Sex," "AIDS," "Abstinence," "Pregnancy and Teens." She wanted to pick up several of the pamphlets, but then she would have to get up and cross to the other side and she felt too embarrassed, so she just idly looked around.

The receptionist called out her first name, and Lisa felt a small twinge in her throat. She turned to Jeff, and he gave her a half smile. At the window the lady quietly asked if she'd like to have the young man accompany her for the consultation. Lisa looked over at Jeff, but he was engrossed once again in his magazine.

"No, I guess not," she said.

Once inside the door the lady asked her for information: name, address, phone, birth date, age, and how she was going to pay for the consultation and the exam; did she have insurance?

"Yes, I do from my parents, but I'm not using it. I'll be paying cash for this." Lisa could feel her whole face turn red, and she hoped the woman wasn't going to give her some smirky smile. "How much is it?"

"That will be $50 unless you're on Medi-Cal, in which case it is $25. The fee includes a pap smear, breast examination, a test for anemia, the HIV test, and three months of birth control pills. Oh yes, and of course the consultation."

Lisa reached into her purse and took out the money; she and Jeff had decided to split the amount. She looked over the forms that had been filled out. Her heart was pounding, and she felt like she was doing something sneaky, breaking some rule, though she knew it was all perfectly legal. Well, she was sneaking, in a way. They had gone to another town, and she sure didn't want her folks to find out.

Another woman, a technician, showed her into a small room with a chair, a padded examining table covered with white paper, a cabinet with supplies on top, and a changing area. "Just have a seat, and I'll draw a blood sample to test for HIV."

"Does it hurt?" Lisa asked.

"No, just the prick of a needle," she said as she first took Lisa's blood pressure. "120 over 80. Perfect! Now, if you'll push up your sleeve." She took out a long piece of rubber strap, tied it around Lisa's arm, then checked for a vein. "Here's a good healthy one." She inserted the needle and deftly drew a small vial of blood. "There you go. All done and you'll get the results in about a week.

"Now, please take off your clothes and put on this paper gown. It opens down the back. You can sit on the table and wait; a nurse practitioner will be here in a few minutes." She smiled again at Lisa. "Is this your first pelvic examination?"

Lisa nodded.

"Don't worry, it won't be hard. It just takes a little getting used to."

Lisa murmured, "Okay, thank you," as the woman left closing the door behind her. The thin paper gown provided little warmth and Lisa felt chilly. The room, the experience, all felt foreign. She knew she should try to take it easy. After all, she was doing the right thing.

The nurse practitioner came into the room wearing slacks and a striped shirt with a white jacket. She had a stethoscope around her neck, her hair in a pony tail, and dangling earrings in iridescent colors.

"Hi," she said cheerfully. "You're Lisa, right?"

"Yes," Lisa replied.

"I'm Marlene Brown and I'm a nurse practitioner. Tell me a little about yourself." She glanced down at the chart. "You're 16?"

"Un-huh."

"Your last doctor was a Dr. Blackford in Eugene, Oregon. Is that where you're from?"

"Yeah. I was born there. We just moved down here last summer."

" I love it up there. I have an uncle who lives about 40 miles from Eugene," the nurse went on. "So, are you liking your life here in California?"

"I like it now. It was kind of hard at first."

"Well, how can I help you today?"

"I'm interested in getting some birth control," Lisa mumbled.

"Are you sexually active now?"

Lisa hesitated. "Well. . . uhm. . . "

"Have you had sexual intercourse?"

Lisa thought sexual intercourse was such a weird term; it sounded like a business meeting. "No, not yet. We've been close, though."

"Well, you're making a wise decision to get birth control. I've worked with too many girls who find themselves pregnant and then have an agonizing decision about whether or not to keep the baby." She was silent for a few moments. "Have you ever had a pelvic exam before?"

"No."

"Well, the first time is sometimes a bit awkward. It will be the first of many you'll have in your life. I know some girls won't come in for birth control because they're afraid to have a pelvic. But I feel that if a girl is ready to have sex, then she's ready to have a doctor or nurse look at her privates; besides, it's easier to have a pelvic than to have a baby." She smiled at Lisa. "So, let's check you out."

The nurse did the typical routine of checking her eyes and ears. She listened to Lisa's breathing and asked questions about her medical history and her menstrual periods. She asked her to lie down on the table and lowered Lisa's gown and gently pushed on her breasts checking for any lumps. "Do you examine your breasts yourself?"

"No," Lisa answered.

"It's a good habit to get into at least once a month. You just push gently on them all the way around each one, letting your fingers explore for any bumps. I'll give you a brochure that explains it all. Your breast exam is normal. But breast cancer is very high in the U.S. Not so often in young women your age, but still it does happen, and that's something you don't want to have to deal with.

"Okay, now comes the fun part. You need to scoot your bottom down to the end of the table here and put your feet in these metal holders. We call them stirrups, but this experience is nothing like riding a horse."

The stirrups felt cold against Lisa's bare feet. Her knees fell apart, the brief gown riding up.

"Just relax now," the nurse practitioner said spreading Lisa's knees further apart. Lisa looked up at the ceiling and was surprised by a poster that said "You have to kiss a lot of frogs before you find your prince!" She let out a laugh.

"That's a good one, isn't it?" She pulled on some latex gloves and picked up a long metal object that looked like the device they put on oil cans when servicing a car.

Lisa winced.

"This is a speculum. I place it in your vagina and it gently spreads your vagina apart enough so that I can take a good look around. It may be a little cold. It might hurt a bit and will feel a little like cramps. Just relax and breathe easy. Don't hold your breath, that will tighten your muscles"

Lisa kept her eyes glued on the ceiling. God, was this what women went through when they had a physical? The metal did feel cold, and she had some tight pains in her lower abdomen; she tried not to flinch and reminded herself to breathe.

"Just a minute more now," said the nurse, lowering the lamp to get a closer look. She took a thin stick with cotton on the end and swabbed the inside of Lisa's vagina. "This is called a pap smear. There we go. It all looks good, but we'll have the smear examined to make sure there are no problems," she said, taking out the metal speculum. Next she inserted her gloved fingers inside Lisa's vagina and explored her insides.

Lisa looked over at the nurse, who read the unspoken question in her eyes. " Just checking for abnormalities," she said. "It all feels just fine," and she withdrew her hand taking off the glove and throwing it in the wastebasket. "Well, Lisa, you've successfully come through your first pelvic. The first one is the hardest," and she gave Lisa a big smile. "Do you feel okay?" Lisa nodded. "You can get your clothes on now and then we'll talk. I'll be back in a few minutes."

Lisa got off the table and stood up. She picked up her sweatshirt and held it to her face. For some reason she felt like crying, and she let out a big sigh. So this was what her mother did on all those doctor visits. She wished she could talk to her right now.

Ms. Brown came back in. "Glad that's over?" she asked brightly. "Now, about birth control. Do you have a regular partner?"

Lisa was embarrassed by the question; of course she did.

"Yes," she said.

"Is he in favor of birth control?"

Lisa nodded. "That's always good to hear. Well, there are several methods: there's Norplant, which will protect you for five years. There's also Depo-Provera, which gives you protection for three months at a time. And then there are the birth control pills, which you take every day for 28 days, and they protect you on a daily basis."

Lisa was only familiar with the pill. "Can you tell me more about them?"

"Certainly. With all of them you may experience some change in your periods— some spotting, for instance. As I said, Norplant will protect you for five years at a time. It is made of six small, soft thin tubes called implants. These implants are placed just under the skin in your upper arm. They slowly let out a small amount of hormone that keeps you from getting pregnant. You can have them taken out at any time. Once in a while, some women experience headaches, and sometimes they object because they can feel the implants when they touch their arm or see a small scar on their arm. The most bothersome side effect of Norplant is frequent spotting during the first 9 to 12 months.

"Depo-Provera is administered with a shot in your rear end, and you need to come to the clinic every three months, but, on the other hand, you don't even have to think about birth control every day. The shot has a hormone that keeps the woman's eggs from leaving her ovaries. It also thickens the mucus at the opening of the uterus, so the man's sperm cannot get inside. Again, there may be some side effects like headaches or weight gain, but not every woman has these problems.

"Then, there's the pill. It's very simple. You just pop one in your mouth every day. There are very few side effects, but you must remember to take every pill in your pack. That is vitally important."

Lisa had been listening carefully. "Well, for now I think I'd like to get the pill and maybe I'll try one of the other ones later. What about this new thing from France? RU -something?"

"RU 486. Yes. The French have had it for ten years. Being able to take a pill in the first few weeks of pregnancy is certainly preferable to having an abortion. But RU 468 is not a method of birth control; it doesn't *prevent* pregnancy."

Lisa listened and then thought again of the pill. "I've heard that sometimes girls gain weight when they start taking the pill. Is that right?"

"Once in a while that happens, but if it does, we'll just adjust the dosage. Or perhaps we'll use another brand. Gaining weight does not have to be part of the picture. I know that there are girls who say they don't want to take the pill because they're afraid of gaining weight."

Lisa shook her head. "I don't get it. Even if a person did gain weight, isn't putting on a few pounds better than getting pregnant?"

The nurse smiled and then reached behind her into a large white cabinet, "I'll give you a three-month's supply, and after that we'll talk to see how you're doing with them. Each month's supply comes in an individual case. Start taking the pills the first Sunday after your period begins. There's nothing magical about Sunday; we just feel it's easy to remember. You just select the pill marked 'Sunday.' You take one a day for twenty-eight days, and you'll begin your new pack on Sunday also. Your period should come during the last week of your pill pack. Be sure not to have any sexual intercourse between now and the time you start taking these pills. In addition, you'll need to use condoms and foam as a back-up for the first cycle or pack of your pills. It takes at least two weeks for the pill to become fully effective.

"Also, if you should take an antibiotic or Valium, you should also use a back-up method. Of course, I hope you won't be needing a Valium; I certainly don't recommend it for teenagers," she said with a smile.

"We'll give you extra condoms as well, since safer sex now means not getting pregnant as well as not getting STDs or HIV. Do you think your boyfriend will be willing to use a condom?"

"I'll talk to him," Lisa said.

"I'm glad to hear that. So often boys and men think somehow it's not manly to use a condom. Mostly, I think they're just embarrassed to put one on, and they use that masculinity thing as an excuse. So, good for him. I'd be happy to talk to him first, or we have a male nurse on the staff, as well. Perhaps he'd feel more comfortable with a man.

"There are a couple of things you need to know about condoms. Be sure you get the latex kind and be sure to get a water based lubricant to put on the outside of it. Also, and a lot of adults don't even know this, a half-inch space needs to be left at the tip. That's to make sure there's room to hold the sperm."

"I'll talk to him," Lisa said.

The nurse picked up a plastic bag containing all the birth control supplies and handed it to Lisa. "Now, regarding the HIV test, you'll need to come back in person to get the results. We do this to preserve confidentiality, which is very important when it comes to AIDS, or birth control for that matter. We get a lot of girls in here whose parents would be very punishing if they knew their daughters were using birth control. However, I think the girls are being very mature. She put out her hand and said "Lisa, this may seem overwhelming right now, but you are making a very responsible decision. Good luck."

"Thank you." Lisa shook her hand.

Opening the office door, she felt like she was stepping back into another world.

Thankfully, no one else was in the waiting room except Jeff, who was slumped in a chair still reading a magazine.

"Hi. How'd it go?" he asked.

"Whew! Okay. I'm glad it's over. The nurse was really nice. Did you get the test?"

"No, they were busy."

"Jeff, come on! They don't look busy now. Don't come all the way over here and not take advantage of getting the test." She felt irritated. "You should see what I've been through. Go on. Get it over with."

Reluctantly, Jeff got to his feet and went over to the receptionist's window. "Uh, excuse me. How do you get an AIDS test?" he mumbled.

"You mean a test for HIV?"

"Yeah."

"We can do it right now. It costs $10.00."

Jeff turned to Lisa. He had a scowl on his face and let out an exasperated sigh. "I'm out of money," he said. Lisa looked in her wallet.

"Here's $10.00," she said. "It's a good investment."

The receptionist took the money and wrote out a receipt. "You'll need to come back in a week to get the results. If you'll come with me now, it won't take but a few minutes. He'll be right back," she told Lisa.

Lisa didn't even have time to read a brochure on "Teenagers and Sex" before Jeff was back.

"So, how was it?" she asked.

"Nothing to it. They just took some blood. I don't know why people make such a big deal out of getting tested."

Lisa couldn't contain a smirk. "Yeah, some people are strange."

"So, are we ready now? Let's get out of here. Come on, I'm starving." Out in the parking lot Jeff asked, "When will it be safe?"

"Safe for what?" she said teasingly.

"Oh gee, I dunno. Safe to cross the street! Come on, when?"

"Boy, are you anxious! Calm down, boy. I'll start taking the pill in about two weeks. But even then we'll have to use foam and condoms for a while."

"Two weeks! You're kidding! Why so long?"

"First, I have to get my period."

"Oh. Well, what about the foam and stuff?"

"That's just to be really safe. You'll see, the time will fly by."

Jeff put his arm around her. "Well, none of it's easy, but I am glad we've done it," he said kissing her on the temple.

"Me too," she said reaching up to kiss him back.

○

Her period came and was over in five days. Two days later brought her to Sunday, the day she could begin the birth control pills. Lisa took the small plastic case out from under the pile of sweaters in her drawer. She had read the directions over many times and she opened the lavender colored case and turned the dial to Sunday. A small pink pill appeared and she popped it into her mouth. She looked at herself in the mirror and smiled. Well, it was done. She was on her way.

○

The following Thursday night Jeff called Lisa on the phone. "I've got the news you've been waiting for, or I should say 'we've' been waiting for!"

"What? Tell me!"

"Guess what?"

"You've been selected to play on a pro basketball team!"

"Right! No, this is better! I got my test results. No HIV! You see, I'm clean as a whistle!"

"Jeff, that's great! I'm so pleased. I really didn't think you did have it, but I feel so much better knowing for sure. Besides, I like a smart man!"

"Okay, that's just one good news. There's one more."

"Jeff, stop. Just tell me."

"Okay, listen. Pete Cline's folks have this cabin at Tahoe and they said we could use it next weekend. Can you go?"

"I hope so. I'll have to ask. How fun!"

"That's not all. Pete can't make it up till Saturday, but he said I—I mean we—could go up Friday night." He paused. "It'll have been two weeks. What do you say?"

"Jeff, I'll do everything I can. I'll have to do some fast talking. My god, I'm so excited!"

"Well guess what? I am too. So, call me later, okay?"

"Right. I will. This is too much!"

○

Friday night of the next week Jeff and Lisa were on the way to their friend's cabin at Lake Tahoe; the rest of the kids would arrive on Saturday. Lisa sat as close as possible to Jeff on the long drive north. They talked and listened to their favorite tapes. Despite the heavy traffic of skiers heading for the mountains, the drive went smoothly, and no chains were required. There was a special warmth between them and it showed in their careful conversation. They took turns telling each other stories from their pasts, stories about childhood experiences, favorite grandparents and the family dog. Occasionally Jeff reached over and touched Lisa's thigh or put his arm around her. Lisa told him about Oregon and

86

all her friends.

During the quiet times she thought about how wonderful it would be to live with Jeff some day and have their children. She liked his kindness, and she especially liked the way he had not pushed himself on her, how he had respected her feelings and her hesitations. She felt excited and scared. She probably should have told her mother. She'd tell her soon, in a few days, but for now she wanted this to be between her and Jeff.

The cabin was freezing cold when they arrived, and they spent the first hour figuring out how to turn on the heat and just looking around. When they came to the biggest bedroom and saw the large queen sized bed, Lisa giggled.

"What do you think?" Jeff asked looking at the bed.

"It looks a little scary."

"Are you scared of the bed or me?" he said, hugging her.

"Ah, neither. I'm scared of 'it!'" and she stepped away. "Come on, let's check out the upstairs and then eat."

Jeff made a fire in the living room while Lisa put water on to boil for spaghetti and heated the garlic bread. "We'll probably be eating spaghetti for the whole weekend," she said. "That's about all I know how to make."

They sat down by the fire. The long trip and cold mountain air had made them ravenous, and there was nothing left in any of the bowls when they finished.

Jeff put on an R.E.M. tape and the song "Losing my Religion," a song they both loved. He sat down and put his arm around her. They kissed for a long time, both of them becoming very turned on.

"Do you want to go upstairs?" Lisa asked.

"Hmm. I don't care. I kind of like it here by the fire," Jeff said kissing her temples, his hands moving under her sweater.

"Me, too. I'll be back in a minute," Lisa said, getting up.

"Where are you going?"

"Remember? It's not entirely safe yet."

Jeff groaned. "God," he muttered.

"Come on," Lisa said. "You do your part and I'll do mine."

She grabbed her purse and went into the bathroom. Searching through her bag she found the container of spermacidal foam. Her fingers felt cold and she was glad she had read the directions beforehand. She pulled down her jeans and underpants and took the container, filled the applicator with foam, and inserted it into her vagina. It felt slightly chilly at first, then moist; she actually kind of liked the fluffy feel of the foam. She wiped herself off, pulled up her pants and glanced in the mirror, running her fingers through her long hair. This part sure wasn't very romantic. But then she gave herself a half smile; she was ready.

Jeff had turned the lights off, so only the fire's orange glow lit up the room. He was lying on the rug against some pillows and gave Lisa a long, sweet smile as she settled down next to him. She laid her head on his chest and sighed deeply. They were both quiet for several minutes just listening to the music and the crackling of the fire. Jeff bent his head down. "Lisa," he said, "I love you."

"I love you too, Jeff," and they kissed each other very tenderly. It was a kiss Lisa wished would go on forever. Gently his tongue came into her mouth and Lisa felt her entire body moving up toward him. She could feel the whole wonderful length of his body, his muscular arms about her, his chest pressing against her own, his penis hard on her leg.

"Take off your clothes," he whispered, and Lisa willingly slipped off her shirt and wiggled out of her jeans while Jeff did the same. Except for their socks, they lay together completely naked, entangled in each other's arms. There was a warm, nutty smell about Jeff that was delicious. The feeling of skin on skin was almost magical, so soft and so moist, and it brought them utterly close to one another. Pushing back her hair, Jeff looked down at her and smiled. "This is good," he said. "I'm glad we waited."

Lisa felt completely safe and warm. Her nervousness dissolved as Jeff caressed and kissed her. His hand explored her crotch, and she felt his fingers pushing their way inside her. She was very wet and felt like she was unraveling as they began moving against each other. Then slowly, Jeff reached under one of the pillows and Lisa heard a crackling sound. Jeff turned over, and Lisa knew he was putting on a condom, and she felt even closer to him. He turned and they kissed again, this time with an urgency. Next she felt his hand moving his penis inside her. He hesitated.

"Does it hurt?"

"No, it's okay. Don't stop," and she reached up and touched the hair on his forehead.

The firelight flickered on his face so that sometimes he was a dark featureless shadow and sometimes she could see the outline of his lips and nose, the light in his eyes. He moved all the way inside of her, and she felt a sharp, almost pinch-like feeling. Involuntarily she let out a small gasp. Jeff stopped moving again and looked questioning. "I'm all right," she said, tightening her arms around him. He hugged her close and continued moving with a gentle thrusting.

"Oh Lisa," he said, moving more and more rapidly. "Lisa."

Lisa tried to move with him but she couldn't keep up. The next thing she knew Jeff let out a loud groan and his whole body shook. He gasped and clutched Lisa and held her tightly.

"Ohhh, god," he said, and she felt the whole weight of his body. Lisa lay quietly, holding him. Her own breathing was rapid. She marveled at what had just happened. So this was sex. How could anyone do this without completely loving the other person? Her senses took in the light, the sound of the fire and Jeff's breathing. She closed her eyes and drifted off.

A few minutes later Jeff reached down to hold his penis so that the condom wouldn't come off. He glanced over at Lisa and she smiled back at him as he removed the condom, tied a knot at the open end and plopped it onto a wad of tissue.

"This is the gross part," he said, and she laughed.

"It may be gross," she said, "but it beats being pregnant."

He settled back down next to her.

"You did like that like an old pro," Lisa said.

"Which part?"

"All of it. The condom and. . . and you know."

"You mean the fucking?"

"Jeff, don't call it that. It wasn't fucking. It was wonderful."

"Was it?"

"Oh yes. Wasn't it for you?"

"It was the best," he said, reaching over to hug her. "Are you okay?"

"Of course I am. I feel great, but I'm getting chilly. Let's go upstairs and go to bed."

"I hate to leave this," he said, moving to kiss her. "Okay, let's go."

The room upstairs was chilly too. Lisa hurried into the bathroom and put on her nightgown. She looked at herself in the mirror. Her face was flushed and she looked happy. No girl could ever have had such a great first time.

Her self-consciousness gone, she got into bed and snuggled up next to Jeff. They held each other to keep warm and because it felt so right and slept soundly the whole night. When Lisa woke up the next morning she found Jeff's arms around her. She moved a little closer to him and was surprised to feel that his penis was hard against the small of her back. She smiled and he hugged her tightly.

"G'morning," he murmured. "I had a great dream that we finally had sex. And we were in front of a big fire, lying on the floor."

"I had the same dream."

"And then," Jeff went on, "I had a dream that we had sex again in the morning in a comfy bed in a. . . ," he paused and looked around the room. . . "in a blue and white bedroom."

"Sounds like a great dream," Lisa said. "Can I join it?"

"You'd better," Jeff said, and he kissed the back of her neck while his hands moved to her breasts.

Lisa felt all tingly, but an alarm went off in her head. "Jeff. Hang on. You're forgetting something."

"What? Forgetting what?"

"Jeff, don't play dumb." Why was she always the one to have to bring up safety? "Jeff, I've got to get up, and you have to get a condom."

Jeff groaned. "God, I know you're right, but it's such a drag."

"Well, would you rather quit school and raise a baby with me or get up now for five seconds?"

"All right. All right. Shit! I left them downstairs." He got out of bed, tugging on his boxer shorts and T-shirt. "I'll be right back. Do you want anything?"

"Just you and that little latex thing." Lisa got out of bed too and went to the bathroom. She was freezing. First she went to the toilet, then took the container of foam and inserted a heavy dose inside of her. She was getting better and better at this. Then she scrambled back to bed, pulling the covers up to her neck.

Jeff came back and jumped in bed, his teeth chattering. "I turned on the heat. It'll warm up. Boy, there's nothing like a quick jaunt in an icy cabin to cool a guy off."

"Did you get one?"

"Yep."

"Well, put it on," Lisa said giggling.

"Uh, I'll need some help now. I didn't need any help before, but I do now." He took Lisa's hand and put it on his penis. "Here, hold him. He's cold."

His penis was soft. Lisa wanted to look at it but was too embarrassed. It was so different from anything she possessed, and she'd never felt Jeff's penis when it was limp. Within a few seconds, though, it was growing larger and hard.

"I think he's warming up," she said.

Jeff turned around, put on the condom and then moved on top of Lisa, kissing her lips and face and putting himself inside of her. Lisa moved a little, adjusting to his body and spreading her legs apart. Jeff was moving on top of her, and their kisses were frenzied and passionate. Suddenly Jeff let out an enormous groan and clutched Lisa in an intense, almost desperate way. Lisa was surprised at how fast it had all happened, but the feeling of lying next to Jeff and feeling his excitement and relief was very satisfying. She relished the moment. In a couple of hours the rest of the kids would arrive, and she and Jeff would be together with the group. For now, though, it was a special time just for the two of them.

O

Almost two months had passed since their time at the cabin. School had gone on as had basketball and play rehearsal. There was a kind of routine to the weeks. Jeff and Lisa managed to be together at least once a week, sometimes two or three times. Because they were monogamous and had no history of HIV or any sexually transmitted diseases, they were able to have sex without the foam and condoms now and they simply relied on the pill. Life was busy and sweet.

Spring vacation was coming up, and Lisa's family planned to go to Disneyland. They hadn't had any kind of a break together for over two years, and her parents figured they could finally afford a short vacation. From what Lisa could tell, she was about the only teenager living in California who had never been to Disneyland. She was excited about it and also hoping to hit the warm beaches in the southern part of the state. The only drawback was Jeff. She wouldn't see him for nearly a week.

"Damn!" Jeff said. "A bunch of us are going to Tahoe. I was hoping you could come too."

"Jeff, I'm sorry. What can I say? I want to go with you, but I also want to go to Disneyland. I mean, can you believe I've never been there?"

"I know. I know. You'll have a great time. Well, think of me in the spring snow while you're doing Splash Mountain or lying on the sandy beach." He tightened his arms around her. They were sitting in his room listening to music while his parents were in the living room talking to friends. Jeff reached down and kissed her. "Come on. We've never done it when my folks were home," he said teasingly.

Lisa kissed him back with a full open mouth. "Is this what you mean? You're a devil, you know, but guess what?"

"What?" he said running his hands over her breasts.

"I've got my period. Sorry, Charlie," she said with a laugh.

"Shit! So I won't get to see you then for a week? You'd better be good down there. Don't run off with any of those surfer studs."

"Or you with any snow bunnies."

○

The trip to southern California had been a ball. Lisa, Stephanie and their parents had gone on most of the rides, had time to relax together, and the two sisters had hardly argued. It was finally easy for Lisa to spend time with Stephanie. The two of them went to the teen nightclub at the hotel and giggled at night in bed about all the goofy boys they'd danced with. The weather had been surprisingly warm for April though the water was chilly. The beach was pure pleasure: hot, golden sand and lots of sun. They all came home brown and refreshed.

Lisa hadn't been in the door more than five minutes before she called Jeff. "Hi!" she said. "We're back!"

"Hi. So how was it?"

There was something different about Jeff's voice—something distant. "It was great. I loved it. We all did. . . So how was your snow trip?"

"Hmmm. It was good. Real good spring snow and lots of sun."

"Were there lots of kids?" Lisa asked.

"About 12, I guess."

Lisa waited for Jeff to say he was coming over. He didn't.

"Well, when will I see you?" she asked, picturing him wearing her favorite blue sweater and baggy shorts.

"How 'bout tonight? I've got to finish some homework. Did you finish your paper for Mr. T.?"

"You mean the one on *Death of a Salesman?*"

"Yeah. That one. I haven't even begun."

"I just have to type mine. It was a hard assignment. You have to have a minimum of 10 quotations."

"Ten? You're kidding! I've got to get going. I'll call you and maybe come over."

His voice had warmed up some, but there was still something strange.

"Okay. I'll see you tonight."

Lisa heard her mother call her to come help unpack the car. She put down the phone and sat still for a minute. Her heart was beating very quickly and her head felt fuzzy.

A couple of hours later Lisa borrowed the car and went over to Kathy's. She wanted to hear about the snow trip from someone besides Jeff.

Kathy opened the door with a surprised look. "Hey Lisa! Come on in," she said.

They chatted for a while before Lisa asked about the trip. Kathy said it was great but she looked uneasy.

"Kathy what's going on? I talked to Jeff, and he sounded funny, and now you do too. What is it?"

"I dunno. I guess I feel a little awkward." She paused. "God. I don't want to sound like a snitch."

"Go on. Please."

"Well, this snow trip. . . Remember my telling you about Molly?"

"Molly? Not really."

"My best friend who moved away? Jeff's old girlfriend?"

"Oh yeah. I remember." Lisa felt something tighten in her chest.

"Well, Molly came on this trip and. . . "

"Jeff got together with her?"

"Yeah, kind of."

"What happened? What did they do? God. I can't believe this!"

"I don't really know if anything happened, " Kathy said. "They spent a lot of time together."

"Did. . . did they have sex?" Lisa asked.

"Lisa, I don't know. I don't think so. I feel terrible. I like all three of you. I feel so in the middle."

"How could he do that? I mean everything was great when I left for L.A."

"I don't know. I don't think he planned to do anything. He didn't even know Molly was going on the trip. It was a last minute thing, you know. Look, don't jump to conclusions. Talk to him."

"I will! But what about me? What about us? I thought we were so solid."

"I know. He really feels bad."

"He is such a shit! I'm going over there."

"Please don't tell him I told you. I know he wanted to tell you himself."

"When, I wonder. In two months?" Lisa shouted back. " I feel like such a fool!" The tears were stinging her eyes. "I'm going over there now. What a jerk!"

She sat in her car for a few minutes trying to calm down. How could he have done this? She started the car and drove slowly, telling herself to take it easy.

Jeff answered the door with a surprised and guilty look on his face.

"Hi, Lis," he said. "Hey, you're all brown."

"Don't I even get a kiss?"

"Hi, again," he said putting his arms around her and kissing her on the lips.

"Oh Jeff," she said and the tears started rolling down her cheeks. "Jeff, I know.

I know about you and Molly." She felt his whole body grow tight.

"Who told you?"

"It doesn't matter. I would have found out."

"But I wanted to be the one to explain things."

"What happened? Did you two have sex?"

"Lisa, don't jump to conclusions. We just spent time together."

"Did you kiss?"

"Yes," Jeff said and he uncomfortably shifted his weight from one foot to the other. "Lisa, come on. Let's go in my room and talk."

Reluctantly Lisa followed him. His house seemed quiet. Maybe no one else was home. Closing his bedroom door, Jeff said, "Look Lisa. It wasn't what you think. I didn't forget about you, about us. And we didn't have sex."

"Did you come close?"

Jeff looked down. "Well, not exactly."

"Not exactly? What does that mean? Jeff, how could you? Why? Everything was fine when I left. At least I thought it was. Wasn't it?"

"Of course it was."

"Well then, why?"

"I dunno. It was just fun seeing Molly again. We skied together and kind of got paired off. Anyway, she has a boyfriend."

"Oh swell! She sounds like a great girl! A real jewel. She sounds like a slut to me. And what about you? Don't you have a girlfriend? What about the bracelet you gave me? Remember our talks? Remember the cabin? The clinic? What about all that?"

"Lisa, don't. I love you."

"No, Jeff. No, you don't," she said trying to talk through her tears. "Someone who loved me wouldn't go off and nearly have sex with another girl, especially an old girlfriend." She stood glaring at Jeff. He looked miserable. "Or maybe you're just not mature enough to know that yet. I'm leaving," she said.

"Lisa, wait."

She walked out of the house to the car and hoped he would follow her, but he didn't. Finally, she drove off, barely able to see the stop signs. Oh god, she just wanted to get home. Shakily, she pulled into the driveway and turned off the engine and put her head down on the steering wheel. How was she going to make it through this? How could everything be so wonderful one minute and so awful the next? Damn! She got out and slammed the car door as hard as she could.

○

Lisa stayed in her room the rest of the day and evening, and even though Jeff called twice, she wouldn't talk to him. She called Gwen in Eugene, but she wasn't home. Next she tried Kathy, who wasn't home either.

Her mother came in around dinner time. "Lisa, I've tried not to interfere, but

I can see how unhappy you are, so it must be Jeff. Do you want to talk about it?"

"Oh Mom. It's so hard," Lisa said bursting into tears.

"What happened?" her mother said, sitting down on the bed.

"Jeff was with an old girlfriend over vacation. I just don't see how he could have done such a thing. I thought we had something so special."

Her mother was quiet for minute, "You probably did have—or do have—something special. I've seen the two of you together, and I think you do. But it's not always easy at your age to stay faithful."

"Mom, don't protect him! I wouldn't have done anything like that. We were so close. We made promises."

Her mother sighed. "I'm so sorry. I'm sorry you have to hurt like this."

Just then Stephanie called out, "Mom, it's time to go."

"I forgot, I have to drive Stephanie to Maggie's house. I'll be back in a few minutes," she said, patting Lisa's back.

"Okay." Lisa buried her face in her pillow.

With her mother gone, Lisa thought about being faithful and promises. She closed her eyes and was quiet, then reached over and picked up the phone to call.

"Zeke? This is Lisa. What are you doing?"

"Lisa!" his voice sounded very upbeat. "I'm great. What's up?"

"Nothing much. Listen, could you come over? I'm having a hard time."

"Sure. Are you crying?"

"Yeah."

"Is it Jeff?"

Lisa was silent. "Please just come over."

"I'll be there in 10 minutes."

○

Seeing Zeke in an old 60's shirt with the Beatles and yellow submarines on it made Lisa smile.

"Hi, thanks for coming—."

"Never fear. Superfriend is here," he said putting his arm around her and hugging her.

"Come on in my room." Lisa led the way and left her door open.

"Now sit down and tell your Uncle Zeke what's going on, and I'll even give you a free foot massage."

Lisa sat on the bed and plopped her foot in Zeke's lap. He firmly rubbed her soles and pulled gently on her toes. Slowly she could feel herself relaxing as Zeke worked the tightness out of her feet.

"So, the truth is that Jeff spent time with another girl but still loves you—right?"

"That's what he says."

"Well, do you still love him?"

"Of course I do. But I'm so hurt and angry right now, and I'm so blown away!

94

How does something like this happen? How can you love someone one minute and then go off and make out with someone else?"

Zeke was quiet. "Well, I did it once. The whole thing was stupid."

"You mean you had a girlfriend and still went off with someone else?"

"Yeah."

"Did you love your girlfriend?"

"I thought I did."

"Were the two of you close?"

"Yes," he said, switching to the other foot.

"Had you. . . you know, did you guys. . . ?"

"Have sex?"

"Yeah," Lisa said.

"Yep. Lots of times."

"And still you made out with someone else? Why?"

"I dunno. I didn't plan it. It just happened."

"Did you and your girlfriend break up?

"Yeah."

"Were you sorry?"

"Yeah. It was a stupid thing I did. But, oh well!" Zeke sighed. "Live and learn."

Lisa was quiet. "I hate this. Life is screwed up."

"So, what are you going to do?"

"I don't know yet. I can't stand the thought of going back to school tomorrow."

"Lisa, just take it slow. Don't rush anything." He stopped rubbing her foot and looked directly at her. "Any time you want, I'll be here."

Lisa leaned over and kissed him on the cheek.

"Thanks," she said.

○

Lisa managed to avoid Jeff for the next couple of days, but he finally cornered her on Wednesday as she was leaving school.

"We've got to talk, Lisa, " he said.

"I know. You're right," she said. " But not here. Let's go some place, to a park or something."

"Let's walk." They were quiet for nearly ten minutes before Jeff said, "Listen. I want us to still be together. I wish I could change everything that happened last week. You're the one I want to be with."

"Jeff, I've done a lot of thinking." She stopped and they sat down. "I miss you, but when I think of going back together with you, it just doesn't feel right. Something has changed. I just don't think I could be with you in the same way. I'm not sure I could trust you again."

"Lisa! You're making too much out of this thing. Yes, we made out but it stopped at that."

"But why didn't you tell me you were thinking about her?"

"I wasn't thinking about her. It just happened. We found ourselves kind of thrown together and it happened."

"Well, it sure doesn't fit my picture of the way love is supposed to be," said Lisa

"I know but couldn't we try again? Don't be so harsh."

"I need some time, Jeff."

Jeff let out a big sigh. "This really sucks, Lisa. How much time do you need? Will you know by next week? Will you know before the prom?"

The prom! Lisa had completely forgotten about it; that fact amazed her. She'd been thinking about it for weeks now, before this Molly thing. It was going to be a great evening: Lisa in a new black dress, Jeff in a tuxedo—a whole special night for the two of them. She couldn't imagine going with anyone else. Maybe she was making too much out of this, after all.

"Jeff, just be patient."

○

Three days later they were back together. Lisa had mostly recovered her good nature and felt back in balance. The prom was two weeks away, and tryouts for the next play were in three days. Together with Kathy and Zeke, Lisa decided to audition.

The fact that the director had selected *Our Town* as their spring play met with mixed reactions. Some thought it was too boring and had been done too many times. Others thought it was neat because at least it was a play most everyone had read if they were a junior or older.

When the news came that Lisa had been selected, she was thrilled. But she was even happier that Kathy and Zeke had made it too. Kathy would play mother to Lisa's Emily; Zeke would be George.

"You know, Lisa, in this play you and I are going to wind up falling in love and getting married," Zeke said, putting his arm around her while they looked at the posted list of cast members.

Lisa felt her face redden.

"Oh-oh, what will Jeff say?" Kathy said.

Jeff did have a few things to say; he objected to the long hours that rehearsals took, and he noted that Lisa seemed to enjoy her time spent with her drama friends more than time spent with him.

"Jeff, you're making this up. Why else would I be going with you if I didn't want to be with you? It's just that these plays take a lot of time. It's like you with your basketball."

"Yeah, but my basketball is over now. And every time I want us to do something, it seems you have rehearsal. Besides, I heard about you and that Zeke guy."

96

"Heard what?"

"I heard about the two of you at play rehearsals."

"What? He's just a friend. We don't make out, unlike some people I know."

"Oh, just drop it! " Jeff said. "God, you're so bitchy lately."

"Look Jeff. I didn't start this whole thing. Everything was fine before you went on your ski vacation."

"Lisa! I said let's drop it. I gotta go. I'll call you tonight."

"I won't be home tonight."

"Okay. Then I'll see you tomorrow."

"Jeff? C'mere. Let's just both take it easy," she said, reaching up to kiss him.

"Yeah, you're right," he said with a tight smile.

O

Her black prom dress was stashed in a brown shopping bag along with her heels, panty hose, and strapless bra. Lisa was in her sweats as she sat in the back seat with Jeff and another couple heading toward the ocean. She leaned against Jeff's shoulder and closed her eyes.

The dance had been pretty cool. The d.j. played a lot of good music and Lisa had danced until her feet were sore. They'd gone to dinner earlier and had laughed uproariously at stupid jokes. There were eight couples in all and they had not made life easy for the waiter, but he had been good natured. About six of the kids had been loaded and the rest had to keep telling them to shut up, but everyone kept a good humor. One of the girls threw up in the bathroom, and Lisa and Kathy had done their best to clean her up. Lisa was exhausted.

The beach was foggy and cold, and everyone piled out of the car dragging sleeping bags and food. The salty air stung her nose, and Lisa felt suddenly exhilarated.

"We need a fire," someone called out. "Everyone look for wood." They bumped around in the dark, feeling through the damp sand. Luckily there were the remains of an old beach fire with warm ashes. Wadded up paper and dry sticks got a small blaze going and, little by little, people straggled in with more wood. The group gathered around huddling together, the firelight flickering on their faces.

Someone brought out beer, but most claimed it was too cold to drink. They warmed their hands, told a few jokes and reminisced about the night. A few kids had been expelled from the dance for showing up drunk. And several kids had thrown up in full view of the vice-principals. Most agreed it had been a good evening. Bringing out a joint, Neil said, "And now for the highlight of the prom, Mr. J; take a hit my friends." The joint was passed around, most everyone taking a drag or two.

Following Jeff, Lisa inhaled deeply but sharp heat burned her lungs and she coughed. The joint went round and round, but she didn't take another toke. Along with the other guys, Jeff took many hits and within an hour the group was singing "Itsy, bitsy spider," and laughing and rolling in the sand The fog continued to circulate around them forming almost a protective shield. Some of the couples paired off to sleeping bags, leaving the rest of the group to their "music making."

Jeff and Lisa snuggled down under a big quilt.

"Hold me close, Lisa, I'm chilly," Jeff said, putting his arms around her, his hands moving under her sweatshirt. He started to undo her bra.

"Jeff, just take it easy," Lisa said. "I'm freezing. I want to get warmed up."

Jeff moved his hands away, but within a minute or two they were wiggling into the top of Lisa's sweats, sliding down inside her underpants.

"Jeff! Damn it! Stop it! " Lisa said, pushing him away

"Lisa, for Christssake! What's the matter with you? We haven't been together for a long time."

"Yes, we have Jeff. We've been together. We just haven't had sex."

Suddenly there was a series of loud bangs almost like the sound of gunfire.

"What's that?" Lisa said sitting up and looking all around. "Paul? What happened?" she called out.

"Aw, Nick threw some firecrackers in the fire. Don't worry; it's okay."

"God, I'm glad it wasn't a gun," she said with a big sigh and snuggled back down under the quilt.

"Come on back here," Jeff said squeezing Lisa, kissing her face and neck, his hands moving up inside her sweatshirt.

"Jeff! For god's sake! What is it with you ? You're acting nuts," she said, pulling away.

"Lisa, don't be so cold. Come on. I'm horny."

"I don't want to do it now. Not like this. You're stoned. I don't like it." She sat up. "This is stupid. I want things to be nice, you know, and special."

"Why does it always have to be special?" Jeff said. "Why can't it just be plain or ordinary?"

"Because it is special, that's why. Sex is special. That's the way I want it."

"Lisa—"

Just then two pairs of headlights flashed out over their heads to the water beyond. They heard a loud speaker and saw some red lights.

"Jesus! It's the police!" Jeff said. He jumped up from under the quilt and hurried around, waking some of the kids and telling others to get rid of any dope or alcohol.

Lisa sat up, feeling her heart pounding. Shit! What would happen now? She visualized her parents having to come to the jail and pick her up.

Two tall men wearing large-brimmed hats cautiously approached the small fire. Both had their guns out. "Okay, kids. We heard gunshots. Who's got the gun?"

The kids all looked at each other questioning.

"No one has a gun," Paul said. "It was just some firecrackers."

The sheriffs looked them all over carefully. One put his gun away while the other kept his trained on the group. "Let's hope that's so. But as you know, firecrackers are illegal." He shone his flashlight around, illuminating the empty beer bottles. "Where's the dope? We can smell it."

No one said a word

"What are you kids doing here, anyway? First of all, you're not supposed to be sleeping on the beach and certainly not using alcohol or dope."

Jeff spoke up. "We came over from Galt High School. It's prom night."

"Swell," said the partner, putting his gun away. "There'll probably be a few traffic fatalities tonight. Let's see your I.D.s."

Some of the boys reached in their pockets, but most of the kids didn't have one with them.

The officer shone his light on each kid's face to see if the I.D. matched. "There's no way you're 21, son," he said to Nick. Nick stared down at his bare feet, his hair flopping in his eyes.

"Okay, we're hauling you in." He shone his light all around the group, checking their faces and the ground around them. "Who here is in good enough shape to drive?"

No one stepped forward. Finally, Lisa said, "I am."

"Come over here, miss. Let's check you out." He shone the light in her eyes and had her walk a straight line. "Okay, you can drive one of these cars. Four of you go with her. The rest of you come with us. Bring your stuff and follow my car."

Lisa felt shaky driving Paul's car, following the sheriff's tail lights. What a mess. What a big shitty mess. The tears were stinging her eyes.

They weren't strip searched, but each of them had to empty their pocket or purse. Only two, Nick and Paul, had any traces of dope on them, and the officer said they'd found a joint and a six pack in Nick's car. The two boys were booked for possession.

"We're going to let you kids go," he said to the rest of the group. "But we're calling your parents, and they'll need to come and pick you up."

Lisa glanced over at Jeff and then at the clock. It was Sunday, 6 a.m. Her parents would be sleeping.

When they finally walked in the door, Lisa felt her entire body stiffen. She wanted to run to them and be comforted, but she didn't dare. Her mother stood at the front desk looking at her while her father talked to the officer. Her name was called, and she was released. Her dad put a heavy hand on her shoulder as they walked outside. Going down the steps, they met Jeff's parents coming in.

"Hello, Lisa," his mother said.

"Hi," she murmured.

The five of them stood awkwardly. Lisa wanted to shrink down and crawl away; instead, she introduced them. "Mr. and Mrs. Branley, these are my parents." The four shook hands.

Finally, Jeff's dad said, "Looks like these kids have gotten themselves into a pile of trouble."

"They're lucky they weren't arrested. Maybe they should have been. There will be some changes at our house, I can tell you that," her dad said grimly.

"Damn it, Lisa! " her father said, slamming the car door. "What were you kids doing out on the beach all night, drinking and smoking dope? I thought we'd seen the last of that kind of thing from you!"

Her mother turned to her saying, "I can't believe I can't trust you any more. How much pot do you smoke? How often?"

"It's not like that," Lisa began. "Some of the kids smoke a lot but I don't. I didn't drink anything. I had only one hit—that's all, just one."

"Well, it's one too many. I didn't know you were running around with a bunch of pot heads," her father said.

"They're not pot heads. Well, maybe a couple are, but not most of them."

"For god's sake! Don't they have anything better to do with themselves? And what about Jeff? Does he smoke and drink too?"

"Not usually."

"Tonight?"

"Some," she said, thinking about how difficult he had been before the sheriff arrived.

"Why do you kids think you have to smoke and drink to make it a special night?"

"Well, you do. You drink to celebrate," Lisa said. She was getting so angry that she was close to tears.

"Lisa, we're over 21. It's legal for us to drink. It isn't for you. And it's not legal to smoke pot, period!"

"Well, that's a stupid law. Besides, what did you do when you were 16? Didn't you ever drink?"

"That's not the issue here. You and your friends were the ones hauled in by the sheriff, and that's damn serious. As far as I'm concerned, you're grounded. . . no dates, no going out, no telephone until after school's over."

Lisa's mother looked sharply at her husband.

"Dad, that's nearly a month! That's ridiculous! I didn't even do anything."

"Lisa, number one, you lied," her father said staring into the rear view mirror at her. "We thought you were going to spend the night at Kathy's. We certainly did not think you were going to spend the night on the beach! Number two, you and your friends were smoking and drinking. And that's true, whether you took one toke or twenty. And number three, we had to come to the police station to pick you up at 7 a.m. So don't tell me you didn't do anything!"

"You know what pisses me off?" Lisa shouted at the same time she was choked with tears. "You don't give me any credit for doing the right thing. For having some common sense, for using my head!"

"Listen, young lady, I don't call sleeping on the beach all night with a bunch of pot heads 'using your head.'"

"Shit," Lisa mumbled.

There was a long moment of silence.

"We're all upset. We'll talk about this later," her mother said as she looked at her husband and at Lisa. Then she turned and looked out the window.

The rest of the trip home, no one said a word.

○

Lisa was able to talk to Jeff the next day at school. She and her parents had compromised on three week's grounding instead of a month. She couldn't talk on the phone for the first week, but after that she had phone privileges. She could continue with drama rehearsals and be in the performance. Jeff, in contrast, was on restriction for only a week.

"Three weeks?" he said. "That sucks!"

"Well, it was going to be a month—till the end of school."

"But Lisa, you didn't even do anything!"

"I know, but my dad is all worked up over this. It's going to be such a drag."

"Don't worry," he said, putting his arm around her. "You'll make it through. But I sure am going to miss you and your warm body."

Lisa let herself be hugged, but she didn't feel very loving.

○

The truth was that the first week was hard, but Lisa noticed that it wasn't as awful as she'd thought it was going to be. She had lots of time to get her homework done, and play rehearsals were going well. Though slightly boring, there was a calmness to life that she hadn't experienced in a long time. One night she, her parents, and Stephanie even played Monopoly together.

The other benefit was that she had time to think. She thought about Jeff and that night at the beach. He had been aggressive and not his understanding self. Of course, it was the pot, something Jeff didn't do often; still, Lisa didn't like it.

And then there was Zeke, who was becoming more and more of a friend. During rehearsal breaks Zeke and Lisa talked constantly and found themselves horsing around. Sometimes Kathy joined them, and once they all went out for coffee when rehearsal ended early, which still gave Lisa time to be in the door by 10:30.

At rehearsal, a week before opening night, Lisa and Zeke walked close together, their arms about each other's shoulders.

"Look up," Zeke said, "there's the Big Dipper." Lisa stopped and took in the big dark sky with its millions of small bright lights. Just then a shooting star cascaded over-head. "Look! It's good luck." Zeke turned to Lisa who moved toward him and he simultaneously slipped his arms around her, their lips meeting in a warm, gentle kiss. They stepped back and stared at each other, then Zeke pulled Lisa close and kissed her again, and this time there was an excitement between them

"Oh Zeke," Lisa said, "what are we doing?"

"I don't know. But it feels good," Zeke said. "Let's keep on."

Lisa laughed and they walked back to the drama building holding hands.

O

Kathy called Saturday morning with the news. "I don't know how to tell you this and I feel like a snitch, but I guess that's just my role."

Lisa held her breath. It had to be news about Jeff.

"Last night there was a party at Dillon's house again. Everyone was there. Well, everyone but you. It got pretty wild. The police even showed up later on."

"Well, it's a good thing I'm on restriction. I don't need any more of that in my life," Lisa said. "So what happened? Are you going to tell me something about Jeff?"

"Yeah."

"And a girl?"

"Yeah."

"Who was it?" A whole series of names zipped through Lisa's mind.

"She's a sophomore. Her name is Tiffany."

"Tiffany Bottsdorf?"

"I think so. Do you know her?"

"No, I don't really know her. She was in my Spanish class. What happened?"

"They danced a lot. I saw them outside making out."

"God! He is such a shit. He's changing. I don't know what's going on."

"I'm sorry to tell you. But I figure better you hear it from me and I don't want you to be made a fool of. Don't tell Jeff I told you."

"No, I won't. Thanks, thanks for calling."

There was an awkward silence, then Kathy said, "So listen, the play's going great, don't you think?"

"Yeah, I do. It's going to be good. You know, Kathy, it's funny. I'm not as upset about this as I thought I would be."

"You mean the play?"

"No, Jeff. . . maybe I've kind of sensed something was going to happen. We're not nearly as close as we used to be."

"I thought so. And you and Zeke seem to be spending a lot of time together."

"Oh, we're just friends."

"Are you sure about that?"

"Sure I am," said Lisa. "Well, listen, I gotta go. I guess I'll call Jeff."

"Good luck, Lisa. Bye."

Lisa sat for a moment. It was a crappy thing that Jeff had done. Were they going to break up? Should they break up? Was that what was next? A wave of sadness swept over her and tears filled her eyes. Life without Jeff. The words sounded awful. She imagined walking around at school without him, parties without him, and the idea left her feeling desolate. She lay on the bed crying softly. Jeff had been her first love, her first real love, and she remembered that night they had made love in the mountain cabin. It had been so wonderful; her heart ached with the memory of it. How could it be ending like this?

She heard a car drive up outside, and she heard her mother let Jeff in the house. There was a soft knock on her bedroom door. "Lisa?"

"Come in," she answered.

He stood in the doorway wearing a Giants cap and his purple-blue sweater. Seeing him there was more than she could bear, and she turned away burying her face in her hands.

"Lisa," he said putting his hand on her shoulder.

"Jeff, how could you?" she said turning to him.

He reached out and drew her to him and held her for a long, quiet time.

"Lisa, I feel like such a dumb shit. I was just stupid."

He paused for a while and the only sound was Lisa's sniffling. She pulled away and reached for a tissue, aware that her face was all blotchy. She blew her nose and finally stared straight at him.

He looked miserable: pale with red- rimmed eyes. "I don't know what's going on anymore."

"You know what I think?" Lisa said reaching for another tissue. "I hate to say this because I think I sound like a parent, but you know what?"

"What? Tell me."

"I think we're not ready for each other. I think maybe we're too young to just stay only with each other. This is hard to say, but I think it's true."

Lisa couldn't believe her own words. She hadn't known she felt this way until she heard herself speaking. She looked over at Jeff. Maybe she was just testing him. He looked so darling; how could she be thinking of not being with him? Still, she went on talking, and she spoke from a deep place in herself that she was barely familiar with.

"Jeff, I hate you for going to a party and making out with some stupid-ass girl! Why couldn't you just be honest with me and tell me you wanted to break up and go out with other girls?"

"I didn't want to go out with other girls. But, I don't know, we haven't been together for a long time now and, I don't know, it just happened."

"That's just plain shit, Jeff! God, this is deja vu. It's just like the last time with Molly. Besides, it's only been a month, maybe a little more. Couldn't you last a month? What is it? Does it all come down to sex? Is that it?"

"Lisa, of course it's not just sex. You know that. I dunno. Maybe you're right. Maybe I'm not ready to just be with one girl. Are you ready to only be with me?"

"Jeff, we slept together. Don't you remember? Of course I am. Do you think I would ever have had sex with you if I hadn't been ready?"

Jeff stared at the floor, and Lisa hoped he was suffering. She sat quietly on the bed and picked at the pillow in her arms. She could hear her mother on the telephone from her bedroom. She looked at the picture of Jeff and her that sat on the desk. It had been taken in the snow, and they were both red cheeked and laughing. She heard a voice inside herself telling her to be honest.

"Jeff, I hate what you did, but I've got to be honest. The truth is I think I *was* ready for you, for us, but lately something's different. I'm not sure I am ready any more. Somehow, things aren't as clear as they used to be."

She glanced over at him. He was looking directly into her eyes and she was aware that she felt older, wiser, like she was saying something he didn't quite grasp. She continued. "Ever since that Molly thing and then that awful night at the beach, we've grown apart, I think. And there's one more thing. I kissed Zeke once, but it was only one time."

"I knew it! So you're not so lily pure, either." Jeff was silent for a long time and his eyes moved back and forth between his hands and the view out the window. "So, what do we do?" he asked softly.

"I don't know. If we break up, I don't want to have to hate each other. I don't want to be enemies."

"Me neither."

"There's three weeks left of school. It would be hard not to be together, and I don't think I could stand to see you with someone else."

"Yeah, but then I'm going to be gone for most of the summer. I just found out that I can go up to my uncle's ranch and work."

"How come I didn't know that?" Lisa asked. "How could you be gone all summer and not tell me?"

"Nothing was decided until three days ago, and we've hardly talked, Lisa. God, you've been on restriction or at rehearsal or something."

Lisa had to admit he was right. She hadn't been very available lately. And if she was truly honest, then she also had to admit that Jeff hadn't been the only guy she'd thought about in the last few months.

"Jeff," she said drawing a shaky breath, "let's just cool it for a while. I don't know what else to do. And let's also promise not to hurt each other."

"So, how do we do this?"

"We'll just be friends."

"Lisa, that will never work. If I see you hanging around other guys, like that Zeke freak, I'll go crazy. And what if I go to a party and talk to some girl for over twenty minutes, are you going to flip out on me? How're you going to feel?"

"Jealous."

"See what I mean?"

They were both silent. "It's hard to care about someone," Lisa said. "It hurts. It's so wonderful when things are going good, but it's so awful other times. Is there someone else you like, that you want to go out with?"

"No, you're the only girl I care about, but I just don't feel free any more—or something like that."

"It's okay. . . well, it is and it isn't. It hurts to hear you say that, but I know what you mean."

"Well, is there someone you like?" Jeff asked.

"No. . . no one like you. Look, let's just stay together till school's out. Then, over the summer you'll be gone and we'll see what happens."

"I dunno. Somehow this sounds too mature or something. Most couples have to get in a big fight to break up."

"I know, but let's not call it 'break up.' Let's call it 'taking a break' or something." Lisa looked over at Jeff and gave a half smile. She pulled his baseball cap over his eyes.

He grabbed her hand and held on. "You're pretty neat, you know."

She smiled. "There is one thing though, Jeff. Even if we still hang out together, you know this means no more sex. I just couldn't deal with it."

Jeff flopped back on the bed with a groan. "Lisa, no, don't say that," he said half in mockery. "I knew this was coming."

"You did? I didn't. But do you understand? I'm just trying to be honest."

"Yeah, I understand. I swear—girls make everything so complicated!"

"You mean it would be less complicated to go on having sex now, even though we're just friends, and then be separated over the summer?"

"Well, sure."

"No way! I can't do it. You're nuts!"

"I know, I know. Calm down," Jeff said, putting his arms around her. "Really, I wasn't serious. So. . . .you okay?"

"I guess so. Are you?"

"Yeah). . . listen, I gotta go," Jeff said looking at his watch. "I told my mom I'd be home for dinner. I'll see you at school tomorrow, okay?"

"Okay." Lisa turned and hugged him hard. "I'll always love you," she whispered.

Jeff leaned down and kissed her. "Me too," he said in a soft voice.

Lisa sat quietly on her bed for a long time, then she got up and looked in the mirror. She searched her eyes, her mouth, looking for some sign that she had changed because inside she certainly felt like she had. The mirror gave her no indication she was different, but she knew otherwise. In a matter of a few hours she had come through something enormous.

○

Now, sitting in English class and anxious to finish the last final of her junior year, Lisa listened to Mr. T. She glanced around the room. Jeff and Kathy were there and a whole bunch of her friends. She was no longer the new girl, and she looked forward to going back up to Oregon for the summer where she had a six week job in a summer camp. She had been hired to do recreation and drama. Lisa liked the way her life was going.

Mr. T's voice broke into her thoughts. He was passing out a paper. "Keep this face down until I give the word. Before you begin this final, I want to say that this has been an extraordinarily good year. I think you all have grown, not only in your ability to express yourselves, but in your development as human beings. I like what I see, and I feel better about the future of our world knowing that there are going to be adults like you out there. I want to wish you all good luck next year and I hope the future will be kind. In the words of the famous *Desiderata*: "For all its sham, drudgery and broken dreams, it is still a beautiful world. Be careful. Strive to be happy."

There was a moment of silence, and Lisa and Kathy glanced over at each other. Someone coughed.

"Okay, you have the full two hours to write your final essay. You will be graded on the content of your ideas, the organization and the presentation of those ideas, and, of course, the correctness of your grammar and punctuation. You may use a dictionary. Now, begin."

There was a shuffling of paper as everyone turned the sheet of paper over and started reading. A few students sighed, one slammed down his pencil in disgust, and almost everyone shifted in their seats. Lisa read the final:

"Throughout the year, beginning with *Our Town*, we have discussed individual and cultural values as a yardstick for measuring the quality of life. It seems clear that without values, life loses its brilliancy and importance. As far as we know, our values separate us from other forms of living creatures.

"In a thoughtful and well organized essay discuss the values that you believe to be important in life and provide specific examples of these values as revealed in at least four of the literary works and presentations we have experienced this year; to refresh your memory, a list of these is posted on the board."

Lisa looked up and read the list:

The Scarlet Letter
Our Town
Huckleberry Finn
Walden
Poetry of Robert Frost, Maya Angelou, Langston Hughes, Gary Soto, Emily Dickinson, e.e. cummings
The Grapes of Wrath
The Declaration of Independence
Beloved
The Education of Little Tree
The Color Purple
Presentations from AIDS and Sexual Harassment Awareness Days

Lisa inhaled deeply. It would certainly take her the full two hours to put all her ideas together. She jotted down several values she thought were important: Friendship, Compassion for Others, Hard Work, Freedom, Family, God. Then she thought of all the literary works posted on the board and was sure she could easily include four of those. Lisa began writing:

"America has been called the land of opportunity, the land of second chances. Throughout American history and literature there is a belief that life can be better. It is what enabled people to take great risks, to travel west from coast to coast and down the river like Huckleberry Finn. It is what kept the black slaves reaching for freedom.

"But change is always scary, and in leaving a safe place, the familiar, there is usually some sadness too."

Lisa paused. Was she sad she was no longer with Jeff, no longer a virgin? Yes, she was. She looked again at Jeff who had his head down and was writing furiously. Suddenly he stopped, put his pencil in his mouth, and looked up and around. He caught Lisa's eye and winked. She blushed and winked back.

No, there was no first time to look forward to any more. But thank goodness the first time had been good; thank goodness she didn't wind up pregnant.

No, not "thank goodness." It hadn't had anything to do with "goodness." It was because they had been smart and used birth control that she didn't get pregnant. And the truth was that it had more to do with her efforts than with Jeff's. Oh, he had been sweet and thoughtful, but all along she had been the one to push the use of condoms and the pill.

Well, she didn't think she'd be on the pill again for a long time. With all the confusion she felt, a relationship didn't seem to fit into her life right now. And certainly not sex; sex was great, but it sure made everything complicated. There would be lots of great experiences later on, and someday there would be other boys, and other men. And someday, a long time from now, she knew she'd have a family.

Lisa sighed and continued writing: "The belief that life can be better is an optimistic view of life, and it is an American value that things can change for the better, that change does not equal bad; it can equal good . . . "

Lisa knew she wasn't the same girl who had walked in the door to her English class last September. Inside, there was a strong warmth that was beginning to grow; inside she felt like a woman.

O

Lisa Howard finished high school and went on to graduate from UCLA with a major in drama. She worked for a while doing small parts in television commercials and now works for an advertising firm in Los Angeles.

Jeff Branley graduated from college and coaches basketball at a high school in Chico, California. He is married and has a two-year-old daughter.

TEEN PARENT

A few days after talking with her mother, Lisa walked through the family room while the TV was on and saw a group of young mothers and their babies being interviewed. The talk show host said the topic for the day was "Teen Motherhood." Five of the six girls had long hair and one still wore braces. Each held an adorable, carefully dressed baby; three of the babies were wearing fluffy dresses, two were in he-man overalls, and one in a Giants baseball suit. The babies (three whites, two blacks and one brown skinned) drooled, sucked bottles, looked around with big eyes, and one slept soundly.

Lisa sat down to watch, glad that no one else was home but also feeling very nervous. She wasn't sure she wanted to watch this. Still, the timing was perfect.

All the girls were thrilled with their babies and Lisa could see why—they sure were cute little buggers! Only one young mother acknowledged that sometimes it was hard and that she was lonely. Two of the six were married, two lived with their parents, one lived with her boyfriend, and one shared an apartment with another woman and her three children.

A woman in the audience asked, "How long are you going to live on welfare? How long are you going to ask taxpayers to take care of you and your baby?"

Three of the young women were living on AFDC, and one responded, "I'm not happy about taking the government's money, but right now I have to do what's best for my baby. I don't plan to stay on welfare. When my baby gets older, I'm going to get a job."

"What kind of a job do you think you're going to get? You haven't even finished high school. You won't be able to make enough to give the two of you a decent life."

Another audience woman stood up and responded, "I don't know why you're picking on them. I was a teenage mother and I did okay. Yes, it was very hard for the first five years, but I managed to get a diploma. I finished two years of junior college and got a decent-paying job. It's been twenty years now, and I own my own condo, and my daughter is beautiful and smart and a good student at college."

The audience applauded and the talk show host asked the woman, "Would you want your daughter to be a teenage mother?"

She paused. "No, not really. It's too hard. But I also want people to know that your life doesn't have to be a catastrophe if you end up having a baby when you're a teenager."

"Did your parents help you?"

"Yes. I couldn't have done it without some help."

The talk show host took over. "Let's talk about the increase in teen moms. The United States has the highest rate of teenage mothers in the whole industrialized world. One in five births in this country are born to teenagers. Why is that? Why don't other countries like France or Norway have large numbers of teenage mothers too? Didn't you girls get any sex education in school? Are

American boys and girls less intelligent?"

One of the young mothers, who held the baby dressed in the baseball suit, spoke. "I don't know about other countries. I just know that this baby made my life better. I know who I am now and I have someone to love who loves me completely."

Another mother said, "My baby gets lots of love and care. She has my parents, my brothers and sisters. We all take care of her and she's doing great."

The host interrupted. "But what about birth control? Didn't you girls know about condoms and the pill? Didn't you learn about all that in school? Or at home?"

All the mothers smiled and one said, "Well, I sure didn't hear about it at home; all I heard was that sex was bad. We studied all that stuff at school. They came and showed us condoms and talked about the pill."

"So why didn't you use it then?" the host asked.

The women looked at each other and giggled a little. One said, "My boyfriend didn't want to use one."

"I thought about it, but I didn't have nothing at the time."

Another mother reached into her bag to get a bottle and said, "The truth is I didn't think it would happen to me; I didn't think I would get pregnant." She smiled in an embarrassed way.

The show took a break for commercials, and Lisa felt the nausea rising in her stomach. She raced to the bathroom and stared at the underside of the toilet seat as she vomited up her morning cereal. Her mouth tasted sour and slimy, and her eyes ached. She sat back on her heels, panting from the retching. God, how she hated this! She stood up, rinsed out her mouth and shakily walked back to the living room where she collapsed on the couch, pulled a blanket around her, and closed her eyes. The talk show host introduced one of the teenager's mothers who looked to be in her 30's. She was dressed in a bright red-and-white-polka-dot dress, and as soon as her grandson saw her, his whole face lit up. She sat down near her daughter, patted her hand, and took the baby on her own lap. The three generations made an appealing picture.

The host addressed the grandmother: "It's my understanding that you wanted your daughter to go ahead and have her baby and that both of them live with you and your husband. Would you tell us about that?"

The young grandmother began, "Well, I was pregnant with my daughter here when I was 16. My parents were furious with me, gave me $200 and forced me to move out. It was a very hard time for me. The father of the baby took off, and I was all alone. Fortunately, I found my way to a state home for unwed mothers. I lived there until after the baby was born, then I found a job taking care of an old woman who let me and my baby live with her. I did that for two years, and then I met my husband-to-be, and we've now been married for fourteen years. He's a wonderful man. He adopted my daughter, and then we had two children of our own. My daughter, Rayella, has a younger sister who's eight. I was absolutely determined that no child of mine would ever have to go through what I did on

110

her own, alone."

"That's quite a story," said the host. "So, you're really one big family, aren't you?"

"That's right. Rayella's baby is growing up with lots of family and lots of love." The mother and daughter smiled at each other.

An audience member said, "You're to be commended. I wish all teenage mothers were as lucky as your daughter. And you've created a good life for yourself. But my question is, how do you feel about your daughter having a baby so young? Is it really all right with you?"

The grandmother answered, "Well, I would have liked her to wait a while because I think life is more difficult now if you don't have an education. But really, it's okay with me. She's a wonderful mother, and I know the baby is going to have a happy life."

"So you're willing to support her all her life?"

"Oh no. Just for a few years until she can manage on her own."

Another audience member said, "You know, I think it's great you're willing to do this, but I wouldn't. I'm 55 now, and if my daughter got pregnant I wouldn't want to take on raising another child. I've already had four children, and now I feel it's my turn."

Many people in the audience clapped.

A woman, who looked to be a grandmother herself, asked, "Does the baby ever seem to be confused about his mother? Does he sometimes think you're both his mother? I'm asking because I have a similar situation at home, and it sometimes causes problems between me and my daughter."

This time the young mother on stage spoke up. "Well, my baby is only nine months old, so he doesn't understand yet, but there are times when I resent my mother. Still, I'm grateful too."

The host looked quizzically at the grandmother, and she replied with a laugh, "Nobody said it would be perfect."

This time a man stood up, and the host placed the microphone in front of him. "You know, whether you think teenage girls should have babies or not, the problem is not with these particular girls having babies. These girls have family support. It's the girls who have no one backing them up, no family to help make it all right. Those teenage mothers are the ones who have such a tough time being a good parent. It's just too much stress to handle at a young age: a baby, no money, and still a kid yourself."

"We'll take a break and be right back," said the host. Lisa closed her eyes and dozed off again.

The angry voice said, "But you mothers are not being fair to these babies. Of course you love them, but a baby is easy to take care of. It's the 8-10-12, and 16-year-olds that are demanding. Everyone loves a baby, but not everyone loves a loud-mouthed kid who breaks into the neighbor's house and is out of control."

Lisa glanced over at the T.V. People in the audience were getting angry. The host spoke out louder to get control. "Folks, come on. What's all the anger about?

These are just young girls up here taking care of their babies." He pointed the microphone toward a smartly dressed black woman wearing a gray suit.

"The anger is about how people in our society are getting sick and tired of teenage hoodlum boys trying to run things with their Uzis and knives and gangs. We're sick of all the graffiti, and the drugs, and our cars being vandalized. Most of these hoodlums are from fatherless homes with mothers who don't have any parenting skills or any money to provide for them."

"Well, what do these teenage moms have to do with that?" asked the host.

"What do you mean? They're creating the problem. They're too young. They're still growing up themselves, and they're not able to raise a child. Being a parent is a lot more than loving a little baby. It's being responsible for that child its entire life. It's sacrifice and hard work, and kids do best when they have two mature, grown-up parents to help them get through this life."

The audience clapped furiously, and the host took another break.

Lisa closed her eyes, feeling the tears slide down her cheeks. Really, the lady was right. She was still growing up herself. How could she be a good mother to a child in a world that already had too many kids who weren't cared about? Lisa relaxed and let out all the tears and the sobs she'd been holding in for days. She felt she'd be crying forever.

○

Two days later Lisa called a teen parent center and asked to talk with a counselor. She was given an appointment for the next day.

She was nearly three months pregnant now and knew she had to make up her mind soon. While it was possible to still get an abortion up to five months, the procedure was much more difficult and the idea even harder to accept. It seemed that the closer the fetus came to being able to survive on its own, the more awesome the decision; Lisa felt like this baby was taking over her life.

The counselor looked tired but she smiled at Lisa when she walked in the door. "Hi, I'm Cindy Schaefer and you must be Lisa. Have a seat." She paused and then said, "How are you feeling?"

"Not very good." Lisa sat in the chair facing the counselor.

"Do you have any morning sickness?"

"Yeah, only it's not always in the morning; sometimes it's the afternoon too."

"It's awful, isn't it? Fortunately, most women stop being sick after three months. So, have you decided to keep the baby?"

"No, I don't know what to do. I was hoping you might be able to help me, you know, tell me what I could do."

"Well," the counselor said, "my job is to help you if you've made up your mind to raise the child. If you'd like to talk to someone about an abortion or an adoption, I can tell you where you can do that."

"No. I know about that. I just wanted to find out what you offer here."

The woman handed Lisa a yellow brochure. On the front it said, "Raising a

Healthy Baby: A Guide for Teen Mothers." "We offer a number of services, and we're here because if you decide to keep your baby we want both of you to be as healthy and happy as possible. It's important to have as few illusions as possible too; if you decide to go ahead and raise your baby yourself, your life—the way it has been up to now—will be over. You'll start an entirely new life, a life as a mother.

"What we have here are support groups where you'll meet with other young women like yourself. You can talk over your problems with them and share your excitement; you can ask questions and get answers, and find out that you're not alone with your worries and anxieties. We also give classes on proper nutrition for you and your baby and help you get into childbirth classes. Later, when your baby is born, we give instruction on parenting and child development. What grade are you in school?"

"I'm a junior."

"Well, there are several paths open to you. You can stay in school and work to graduate and get your diploma; that's the best course. Or, you can study to pass your Proficiency and get out of school early, or you can study to get your GED at 18. You know, it's a sad fact, but most teen mothers never graduate from high school; only about 20% ever get their diplomas. We'll do whatever we can to help you finish school. If you have child care, you can go back to your own high school or enroll in a teen parent program where you bring your baby to school with you. You'll need to sign up early because we have a long waiting list."

Lisa felt overwhelmed trying to take in all this information. She hadn't even decided to stay pregnant, let alone think about waiting lists and schools.

"I don't want to mislead you. It's very, very tough being a mother for the first time, especially if you're alone. Do you have anyone to help you? Will you be with the baby's father, or will your parents help out?"

"I don't know yet. I mean, we haven't decided. My parents said I could stay at home while I finish high school, but they won't raise the baby; they both work anyhow."

"You're lucky to have parents that are willing to do that much. I didn't get any help like that when I was your age."

"You were like me?"

"Yes. It was a long time ago, and there wasn't so much help or understanding back then. My parents sent me to live with an aunt, and that didn't work out very well. I had to wait five years before I could even get my high school diploma, but I did it. Later on, I went to community college and that enabled me to get a decent-paying job. I probably sound like a broken record but I have to say it again: without that high school diploma, you can't really even support yourself— let alone a baby too."

"So, "Lisa said, "if I keep the baby, I can go back to the school I'm attending now so long as I have someone to watch the baby for me. Or I could go to a teen parent school, bring the baby with me, and still graduate?"

The counselor nodded her head. "Yes. You'll probably lose some time but you can graduate. When is your baby due?"

"Around the end of July."

"Well, that's certainly good timing. You could have the summer and then start up school in the fall. If things go well and you work hard, you just might be able to graduate on time, but even if you can't, it's a small matter when you compare it with the importance of taking care of a baby."

Lisa thought about all she'd miss: graduation, the prom, parties, fun times at the beach, the excitement at school. Her dreams of going off to college would have to be put off—maybe not forever, but for a while. She'd heard about a girl in New York who had a baby at 15 and managed to graduate at 18. She was even class valedictorian and won a scholarship to a college. So it was possible to be a success. But she didn't think she was the scholarship type. She'd always been an okay student but then she'd never worked super hard either. Maybe having this baby would bring out the best in her, force her to take life more seriously.

"Want to talk about what's going through your mind right now?" the counselor asked.

"Oh, I was just wondering if I was capable of graduating and still going to college if I have this baby."

The woman watched her with serious eyes.

"All I can figure out," Lisa went on, "is that I have to change a lot. I can see that I just couldn't be like a teenager anymore. I mean, I'd still be a teenager, but I'd have to give up most of the stuff that teenagers do—you know, having fun, dates, hanging out, parties, just fooling around.

"I'd have to be more serious, a lot more serious. I'd have to become like an adult and just forget about the way I thought my life was going to be, the way my life was going to turn out."

After a pause, the counselor said, "I think that realization comes to most of us some time in our lives. Most of us have to finally understand that life isn't going to be the way we wanted it to be. Some people learn this at 25, some at 40, some as late as 60. And then there are some who have to learn it very young, as young as 14. . . or 16. It's painful to grow up so early, but it can be done." She smiled at Lisa and her eyes glistened.

Lisa dug her nails into her palms. She didn't want to cry. "I've got some more thinking to do. . . Thank you for your help. Maybe I'll call you back."

"Goodbye Lisa. I wish you all the luck in the world, whatever you decide."

O

Lisa slept poorly the next few days and was only able to complete a small part of her homework. Her grades had fallen, though she figured she'd still pass her classes if she could just get back to studying. Except for Kathy, her friends had stopped calling, and Lisa found herself with a lot of unoccupied time on her hands. Jeff came over every night, but talking wasn't easy now. Finally, she told Jeff she was thinking about keeping the baby.

Jeff stared at her. "You're *what?*" he said.

"I'm thinking I'll drop out of school and go on independent study. Then, when next fall comes, I could go to the teen parent program and take the baby with me."

"But Lisa, you don't want to be a mother now, do you? What about the rest of your life? What about college?"

"It's still possible for a person to finish school; it just won't happen the way I wanted."

"Lisa. . . we made a mistake. You don't have to punish yourself for the rest of your life."

"Jeff, it's a baby, not a punishment."

"Lisa. . . how can I get married and be a father right now?"

"I'm not asking you to," she said, taking his hand. "We don't have to get married. Just don't leave me. You can still have a life. . . Listen, if I decide to keep the baby, would you go to childbirth classes with me?"

"God, Lisa. . . God, I don't know. Look, I'm sorry, I don't want to hurt you, but I told you. . . I just can't be a father. I mean, not a real father. Shit! This is so bad. I'll probably feel horrible about this for the rest of my life," he said looking off into space.

"Well, it's not what I wanted either, but I can't stand the idea of adoption or abortion, so I guess this is the only thing I can do." Lisa felt such a mixture of anger and sadness. On one hand, she wanted to smash Jeff in the face and on the other she just wanted him to hold her. All she could do was stand and look at him.

"What do your folks say?" Jeff asked.

"They say it's my decision. They say I can live here as long as I need to until I can be on my own. It's hard for them too, you know. They love me and they want to help, but they also don't want the responsibility of raising another child. What about yours?"

"They said they'll help with the financial end of it for at least a year. They want me to graduate, and they want me to go to college, but I don't know how I'd do that and support a baby. What a mess! Lisa, have you thought about an abortion?"

"Of course I have; I just can't do it."

"It would sure make things easier."

"For you, Jeff, not for me."

"Lisa," Jeff said, drawing her close, "I'm really sorry."

"Me too. It really is the girl who gets stuck. It's true."

She let herself be hugged, but she noticed a real change inside. The close, tender feelings she had felt for Jeff all along were different. She felt an edge, a hard edge inside herself. He didn't evoke the same excitement, the same melting feelings. It was like she had more important things on her mind now, something more important than Jeff. She felt an alliance forming between herself and the small creature now growing inside of her.

The idea of having an abortion was barely thinkable. She knew life would be simpler if she had one, but she was afraid she'd never be able to live with herself afterward. The timing was awful. If it were ten years from now or even five, she'd be an adult with some part of her life settled. She'd have an education and a job. She wished she'd never moved from Oregon. She wished she'd never left her old friends. She wished there was no such thing as sex. She wished it was ten years from now. Shit, she could go on wishing forever, but it wouldn't change anything. She was still not quite seventeen and she was pregnant. What else could she do?

She looked up at him. He was wearing that beautiful blue sweater, and she could feel an ache inside her whole body. His eyes were warm and concerned, his mouth held in a quizzical half-smile. He was waiting, waiting for her to tell him what to do.

Lisa was aware of feeling unattached, as though she had been picked up and shifted to a far-off hilltop. She could see the outline of Jeff's figure, but there was a slight fog about him, and he seemed to be drifting away into the distance.

"Lisa?" His voice startled her back to reality. "Lisa?"

"You know, it's amazing," she said with a sigh. "I feel kind of peaceful now. I think I've made up my mind. I'm. . . " — she took a deep breath,— "I'm going to stick with this baby."

O

A couple of weeks later Lisa returned to school to have some papers signed and as she walked about the school halls, she felt strangely removed from everything: the signs for school spirit, the pictures of sports teams, the posters put up by kids running for school office, and the bright yellow signs advertising the Junior-Senior Prom.

Her life now consisted of being at home, homework, and the baby-to-be. Her parents had her keep a list of every expense related to the baby: vitamins, baby clothes, medical appointments. Even though they were paying these expenses, they wanted her to have an idea of how much it cost to have a baby. She wouldn't have to worry about paying her own bills yet, but in her Childhood and Family class she'd had to make out a monthly budget as though she were self-supporting. The amount of money astounded her; including car insurance, utilities, food, rent, clothing, entertainment, and medical coverage, she figured she would need to earn a minimum of $1500 per month just to live! If she worked full time, she'd have to earn at least $10.00 an hour *after* money was withdrawn for taxes and social security. And that didn't count child-care expenses. How could she possibly get a job where she could earn enough?

Lisa had read that two thirds of the families headed by teenage mothers lived below the poverty level, and now she could see why. If Jeff and her folks didn't help, she'd never make it. She felt doomed unless she could finish school and go on to college or a vocational school—or marry a man who was rich!

Lying in bed at night, Lisa was afraid when she thought about the future. Her former life—the life when she worried about boys, what to wear, clothes, or whether or not some girl would be her friend—seemed ages ago; sometimes she felt like she'd never been young in her whole life.

Then, in the morning, the world looked better, and she figured that so long as her parents helped her finish school and get some training, she would make it after all. If Jeff paid some child support, she and the baby would survive. Of course he'd pay child support. He had to. Besides, he was a good person; he wouldn't not support his own child! Would he?

Then she would feel this rage mounting inside of her as she thought of Jeff at college, going to classes and parties, living a carefree life, surrounded by friends, laughing and sharing some joke. How unfair it was that her life was reduced to this stupid small world of a baby and never having enough money and worrying all the time while he was off just being young and having fun!

Her anger toward Jeff engulfed her, and then she got angry at herself as well. After all, she was responsible for having this baby too, and she was the one who chose to keep it. Only sometimes it didn't feel like a choice at all!

○

The high point of Lisa's month was her doctor's appointment. It was funny that what had once been traumatic—going in for a pelvic exam—now brought her excitement. She'd been able to find a woman doctor who helped her feel good about herself. On her very first visit the doctor had said to her, "Look, Lisa, I'm not happy about girls your age having babies, but since you've decided to go ahead with this pregnancy, you need to feel as good as possible about it. You need to take good care of yourself and be proud that you're going to be a mother. It's only from a full heart that you'll be able to give your baby all the love it's going to need. And, after all, you're only doing what women have done for centuries—having a baby when you're young and strong."

Now, sitting in the waiting room, Lisa glanced over at the teenage girl next to her. She had long dark hair and nails bitten down to the quick. She was constantly fidgeting and seemed very nervous.

"Are you waiting to see Dr. Osborne?" Lisa asked.

Surprised, the girl looked up. She glanced down at the paper in her hand and said, "Yeah, that's her name."

"You'll like her. So, how far along are you?" Lisa asked.

"Uhmm. . . six months. I'll be so glad when it's over."

"I know what you mean. Were you sick a lot?"

The girl nodded her head. "All the time. It was so awful. I couldn't do anything."

"Are you still going to school?"

"Yeah, kind of. I'm on Home Study because I was sick so much. It sucks. I hate it. It's all stupid. I'm not going to use half the stuff I have to study. Besides,

I'm so far behind in school, I'll never graduate." She reached in her pocket and pulled out a picture. "Want to see my boyfriend?"

Lisa looked at his face. He was young, had long hair and a goofy smile.

"He's the father," the girl said. "Me and him are going to get our own apartment as soon as the baby's born. He's already got a job at a gas station. He makes six bucks an hour. He's been there three years."

"Is that what you're going to live on?"

"That — and if I don't let on that we're living together, I can get WIC and AFDC. We're going to find a place that's really cheap. I figure we'll be okay. How 'bout you?"

"Oh, I'm not getting married, not now." Lisa lowered her eyes. It was hard to admit. "I'm still at home with my parents."

"They're letting you stay there?" the girl asked, her eyes widening. "That's really cool. My mom kicked me out as soon as she found out I was pregnant. But I wouldn't have wanted to stay there anyway. I hate her boyfriend; he's a real ass and a druggie."

Lisa noticed the girl smelled of cigarettes and wondered if she was smoking even though she was pregnant. She shuddered at the thought but didn't say anything.

"Yeah, well they're not happy about this whole thing but they want me to be okay. I don't know how you can do it."

"Oh, it's not so bad. Actually, I like living with my boyfriend and his friends. He's straightened himself out from a few years ago. I've known him since I was 13. He used to be my neighbor. Still, it's cool you get to stay at home, if that's what you want."

"I do. I mean it's hard sometimes. My mom and I argue once in a while, and my dad's real disappointed, but there's a lot I don't have to deal with—like money."

The girl let out a big sigh. "I'm so sick of money. You're lucky. I'm never going to kick a kid of mine out of the house. I don't care what she does." She fidgeted in her seat and looked in her purse.

Lisa looked again at the girl's stringy hair and scuffed boots. There was a scrappiness about her that Lisa admired; she would need all the toughness she could get.

"So, what are you going to name your baby?" the girl asked.

"Oh, I haven't figured that one out yet," Lisa said.

"Really? God, that's the first thing I knew. It's going to be Autumn if it's a girl and Jason if it's a boy."

Lisa smiled. "Those are neat names."

"Camille?" the receptionist said

The girl looked up. A half smile crossed her face, but her eyes looked scared. "That's me. Well, nice talking to you," she said getting up and turning to Lisa. "I hope everything goes okay."

"You too. Good luck," Lisa said. *Good luck to both of us* .

○

Jeff drove up with screeching tires, slammed the car door, and came in Lisa's house through the kitchen door. Lisa was buttering some toast and looked up with surprise.

"Hi."

"Hi. Listen. Can we talk?"

"Sure. Aren't you supposed to be in school?"

"Yeah. Well, it's one of those days when they have a lot of different speakers come on campus, and I just didn't want to stay." Jeff looked around. "Who's here?"

"No one. Everyone's gone."

Jeff kept picking up silverware, putting it down, adjusting his baseball hat, poking his finger into the peanut butter jar.

"What's going on?" she said.

"Well, I've been thinking and talking to my folks. You know, I feel like such a shit. I mean, you know I don't want to be a father, but I guess I'm going to be and I can't pretend I'm not. I figure I need to do the right thing, and we should get married."

Lisa stared at the yellow glob of butter that was refusing to melt on her toast. She couldn't quite grasp his words.

"What?"

"We should get married."

"Why?"

"'Cause we're going to have a baby. Remember?"

"Wow. I can't believe this. Is this what you want to do? I mean, we never even talked about it before. How come now, all of a sudden?"

"I figure I should grow up."

"But what about finishing high school and college?"

"My folks say they'll help support us till I graduate, and I'll have a job anyway. Then I'll get a full-time job and then maybe I could go to college when I'm older— you know, 25 or something."

Lisa felt her throat tighten. She looked up at him and wanted to throw her arms around him. "Jeff . . . God, I don't know. I have to think."

"What do you mean? Don't you want to get married? I thought you did."

"I guess I did for a while. . . but I just never thought it would happen. I knew you weren't ready for that. Well, I wasn't either." Lisa sat down and started to eat her toast, the crust sticking in her throat. "I just can't picture myself being married . . . not like this."

"Can you picture yourself being a mother?"

She glanced down at her growing stomach. "Well, yeah. I'm kind of being forced to."

"God, I thought you'd be happy."

"I am. I guess. It's just that it's a big decision. I have to think."

"It's not as big a decision as having a baby."

"Yeah, well, we didn't *decide* that," she said.

Jeff was quiet for a moment. "Listen, I'm starving. Got anything to eat?"

Lisa got up and looked in the refrigerator. "Here's some pasta from last night. Want that?"

He nodded, and as Lisa put it in the microwave, Jeff came over and put his arms around her.

"Look, I know it's not the most ideal situation but it's the best I can do."

Lisa looked up at him. "I love you for trying," she said. "We'll talk, okay?"

He wolfed down the food. "Okay. Thanks for the pasta. I gotta get back to school before I get another cut. I'll call you tonight." He kissed her quickly and was gone.

She watched him drive away. He was so sweet. He was trying. He was still a kid, but he was trying. Lisa sighed deeply and finished her toast, washing it down with a glass of milk.

O

Before going to bed that night she went into her parents' room. They were both in bed reading.

"Could we talk for a minute?" she said.

They both shifted their positions and took off their reading glasses.

"What is it? Are you feeling okay?" her father said.

"Oh yeah, I'm fine. Jeff and I have been talking about getting married." Lisa waited for them to say something. "Jeff thinks it's the right thing to do. It is, I guess. . . " She looked about their room at the family pictures of her grandparents and of herself and Stephanie on a camping trip up in Oregon six years ago.

"But how would you live? How could you support yourselves?" her mother asked.

"His parents said they'd help support us till he graduates. I guess we could both work. And then later Jeff could go to college, maybe."

"How are you going to work when you have a baby?"

"Well, I'd only work till the baby's born. And then I'd stay home."

"Lisa, do you have any idea how much it would cost to live on your own?"

"Yes, I do. Why are you only talking about money? Why is it always money?"

"I guess it does sound like we're placing too much importance on money. But you can't live on love, you know. And starting out a relationship with a new baby and not enough money is really asking too much of yourselves."

"Dad, age doesn't have anything to do with this. Of course this isn't the way I wanted to get married. I never planned to get pregnant at 16, or have a baby or get married." Her throat was feeling thick. "I always thought I'd graduate from high school like everyone else and go to college and get a job, and then meet someone and get married and have children."

"Lisa, it's not too late to have an abortion. It is a choice, you know."

"Of course I know! Don't you think I've thought of that? I just can't though. I just can't."

"Lisa, come here," her mother said patting the bed beside her.

Lisa shook her head. It felt like there was a huge river between her and her parents, and, no matter how she tried, she just couldn't get over to their side again.

Her mother reached for some tissue, handed some to her husband, and some to Lisa. They all dabbed their eyes, and Lisa's mother finally blew her nose and then started laughing.

"Here we all are crying together. It's so sad, but . . . "

Lisa looked up at her parents and the three of them smiled.

"We love you, kiddo," her dad said.

Lisa nodded and then collapsed in their arms. God, it felt good to be taken care of.

O

Several weeks later the Branleys came over to talk. Awkwardly, they all sat around the dining room table sipping coffee.

"How are you feeling, Lisa?" Mrs. Branley asked.

"I'm okay now. I'm not getting sick anymore."

"Oh, I was sick my whole pregnancy with Jeff," she said. "Of course, I was 33 at the time."

Lisa quickly looked at her mother who said, "Sometimes younger people have an easier time of it. I was very fortunate myself; I felt great the whole nine months."

The men sat silently. "Well"—Lisa's father cleared his throat- "we're here to talk about a wedding. Personally, I'd like to see these kids wait a while, at least a year."

"We would too," the Branleys said. "We still can't believe the two of them got into such a mess."

Mrs. Branley looked at Lisa. "I just don't think my son should have to pay for one mistake for the rest of his life."

"His life? What about my life?" Lisa said. She looked at Jeff, then her parents. "I'm the one who's stuck. I'm the one who has to give up everything and drop out of school."

Jeff reached over and took her hand. "Mom, that's not fair. We've already decided. We're going to have a baby and we're getting married."

"Look, marriage is a complicated decision, and once you're married you're tied together legally, and you're both so young," Mr. Branley said.

"We're already tied together," Lisa said sharply.

"You certainly are," said Jeff's mother with an edge to her voice.

"Let's try and figure out what's best," Mrs. Howard said. "I really think Lisa would be better off at home—at least till the baby's older. Then, if things go well, you two could get married and live together."

"But then Jeff wouldn't be a part of everything and we'd never be together."

"Lisa, having a baby is so much work. You have no idea."

"I've taken care of babies."

The two women glanced at each other. "Not 24 hours a day, seven days a week," Lisa's mother said.

"Besides," Mr. Branley cut in "you'll have a very difficult time supporting yourselves. We said we'll help but we can't do it all. Jeff, you know you'll have to get a job, and that means no basketball. Could you help out too?" he said turning to the Howards.

"We've talked about it, and we could use the money we've saved for Lisa's college. It's not much, but it would help for the first year or two."

Lisa and Jeff looked at each other. Did he feel the same odd mixture of excitement and loss? She saw her future moving further and further away from her, out of her grasp, while the present grew larger in all aspects. Her future was right in her belly, and she clasped her hands in front of her.

"You know, I hate to sound so pessimistic, but even with both families helping and your working, Jeff, it's going to be very, very difficult," Jeff's mother said. "You'll never really have time for the two of you to have a relationship."

"That's all the more reason why we should get married now. We know it will be hard, but other people have been through it, and they've made it."

"But most teenage marriages don't make it, Jeff, and it's not what . . . what we wanted, what we hoped for you."

Lisa's father said quickly, "Look, we've all got our lost hopes and our anger and disappointments, but we can't dwell on that. We want to help Lisa and Jeff and the baby, not hinder them. I'd like to see you two wait to get married, but" —he turned to Lisa's mother— "we'll help you out. Of course we will."

"Well, we will too," said the Branleys.

Jeff stood up and shook Mr. Howard's hand and then his father's. "Thank you. We really appreciate it," he said putting his arm around Lisa.

Lisa leaned against Jeff. Why didn't she feel happier? After all, she was getting married!

O

It was a warm spring night with only two weeks left of school, and the air was sweet with the smell of blooming star jasmine and honeysuckle. It was the kind of night to sit and talk and share long sweet kisses with your boyfriend. Lisa sighed. She had finished her week's homework and her back ached. She longed to just fall into bed, but she was waiting for Jeff to show up so they could talk about the wedding plans. They had decided to get married at the end of June. It would be a wedding for just their families. Lisa had asked Kathy to be her maid of honor and Jeff had asked Dillon to be best man. They were going to be married by a judge in the Howards' back yard.

Where was he? He was 45 minutes late. She looked up at the off-white, loose-fitting wedding dress she'd found last week. It was pretty, she guessed, but not exactly how she'd imagined it. She had wanted to be a bride and be alone with her husband for several years. Well, maybe they'd have a few weeks. She sighed and looked at her list of things to do: order a bouquet of flowers plus corsages and boutonnieres; find a restaurant so they could all go have lunch after the ceremony; get blood tests and legal permission; order announcements to send out after the wedding. She imagined the expression on her friends' faces when they opened the envelopes in Eugene. She also needed to write a thank-you letter to her grandmother, who still lived in Oregon and who had sent them $300 as an early wedding present.

She looked again at her watch—ten o'clock. An hour late. Just then she heard Jeff's car drive up, and a few minutes later he opened the door to her room.

"Hi," he said with a little hesitation.

"Hi." He reeked of beer. "Jeff, you're an hour late. What's going on?"

"Don't make a big deal out of it. I was just shooting some hoop. God, it's such a great night."

She wouldn't look at him and instead stared at her list. Finally, she said, "That's not the whole story. You've been drinking too."

"Come on. I just had a couple."

"Jeff, what are you doing? It's a school night. Besides, you've been drinking a lot lately."

"Gee, Mom, do you have anything else to lecture me on?"

Lisa was quiet. She knew anything she said now would only cause more problems. The strong silence sat between them. He didn't get it. He thought he could just go on with his life the way it was; go to school, play basketball, party. He didn't have a clue what it meant to be a father.

"So, let's talk," Jeff said.

"Oh, go home. I don't want to deal with you now."

"Yes, your majesty. Whatever you say, your majesty. Why don't you stop trying to run my life? You can't have everything just the way *you* want it."

"Me?" Lisa could feel the rage growing inside of her. "The way *I* want it? Do you think I want this? Do you think I want to give up my life right now? Drop out of school? Never have any fun? Shit! I'm not even 17! Why don't you grow up? Stop being a kid!"

"And why don't you stop telling me what I can and can't do!"

"Why don't you just shut up!" Lisa screamed.

"Fine! I'm outta here!" He spun around and was out the door before Lisa could say another word. The next thing she heard was the squeal of his tires as he took off. She collapsed on the bed and tears burned her eyes. *I hate him. I hate him so much!*

○

It was already hot by 7:30 a.m. the next day and the bright sunlight woke her. Lisa heard a knocking on her window and raised her head. She saw Jeff's Bulls hat and got out of bed. Glancing in the mirror, she saw her puffy, red eyes.

He grinned and held out a rose. "Hi."

She wanted to be mad but felt only exhaustion.

"Hi."

"Here, this is for you. It's a peace offering. I'm sorry I was such a jerk last night."

She sniffed the rose, which looked beautiful but had no fragrance. She knew he had just stopped at the supermarket on the way over.

"This is so sweet," she said.

"So, how are you and junior this morning?"

Her face broke into a big smile. "Well, it wasn't an easy night, but we're okay."

"Listen, I got to get to school. I just wanted to . . . well, don't worry, okay? Everything's going to be all right."

She nodded, blinking rapidly to keep back the tears.

"I love you," he said.

"Me too."

"I'll see you after school."

Lisa watched him drive off, then put the yellow rose on her pillow and lay down. She hoped, she prayed he was right.

○

Lisa sat in the Independent Study classroom. It was the last day of school in June and there was only one other student in the room with her. Her teacher and three others were busy making out grades, and the room was quiet and hot. This was her last final, and Mr. T. had sent it over for her. The night before she had talked to Jeff and he had told her what to expect: "Just be ready to write a lot. It covers the whole year, but you don't have to memorize anything. You'll do fine. Don't worry."

Lisa sighed. She wanted to do well, but it was hard to get too serious about a final when she was eight months pregnant. She looked down at the typed pages before her and saw that Mr. T. had written a note:

"Lisa, I understand you've got a whole lot going on in your life. I want you to know that I respect the decision you've made. Good luck to you in all you do. In the words of the famous *Desiderata*: 'For all its sham, drudgery and broken dreams, it is still a beautiful world. Be careful. Strive to be happy.'

Sincerely, Mr. T. "

Lisa smiled and pictured Mr. T. in her mind as she continued to read the paper: "You have two hours to write your final essay. You will be graded on the content of your ideas, the organization and the presentation of those ideas, and, of course, the correctness of your grammar and punctuation. You may use a dictionary.

"Throughout the year, beginning with *Our Town*, we have discussed individual and cultural values as a yardstick for measuring the quality of life. It seems clear that without values, life loses its brilliancy and importance. As far as we know, it is our values that separate us from other forms of living creatures.

"In a thoughtful and well organized essay discuss the values that you believe to be important in life and provide specific examples of these values as revealed in at least four of the literary works and presentations we have experienced this year; to refresh your memory, a list of these is included."

Lisa read over the list:

The Scarlet Letter

Our Town

Huckleberry Finn

Walden

Poetry of Robert Frost, Maya Angelou, Langston Hughes, Gary Soto, Emily Dickinson, e.e. cummings, *The Grapes of Wrath*

The Declaration of Independence

Beloved

The Education of Little Tree

The Color Purple

Presentations from AIDS and Sexual Harassment Awareness Days

She inhaled deeply. It would certainly take her the full two hours to put all her ideas together. She jotted down several values she thought were important: Friendship, Compassion for Others, Hard Work, Freedom, Family, God. Then she thought of all the literary works posted on the board and was sure she could easily include four of those. Just then the baby kicked and Lisa's hand automatically went to the place just above her ribs on the left side. She smiled and felt a secret pleasure.

She guessed the baby wanted to be included. She had to add "Children" to the list. And "Life." To give a child life. And that included sacrifice and nurturing. "Nurturing" would be a value she could put down; taking care of what you love, helping life—all of life—to grow in healthy ways; and that would include the environment as well as children.

She looked again at her own list and narrowed her list of values to Hard Work, Freedom, God, Life, and Nurturing. The baby kicked again. *Thanks, little one. We're in this together, you know—forever.* Lisa began writing the essay of her life.

○

Lisa and Jeff were married that June and in mid-July they had a healthy baby boy whom they named Erik Michael Branley. Jeff graduated from high school the following June, and Lisa was able to finish six months later. They lived in a small two bedroom apartment for a year but then Jeff moved out and Lisa moved home with her family. Jeff now works for a construction company making eight dollars an hour and is taking classes at the community college two nights a week.

Lisa also takes a night class and hopes eventually to work in a nursery school where she can enroll Erik when he's older.

Jeff and Lisa go to counseling twice a month to see if they can learn to communicate better with each other and perhaps save their marriage.

ADOPTION

The meeting room was small with chairs set in a circle. There were six teenage girls and three older women who, Lisa guessed, were mothers like her own. They had all come to hear a woman speak on adoption.

Megan, the counselor, introduced Shirley who looked to be about twenty-seven. She was an attractive blond woman dressed in jeans and a flowered blouse. She had manicured pink nails and large earrings; she also had a big smile.

"I'm glad to be here tonight," she said. "The first thing I have to tell you is that just about 10 years ago I found out I was pregnant. I was 17 and a junior in high school. I had a boyfriend and we'd been together for over six months. We'd had sex five times and I guess it was that fifth time when I got pregnant. Getting those test results was one of the hardest days of my life. I never was particularly religious, but for awhile I did believe I was being punished by God."

Lisa felt sweaty all over. This woman's story was too close to her own, and if she'd been able to leave quietly, she would have. She glanced over at her mother, who gently touched her arm and kept her eyes on the speaker.

"I agonized over what to do. My boyfriend and his parents wanted us to get married, but I just didn't feel ready. I wanted to go to college, get a job. My sister wanted me to get an abortion, but I just couldn't see myself doing that. My parents were very upset, but they didn't kick me out of the house. They did say that if I decided to keep the baby I would be the one taking care of it. They said they'd help me with my education and let me live at home for a while, but that I would have to figure out how to juggle high school and be a mom. They said they'd be happy to be grandparents but that they wouldn't be baby-sitters."

She paused and smiled. "I'm glad they were able to be clear about it, but at the time I thought they were very harsh. I wasn't able to accept that if I chose to go ahead and keep my baby, I could no longer be the one who was taken care of; I didn't want to acknowledge that once I became a parent, my baby would get to be the child.

Of course I agonized over my decision. In the end, I just felt I couldn't be a good parent to that child. I was too young, and I didn't think it was fair to me—and especially not to the baby.

"It took a lot of convincing of my boyfriend, but he finally agreed to consider adoption. We went to an agency, and it was amazing how there were so many couples dying to be parents and give a child a good home. A lot of people said I was selfish, and maybe I was. But I must also tell you that I have witnessed the complete happiness of the family that my child is now a part of. I know in my heart that I did the best possible thing for my baby."

The room was silent.

"I'm sure some of you have questions. Please don't be afraid to ask them. That's why I'm here."

A young girl with long dark hair raised her hand. "What happened to your boyfriend? Did you get married?"

"No. We stayed together for a while, but then after we graduated he moved to another town and I went to college.

"How did you handle going to school while you were pregnant?" said a girl who looked like she could deliver at any moment.

"I stayed in school until I was about four months pregnant. I wanted to stay the whole time, but I just couldn't stand being around all the other kids who were active and going to games and parties. I felt very isolated, so I went to an independent study program and finished the year. I found out who my real friends were—a couple of girls and my boyfriend. I was lonely in my senior year, but I put my energy into studying. I got good grades and, although some kids gave me a hard time, a lot of others asked my advice and opinion on all kinds of things like sex and boys. I tried to never give off the feeling that I was ashamed of the adoption, but it wasn't easy.

"I want to add that my parents were really supportive. They backed my decision all the way. I also got some counseling to help me deal with the loss I felt after the baby was adopted." She smiled at the girls in the circle.

"Do you ever think about your baby?" another obviously pregnant girl asked.

"Oh yes. I certainly do. In fact, I see him often. He's 10 years old now. He calls me Shirley, his 'other mom.' I have his parents' permission to see him about once a month, but it's more like four times a year since I moved up here. We get along great. I'm more like an aunt, a very special aunt."

One of the older women in the group raised her hand. "What about the harm done to this child when he realizes that his real mother didn't want him? That's a terrible rejection for a child."

Shirley paused for a few moments. "You're right. It's an awful realization. I think that issue will be difficult for him at times throughout his life. I have trouble with the words 'didn't want him.' It wasn't as easy as 'not wanting him.' I did want him, but I wouldn't have been a good parent. When he's a parent himself, he'll know how hard it was to give him up, but he'll also realize that I did a very loving thing for him—I gave him the best life I could—a far better life than I could have created for him on my own. And I did another thing—I gave him parents who love him deeply."

"But no one can love a child like his real mother," the lady said.

"I agree. My baby's real mother is the one who is raising him, who takes care of him everyday, who knows his wants, his fears and his dreams. She probably even knows why he hates the color yellow. She is closer to him than I could ever be."

"Do you ever regret giving up your baby?"

"I can't say that I regret it, though I do regret I ever got pregnant and had to make such a hard decision. It still makes me sad, but I've grown up and changed. There was a time when I couldn't get up here and give a talk like this without crying. Now, I'm happy with my life. I went on to college and had many wonderful experiences. I have a good job and soon I'm going to get married and we hope to have at least two children—all very loved and well cared for."

A young girl with long blond hair said, "I just don't think I could live with myself if I gave up my baby."

"Well, it's a personal decision and I'm here to present you with one of the alternatives available to you. The thing is—when a woman gets pregnant before she's truly ready, before she really wants a baby, then there is no perfect solution; there's no way to come out of this dilemma without some kind of loss, some kind of sadness. The teenage girl, or the woman who decides to keep her baby gives up a lot of hopes and dreams and experiences she'll never get to have in her lifetime. She has to live with a lot of anger and frustration; her baby often has no father; financially, her life is very meager, and she probably feels very dependent either on her parents or on some man or on welfare.

"It's difficult to accept, but getting pregnant before you're ready—whether you keep it, or allow it to be adopted, or even have an abortion—means that you can't come out a complete winner; you have to give up something. Still, out of all this I feel I was able to make something wonderful out of a very sad situation; I know that in letting my baby be adopted I've enabled three people to be tremendously happy—the mother, the father and my—their—son."

There was a moment of silence and then everyone clapped.

"Thank you, Shirley," Megan said. "Are there any more questions? If not, I'll leave these brochures explaining the adoption process. If you contract with an agency, it acts as an intermediary between you and the adopting couple. Often your medical expenses will be paid for before the baby's born and the hospital stay; it also includes counseling before and after the adoption."

Megan looked at everyone. "Thanks for coming. Good luck with your decision."

Lisa and her mother glanced at each other and got up to leave. On the way out they took a brochure. Lisa slid into the front seat and let out a huge sigh. "Whew! I'm exhausted."

"I am too," said her mother, "and I'm not even pregnant. Listening to her story was a real experience."

"I admire that woman so much," Lisa said and she felt the tears sting her eyes. "I just don't think I'd have the courage to do what she did."

Her mother started the car and said, "Courage is the right word. I'm not sure I'd be able to do it either, but I'm sure glad there are women who can. . . otherwise, your Aunt Jenny wouldn't have Troy and Chris. She adopted them when they were infants, and look how great it's turned out. You know, Lisa, if you decide you want to go ahead with the pregnancy and then have your baby adopted, we can help. There are alternative school programs and you could stay at home. Or you could go live with Aunt Jenny up in Seattle. I've already talked to her, and it's definitely an option. She said she'd love to have you."

Lisa thought about it. If she went away, she wouldn't have to deal with the shame and criticism from her friends. But then she also wouldn't have Jeff, and she had just moved six months ago. She didn't want to move again and be away from her family. Maybe she could still go to school. She counted the months again. The baby was due in late July. Maybe she could stay in school the whole time she was pregnant and then have the baby over the summer. She'd heard of girls staying in school and doing that. The one lucky thing that had happened was that the baby's due date was during the summer.

They pulled into the driveway and Lisa went straight to the phone. She hadn't talked to Jeff in such a long time and she missed him.

His voice sounded warm and caring. "How'd it go?"

"Whew! It was really something. This woman had a lot of strength to let her baby be adopted."

Jeff was quiet for a few seconds and then said, "It's weird to think of your own kid out there being raised by someone else. I'm not sure I could stand for some other guy being a father to my own child. I'd always be looking at little kids, wondering if one of them was mine."

"I know," Lisa said, "but are you ready to drop everything and be a dad? Are you ready to get a job, take the GED, and get an apartment with me? You could still go to college if your parents would help you—I mean us. But you'd go with me and the baby. Or are you ready to pay child support to me for the baby and I'll raise it on my own?"

"God, I'm not ready for any of those things." Jeff was quiet again and they both felt the hard tension between them.

"At least with adoption you know your kid is being totally loved and taken care of." Why was she feeling so angry?. She knew Jeff cared, but she still felt very alone in this whole awful ordeal; she also felt he wasn't being realistic. The decision seemed much more hers than his or theirs. After all, it was her body experiencing everything, and she would be the one who felt tied to the baby.

"Have you told your folks yet?"

"No, I'll probably tell them this weekend."

"I can't believe it! I mean this is probably the biggest thing of your whole life and you haven't even told your parents?"

"I'm going to. You don't really know my dad. He's going to flip."

Lisa felt like saying, "Oh grow up." Instead she said, "Well do it soon because my parents want to talk to yours."

"Oh God," Jeff said.

○

In the following week Lisa went to an adoption agency, talked to a counselor there, and brought home some more information about adoption. She was determined to settle this matter with Jeff over the weekend; she couldn't take the indecision any longer.

Jeff said he wasn't ready to deal with her parents, and so he honked the horn that night and Lisa ran out to the car and got in. They drove to a coffee cafe that normally wasn't frequented by teenagers and sat at a table in the back.

"So, do you want one of those cappuccinos?" Jeff said.

Lisa nodded but then added, "Better make it decaf."

Jeff looked at her quizzically. "Huh? I thought you hated decaf."

"I do, but I don't think it would be good to have caffeine now." It took a couple of seconds for her message to translate to Jeff.

"Oh," was all he said.

There were very few people in the cafe, so Lisa took out the brochures she'd received from the adoption agency and put them on the table. "Here, I want you to look at these."

Jeff looked uncomfortable, but he glanced through one while he drank his coffee.

"God Lisa, this is the shits! I don't want to sit here and look at this stuff."

"Look, Jeff, I just can't keep going through this over and over and over. I've got to make a decision. If I wait much longer, I'm going to get too attached. I'm not getting an abortion. I've already decided that, but I—I mean we—have to decide if we're going to keep it or let it be adopted."

Jeff looked back down at the brochure in front of him—"Adoption—A Loving Choice." The pamphlet talked about young children being adopted into caring families, and it showed pictures of smiling people.

"Lisa, I don't know. This is all kind of beyond me. What do you want to do? I mean, this has got to be the hardest on you. Can you really imagine staying pregnant for nine months and then handing the baby over to an agency?"

"Not an agency! To a couple, to a mother and a father. Jeff, you've got to help me here. I really think it would be best for the baby and best for you and for me. You know we're not ready to raise a child, not together or apart. And there are plenty of people out there who want one, who want one more than anything in the world."

"Lisa, I've got to leave it up to you. I'm sorry, I just can't relate to this whole thing."

Lisa looked at him a long time. "Jeff, why can't we decide? I don't want you to leave the whole thing up to me! It's not just my decision."

"Come on, let's get out of here." Jeff stood up and pushed back his chair. They walked outside in silence and kept going. After two blocks Jeff turned to Lisa and said, "Look, I know I should be handling this better. I know I should do the noble thing and probably marry you and get a job and settle down and have the three of us all live happily ever after. But Lisa, I just can't do that. I don't know what the fuck to do. I love you and all, but I can't deal with this family shit. Not now; God, I'm only 17!"

Lisa stood looking at the lines in the sidewalk and at the scuffed toes of her black shoes. "I think," she said in a shaky voice, "I think if we tried to be a happy family it would never work. We'd end up getting divorced or something, or we'd end up hating each other." Digging her nails into the palms of her hand she said, "Let's be strong Jeff. Let's do the right thing. Let's let the baby be adopted."

Her words rang like giant gongs that drowned out all the city noises around them. Jeff took her hand and then pulled her close. He buried his face in her hair and whispered, "Okay, we'll do it. And we'll hang together through this We're going to get a ton of crap laid on us; you know that, don't you?"

For a brief moment Lisa relaxed against him; she nodded her head yes.

○

Jeff and his parents arrived at Lisa's home two weeks later. Everyone felt tense and awkward as they sat around the dining room table clutching their coffee cups. Lisa's father began in a tight voice.

"We all know why we're here. I can't tell you how hard this is for me and Lisa's mother, and I'm sure it's awful for you too," he said looking at the Branleys. Jeff kept staring at the table and blinking his eyes. Lisa wanted to reach over and grab his hand, but she felt paralyzed.

"We've talked at length with Lisa, and she and Jeff have determined they want to place the baby in adoption." He paused and went on, "Personally, I don't see any totally positive way out of this. The whole thing is extremely sad." Lisa's mother's eyes filled with tears and she reached for a tissue.

Jeff's mother dabbed her eyes and said, "Well, I just can't bear the thought of my grandchild being raised by someone else. I just couldn't live with myself. Brad and I would rather raise the baby ourselves then see it given up to strangers." She looked directly at Lisa and her eyes were brittle, her face grim.

"Mom," Jeff said, "Lisa and I have talked a whole lot about this and we both think it'll be the best thing for the baby to be adopted. I mean, we know that we're not ready to give up at least 18 years of our lives right now to be responsible for a child. And it wouldn't work for you and dad to raise it. The kid would be confused. Who would be his mom and dad? Besides, I know you and dad want to be free and be able to do all the things you've talked about. And I'd feel guilty if I let you guys raise it."

"It seems to me you're going to feel guilty no matter what," said his father.

"Listen," Lisa cut in, " a child needs a whole family, a young family, people who are ready to make that child the focus of their lives; you know, people who really want a child."

"Well, I can't accept it," Maureen Branley said. "I won't let it happen."

"I'm afraid we have no say here," Lisa's father said. "According to the law, it's entirely up to the parents of the child; grandparents have no legal rights."

Silence filled the room. Lisa reached behind her and put some of the adoption brochures on the table. "These helped me. They explain a lot. Please, just read one," she said handing it to Jeff's mother.

Everyone picked up a pamphlet although Lisa's parents had already examined one. The room was quiet and Lisa and Jeff quickly glanced at each other. Finally, Lisa couldn't stand the silence any longer. "Look, this agency will help me—us— find a wonderful family. They really make sure that the family that wants to adopt is solid and loving. And it's all legal. We are the ones who select the adopting family. I can even make an agreement with them to see the baby after it's born; you know, have a relationship with it."

Lisa's mother lowered her eyes and carefully examined the print on her flowered skirt. She marveled at her daughter who suddenly seemed so grown up. Where was she finding the strength to go through with this? Lisa reminded her of her grandmother although she had never really seen the similarity before. They were both strong people, able to do what they perceived was right regardless of what other people thought. She glanced at her husband whose eyes were glistening. Their daughter was truly a responsible, caring person; what more could they have asked for?

Jeff's parents put down the brochure and his father spoke. "This is so hard. I had no idea. . . Look, I appreciate the way you've researched this, Lisa. Adoption looks to me like a positive way to go. I just wish you two had been this responsible a few months ago; then we wouldn't even be in this mess."

"Lay off, Dad," Jeff said looking directly at him. "Don't you think we've been over that a million times? We're here to deal with the present."

There was another awkward silence, then Lisa's father spoke. "I know that none of us ever expected a grandchild of ours to be raised by someone else. It's a very difficult notion to conceive of. But really the decision is yours." He looked at Jeff and Lisa. "If you were older then I'd like to think the decision would be different, but that is not the case. This adoption group looks very promising. If you pick people to raise this baby, people who are loving and willing to allow you a relationship with the baby, then perhaps the child will be able to grow up confidently and won't feel rejected. I know adoption can work very successfully."

"We'll be happy to pay half of whatever expenses are incurred," Jeff's father said. "Lisa, I guess I don't have to say that this is going to be the hardest of all on you. You're the one who's really going to feel the enormity of what you both have decided to do. Jeff, I hope, will be a help, but that's probably all he can be. You're the one it's all going to fall on." His smile was encouraging, "It's going to take a lot of strength."

Lisa suddenly realized she had been holding her breath. It was strange to hear someone else verbalize what she knew to be true. She could only nod.

"Well, if there's nothing else," her father said, "I guess that's it."

Everyone got up. The parents shook hands and Jeff's mother put her arm around Lisa. "Take care of yourself, Lisa. Remember, I'll do whatever I can."

Jeff and Lisa walked outside together and Lisa looked up at him. "God, I feel so shaky," he said.

Lisa took his hand. "Me too. Boy, your mom was angry for a while."

"She held herself in check pretty well. I never realized before that this would be hard on them. I guess the baby is kind of a piece of them too."

"Do you still think we're doing the right thing?" she asked.

"Yeah, but it sure sucks."

" 'Sucks' doesn't begin to describe it," Lisa said.

Lisa's decision to keep the pregnancy and go for adoption changed her life completely. She dropped out of Galt High and went to an independent study program which allowed her to continue her education without going to school everyday. Instead, she studied at home alone for 25 to 30 hours per week and went in to see her teacher once a week. It was often boring and she fought the temptation to watch TV, but at least she wasn't behind in school credits and she didn't have to face the other kids.

"There's really only one person who supports me," she wrote in a letter to Gwen, "and that's Kathy. I don't know what I'd do if she didn't stand by me. It's so hard to do the right thing and know that everyone else is against me. The other kids think I'm a slut for giving the baby up for adoption, like I'm doing something to be ashamed of, like it would be better to keep it and be a mother, or that I'm stupid not to have an abortion. I wish I'd never left Oregon."

Gwen wrote back. "Lisa, I don't know how you can do it, but I think you're amazing. You have to come visit when it's all over. Or come when you're eight months pregnant and blow everybody's mind!"

Gwen just didn't get it. The last thing Lisa felt like doing was showing off her pregnancy; it wasn't entertainment. Besides, she couldn't face all of them; everything had changed and there was no place for her. She didn't fit anywhere.

Talking to Kathy, who dropped by one day after school, she said, "I can't get joyful about this baby, you know. I don't even want to. I just want it to be over and done with. I'm so sick of getting bigger and bigger. Other women, when they're pregnant, go out and buy baby clothes and strollers and stuff and they get to feel good that way, but that's just something I won't do. It would make it too awful to get all involved like that and then give it up. It's so hard. I didn't know it would be so hard."

Kathy looked at Lisa's swelling breasts and the large maternity top.

"Lisa, I wish I could help, but I just can't relate to this whole thing. Still, you've got to believe that you're going to come out of this a better person. You've got to believe that. Don't give up on yourself."

Kathy's words helped, but the sense of aloneness stayed. That night Lisa's mother sat with her in her bedroom.

"I've been thinking," she said, smoothing the quilt on Lisa's bed, "why don't we try to get in touch with that lady—Shirley was her name. You know, the one who spoke at the meeting. I bet she could help, Lisa. At least she'd understand what you're going through."

Lisa felt her spirits lift for the first time in weeks.

Shirley invited Lisa to her home and she promptly answered the door when be bell rang at 11 a.m. "Lisa?"

"Hi. Thanks for letting me come over."

"Oh, I'm happy to be of help if I can. Come on in and sit down. Would you like some tea? I remember I loved drinking mint tea when I was pregnant."

Lisa looked at the slim woman facing her who was so confident and together. "That'd be great." She took off her coat and tugged on her large shirt. There was an awkward moment while Shirley poured them each a cup.

Once they settled on the couch, Shirley said, "Why don't you tell me what's going on."

Where to begin? Lisa took a sip of tea. "Do you think about the adoption very often?" she said.

Shirley smiled. "Not really, not now, but I did at first, all the time. You said on the phone you were having a tough time. I'd nearly forgotten that time before the birth. It's pretty awful, I know."

Though she'd vowed she wouldn't cry, Lisa couldn't help it. "I just feel so left out of everything. I hardly have any friends. I just get fat and study all day. Sometimes I think I made a huge mistake." She gulped for air and blew her nose. "Well, I know I made a mistake but, you know, I mean the adoption. And here I am pregnant for the first time in my life and I don't even feel happy about it."

"You're doubting yourself? Is that part of it?"

Lisa nodded. "I made up my mind to let the baby be adopted, but maybe that's not what I should do."

"Lisa, it's okay to doubt your decision. You'll probably go back and forth in your mind a hundred times before it's all over. This is such a big event; of course you're not going to be able to make up your mind once and for all and never think about your other options."

"I mean, what if the people who adopt it are mean, or what if it grows up always feeling unloved or hates me?"

"Lisa, there are no guarantees in life—not for anyone. But the agency is really thorough; the last thing they'd want is for a baby not to be loved and cared for. They'll do everything possible to make sure that the people who adopt it are solid and wonderful. And how could the baby feel unloved when those people will want a baby more than anything in the world?"

"But maybe it will hate me for letting it be adopted, for not keeping it."

"I don't think so. I know my son doesn't hate me. He's fond of me, but not as his mother; I'm more like an aunt, a good friend."

The phone rang and Shirley got up to answer it. "No, no it's fine," she said. "I'll be there by one o'clock."

Lisa looked around the sunny living room: the large vase of flowers on the table by the window, the picture of a country scene by a river on the wall. She was aware of what a pleasant life Shirley seemed to live.

"Am I keeping you?" Lisa asked when she returned.

"No, I just have to be at work by one. We have lots of time. Are you hungry?"

"All the time, but not now thanks." Lisa felt a pressure in her chest and an urgency to talk quickly, as though she had only this one chance to speak her mind. "I'm worried I won't be able to go through with it, that I'll change my mind. So many people think it's an awful thing to do, to give up your baby."

"I know. I know. Young people especially feel that way; perhaps it's because they're young themselves and they can't imagine their own parents ever letting them be adopted. They're just not able to project themselves ahead in time and figure out what would be the best thing for the baby—not themselves, but the baby."

Shirley stood up and paced the room. "Sometimes I get so angry, you know. There are so many people out there who want to have a child and can't. And then there are people who shouldn't have children because they're lousy parents, and those people are able to pop them out one after the other. It's not right!

"You know, whenever I get confused, I just think of my son and what a neat family they are, and I know I did the right thing."

"I told my boyfriend it was the right thing to do, but inside I'm still afraid. I'm afraid I'll get attached and I won't be able to give it up, but then I don't know how I'd ever take care of a baby, either."

"Lisa, maybe you're rushing it a bit. Maybe you're trying to make yourself do something you're not ready for. Take your time, check it out. You know, you can always change your mind right up until you sign the final papers."

Hearing this, Lisa felt calmer. Maybe she was hurrying things. She finished her tea and glanced around the room again. Next to her on an end table was a picture of a little boy who was missing several teeth and holding a basketball. She looked over at Shirley. "Is that. . . ?"

"My son?" Shirley said, reaching over to hand the picture to Lisa. "It sure is. That's Jason. He was eight then. I just love that picture because he looks so totally happy."

"Don't you sometimes wish you were his mom?"

"Well, yes. Once in a while I catch myself having fantasies that I could have worked things out and raised him. But that's what they are—fantasies. I couldn't have given him the life he has now. No way."

"Do you ever miss him?"

"Mostly no. You know what is hard, though, is his birthday. Every year on his birthday I feel very close to him and a little sad. And then it passes. Someday I'll have a child of my own to raise and that will help, I know. I really look forward to that."

In the silence that followed Lisa could hear a ticking clock. She looked around and saw it was already 12:30. "Gosh, I guess you have to go." She pulled herself up from the couch.

Shirley got up too. "Lisa, call me if you need to. I'd love to see you again. I wish you so much luck with your decision, " she said giving her big hug

"Thank you," Lisa said. "I just wish it wasn't so hard. Sometimes I wish someone would force me to do something so I wouldn't have a choice. It's such a big responsibility. I never understood that before."

"Maybe that's because before you were a child, or at least a teenager. You've become an adult now," Shirley said.

"I guess. . . I wish I'd chosen an easier way to get there."

"Lisa," Shirley said taking her hand, "I've learned from my own life that this decision will change your life forever and you'll be a different person as a result. It will color even your everyday existence. It's what they call a life-transforming decision, and it's not meant to be easy. You're going to make it Lisa. Take care and let me know what you decide."

○

Two months later at the adoption agency Lisa found the right family for the baby. Their names were Emily and Tim Davis, and they were in their 30's. Their picture showed two smiling people and their dog, a golden retriever named Daisy, sitting at a picnic table in the park. The information that went with the picture said:

"We are two people who long to have a child share the happiness of our life. Emily is an elementary school teacher, and Tim works for a small computer company. We own our own home, which has a big backyard just waiting for a swing set. We like camping, baseball and reading. Neither of us uses drugs and we rarely drink; we are very committed to leading a healthy life style. Unable to have children of our own, we hope to adopt two children to complete our family."

What Lisa liked best about the picture was the golden retriever sitting between them on the picnic bench. They seemed to have it all except the one thing they wanted most. She called Jeff that night.

"You've got to see this picture, Jeff, and listen to their writing."

His voice was distant. "Yeah, they sound neat."

What was with him? Lately he'd been so uninvolved, more concerned with his basketball and baseball than the baby.

"Don't you care about this, Jeff?"

"Sure I do. It's just that. . . .God, it's taking so long. I want it to be done and over with."

The anger welled up inside of her. "What did you expect? A baby takes nine months! Anyway, you're not the one who's getting fat and having trouble sleeping!"

"Lisa, I'm sorry. I know it's all on you."

"You're damn right it is," and she slammed down the phone. He was such a shit! The phone rang again and she disconnected it. She was sick of Jeff and sick of the baby and being pregnant. She wanted her life back!

About ten minutes later, lying on her bed, she calmed down. Really, what had she expected? Jeff was 17 and a boy. No matter how neat he was, he still couldn't relate to what all this was like for her. For all the changes that men seemed to be going through, all the efforts to help men be more fatherly and family-oriented, having a child was still the female's job. . . And even though she didn't want to get married, she wished Jeff had asked her. He had never once said, "Let's get married." Damn him!

Lisa sat up, her head in her hands. She felt so trapped, as though all the doors in her life had closed. She tried to think ahead to five months from now, when the baby would be born and adopted and happily loved. But she knew she was always going to have a scar, a sad wound left by the first baby of her life. . . the baby who would know another woman as "mother."

○

As the months went by and the end of school was only a short time away, Lisa withdrew more and more inside herself. Everyone knew she was pregnant, but people seldom talked about it, since the rumor had spread that she was going to let the baby be adopted. She went to see her teacher once a week, did her homework and her birth exercises, and once in a while talked to Kathy.

Jeff was around, but only barely. He came over sometimes but always seemed very nervous. Occasionally they went out for coffee, but mostly they talked on the phone. They avoided difficult subjects like parties and the fun stuff going on at school. The prom, especially, was painful to talk about, since they had each decided not to go. They did, however, make a date to be together for that night.

He showed up at the door with flowers and a strained smile.

"Hi, beautiful," he said when she opened the door wearing black stirrup pants and a large pink floppy top that hid her protruding belly.

"Jeff, they're beautiful. Thank you." Lisa felt strangely nervous as she took the flowers and went to the kitchen to get a vase. "So, what movies did you get?"

"I got your old favorite *City Slickers* and some movie with Johnny Depp. So, where is everybody?"

"Oh, my folks took Stephanie and a friend of hers out to dinner," she said putting the flowers in water and bringing them out by the TV. She stopped and looked directly at him. There was a young sweetness to his face, and his eyes were kind. He wore that same blue sweater he had worn the first day of school.

"Hey, what's wrong?" he said putting his arm around her and drawing her close. "What is it? Is it the prom?"

Lisa let herself be held. It felt so good to have his arms around her, but at the same time she was aware of her size and how it came between them.

"No, it's not the prom. Well, I guess it is, in a way. It's just everything. And then you would have to wear that sweater tonight!"

"What's my sweater got to do with it?"

"Jeff, you are so clueless. Never mind, it doesn't matter," she said pulling away from him. "Want something to eat or drink?"

He followed her out to the kitchen and they both looked in the refrigerator. Their heads touched lightly and Lisa laughed.

"Now what?" he said.

She laughed again. "It's too much. I mean, here we are looking in the refrigerator together while all our friends are out to dinner all dressed up in tuxedos and strapless dresses. It just struck me as funny. I'll make some popcorn, okay?"

They put on the movie and talked a little, off and on. Their awkwardness soon melted away and they snuggled up with each other, Lisa resting her head on Jeff's chest. It felt so lovely to have him close by, to hear his heart beat under his sweater. It had been a long time. Jeff was idly stroking Lisa's hair and she raised her head to him almost questioning. He bent down and they kissed a long, sweet kiss. She opened her eyes and looked at him.

"Hi, stranger " she said.

He put both his arms around her and kissed her again, and Lisa felt a warm fluttering inside her and she knew Jeff was feeling it too. Their tongues met in a sensuous way and Jeff's arms tightened around her. He kissed her temples and held her closely.

They were silent for a long time while the movie continued with a lot of whooping and hollering. Lisa pulled back and looked at him.

"I wish it could have been different," she said.

"Me too. You know I do. I feel so bad and guilty sometimes," he said, taking her hand.

Lisa touched his dark blond hair. "I still love you. I think I always will. Thanks for sticking by me. Most guys wouldn't have done it."

He reached over and drew her to him. "Most guys probably wouldn't have gotten their girlfriends pregnant . . . ."

"Yeah, but it took two of us."

"It's funny, isn't it," Jeff said. "I just don't get how life can change so much and so fast. It's weird, you know. Sometimes I don't even feel like the person I was last fall."

Lisa nodded. She felt light years away from the girl who had walked into that English class in September.

○

Lisa had met with the Davis family twice. It was always awkward, but she liked them a lot, especially Emily who had gone out of her way to help Lisa feel welcome. She was 35 years old, and she and Tim had been trying to have a baby for five years with no success. Tests taken a year ago had finally shown that their chances were slim to none at all. It turned out that Emily was one of those rare women who had already gone through menopause. It was hard to believe, but it happened.

"It's ironic," Emily said to Lisa as they drank their tea in Emily's kitchen. "Here you are, so young and able to have a baby you feel you can't take care of, and here I am—only 35— and too old to have one but certainly able and wanting to give a child a good home. I'd do anything to get pregnant."

Lisa nodded her head. She looked around the kitchen: the Davises had a beautiful home with nice furniture and a big backyard. They seemed to have a really good relationship. Tim had been very involved in their first meeting, wanting to be an equal partner with Emily. Once, when he had talked about wanting a child, he had had tears in his eyes. Lisa knew from deep inside herself that her baby would have a wonderful and loving life with these people.

An important change had taken place—she now thought of this pregnancy as a baby. In the beginning, it had been just potential—tissue and fetus—but now, as the months had gone by and she had felt movement, it had become a baby, and Lisa felt even more of an obligation to make sure the baby would have everything it needed in life.

The birth and adoption would happen near the end of July. Lisa was glad she had made up her mind; she couldn't have tolerated still being undecided. This way she had managed to distance herself somewhat from the baby. She was going to let the Davises name it, and she constantly tried to think of it as their baby, not hers. Ultimately she knew this would be the least painful way for her to deal with the whole thing.

The people at the adoption agency helped too. They were supportive of her decision and didn't pressure her. She'd also found another teenager, Carol, who was giving up her baby. The two of them had talked for several hours, and it helped to have another girl who felt as she did, who struggled not to get too attached and who resisted looking at baby clothes. Carol, however, really had no choice; her parents had kicked her out of the house when they found out she was pregnant. That was a reality Lisa hadn't had to deal with; she thanked God for her parents' support.

Emily warmed her hands around the mug of tea and fingered the cotton place mat on the table. She cleared her throat and then said, "There's one thing I need to bring up. It's very hard to talk about, but Tim and I feel we must."

Lisa held her breath and felt the tension rise in her chest. At the same time the baby kicked on her left side; quietly she placed her hand over the spot.

"There's so much in the news these days about struggles between biological and adoptive parents," Emily said. "All the cases are so heart wrenching for everyone. I have to tell you I'm so afraid it will happen to us, that you'll change your mind at the last minute and decide you'll want to keep the baby."

Emily was talking faster and faster. "Of course, I understand that it's your right to change your mind, and I guess I could also understand your position; I mean, I'm not sure I could do what you're doing. But I know I couldn't take it if you. . . if you did change your mind. I couldn't take the heart break and Tim couldn't either. Not after all the disappointments we've had and all the lost hopes." Emily was crying now and stopped to cover her eyes.

Lisa was stunned. She'd never thought about the adoption from their point of view; she'd only considered her own struggle, her own confusion. It was hard to put herself in Emily's spot, to think you were going to have a baby, to plan for it, fix up the nursery, buy the clothes. And then, right before the baby was born—or even in the hospital—to have the baby wisked away! It would be like a miscarriage, like a death.

Lisa felt an enormous burden to be absolutely clear and honest. "Emily, I would never do such a thing. I mean, I know that people change, and I guess I've heard of some women seeing their baby and then deciding that they just can't give it up. But I won't do that. I won't do that to you and I won't do that to the baby. I'm trying so hard to do what's right for the baby." She was having trouble getting the words out and her jaw was quivering, the tears stinging her eyes. "I promise I won't do that. I promise."

Emily reached over and put her arms around Lisa. "Oh Lisa. Thank you. I know you're being as honest as you know how to be. I didn't want to pressure you, but I had to say it. I'm so anxious myself."

Just then, Tim came in the kitchen and a look of concern passed over his face.

"Em, are you okay?"

Emily looked up. "Yes. Don't worry. We talked. It's going to be all right."

Tim put his hand on Emily's shoulder. "Lisa," he said, "it's because of you that we'll get to be the family that we always wanted to be. Believe me, that baby will be loved and you will always be a part of its life."

"I know that," Lisa said. "That's why I picked you."

Just then Daisy came into the room and put her great golden head on Emily's lap. For a brief instant, it felt like a whole family of five.

○

Lisa sat in the Independent Study classroom. It was the last day of school in June, and there was only one other student in the room with her. Her teacher and three other teachers were busy making out grades and the room was quiet and hot. This was her last final, and Mr. T. had sent it over for her. The night before she had talked to Jeff and he had told her what to expect: "Just be ready to write a lot. It covers the whole year but you don't have to memorize anything. You'll do fine. Don't worry."

Lisa sighed. She wanted to do well, but it was hard to get too serious about a final when she was eight months pregnant. She looked down at the typed pages before her and saw that Mr. T had written a note:

"Lisa, I understand you've got a whole lot going on in your life. I want you to know that I respect the decision you've made. I have to confess that I'm not entirely objective because I'm adopted myself and I was lucky to have the best parents anyone could ever have. Good luck to you in all you do. In the words of the famous *Desiderata*: 'For all its sham, drudgery and broken dreams, it is still a beautiful world. Be careful. Strive to be happy.' I hope to see you next year in Senior English. Sincerely, Mr. T."

Lisa felt a surge of joy. How could it be! This was amazing, like a gift! She pictured Mr. T. as she continued to read the paper:

"You have two hours to write your final essay. You will be graded on the content of your ideas, the organization and the presentation of those ideas, and, of course, the correctness of your grammar and punctuation. You may use a dictionary.

"Throughout the year, beginning with <u>Our Town</u>, we have discussed individual and cultural values as a yardstick for measuring the quality of life. It seems clear that without values, life loses its brilliancy and importance. As far as we know, it is our values that separate us from other forms of living creatures.

"In a thoughtful and well organized essay discuss the values that you believe to be important in life and provide specific examples of these values as revealed in at least four of the literary works and presentations we have experienced this year; to refresh your memory, a list of these is included."

Lisa read over the list:

The Scarlet Letter
Our Town
Huckleberry Finn
Walden
Poetry of Robert Frost, Maya Angelou, Langston Hughes, Gary Soto, Emily Dickinson, e.e. cumming
The Grapes of Wrath
The Declaration of Independence
Beloved
The Education of Little Tree
The Color Purple
Presentations from AIDS and Sexual Harassment Awareness Days

She inhaled deeply. It would certainly take her the full two hours to put all her ideas together. She jotted down several values she thought were important: Friendship, Compassion for Others, Hard Work, Freedom, Family, God. Then she thought of all the literary works posted on the board and was sure she could easily include four of those. Just then the baby kicked and Lisa's hand automatically went to the place just above her ribs on the left side. She guessed the baby wanted to be included and she knew she had to add "Children" to the list.

She thought of Emily and Tim Davis and with how much love and anticipation they awaited this baby, what a world of warmth and caring the baby would grow up in. Placing the baby in adoption would be the hardest thing she'd ever do in her whole life; but at least it was right. And it was living in a true way. It was being true to what was right for her—no matter what other people thought.

She paused for a moment and stared at the paper in front of her. The room was quiet. Weren't values what this whole year had come down to? Trying to figure out what really mattered in life and being true to that? Wasn't that part of what it meant to be an American? To have your own point of view and to stand by it? And if you fell down, to get up and start all over. To have a second chance. A second chance to make things right, to change a mistake into something positive. That's what she was doing. She was giving this baby the best chance she could.

She added the words "Second Chances" to her list of values and shifted in her seat, trying to get comfortable. She sighed, then smiled. She was going to ace this final! She began writing:

"America has always emphasized the freedom of the person to choose her own course in life. From *Huckleberry Finn* to *The Color Purple*, the individual struggles with her conscience to be true to herself and to live life accordingly. In my own life, I have had to wrestle with confusion and listen to my own inner voice. Sometimes my values conflicted with one another, and I became lost while trying to figure out what was right for me. Fortunately, America has also allowed people to have a second chance in life and to start over many times if necessary. . . ."

○

In July, Lisa Howard placed her baby boy in adoption with Emily and Tim Davis, who named him Brandon. The Davis family adopted another baby, a Vietnamese girl, three years later.

Lisa graduated with her high school class and went on to finish college. She is married and lives in Davis, California where she is finishing her master's degree in Sociology. She and her husband hope to serve in the Peace Corps for two years in Africa and then start their own family.

Lisa visits Brandon many times a year and always remembers him on his birthday.

Jeff Branley graduated from high school and enlisted in the Air Force. He is stationed in Colorado, is married, and has three children. He writes Brandon frequently and hopes someday Brandon will visit them in Colorado.

ABORTION

Each morning Lisa felt shaky for the first three hours of school. Mostly she sat in class and didn't say much. Mr. T., her English teacher, asked her to stay a few minutes after everyone had left.

"Your work is not what it was, and you haven't turned in the last three assignments. Is there anything wrong?"

She looked down at the floor, telling herself not to cry. "No, everything's okay. I'm just tired. I'll get it together," she said. *Just as soon as I can decide what in the hell to do with my life.*

Kathy was waiting for her as she walked out. "You want to meet after school today?"

"Don't you have rehearsal?"

"It was canceled. I'm sure sorry you dropped out."

"Yeah," was all Lisa could come up with. Maybe she could talk to Kathy. She just had to talk to someone. "Okay. Let's meet in the parking lot."

"Good. See you at three."

O

Lisa got into Kathy's VW and slammed the door. "Want to get a coke?" she asked.

"Yeah, only let's use the drive through."

They got their drinks and drove a few blocks to a nearby park.

"Lisa," Kathy began, "I don't know you very well, but I'd like to help if I can. I know something's going on."

She waited and they both were silent. Lisa fiddled with her straw and took a deep breath.

"I'm pregnant," she said.

"Oh no. Oh Lisa. . . what are you going to do? What does Jeff say?"

"You've got to promise me you won't tell anyone. No one else knows, but I just had to tell someone." She started to cry. "I feel so bad. I'm so fucked up."

"What bad luck."

"Well, it wasn't just luck. It was also stupid. I mean we tried to be careful, sort of; at least we did once. Then I went to get the pill, but I was too late. I even had three months supply and everything. I just can't believe this happened to me."

Kathy sat and shook her head. "How 'bout Jeff? What about your folks?"

"Jeff's just kind of stunned. He's waiting for me to say what I want to do. My parents have actually been wonderful. They say it's my decision and they'll support me. They also said they wouldn't raise a baby."

"Listen," Kathy said after a few minutes, "I don't know how you feel about abortion, but my sister Barbara had one. You could talk to her."

"She did? How long ago? How old was she?"

"It was three years ago. She was 16. It's one reason I'm kind of reluctant to go with any one guy. I don't ever want to go through what she did."

"Was it awful?"

"I don't know if the abortion itself was awful, but she sure was upset and confused for a long time. Our family was a mess. She was sick and nearly dropped out of school. And then, when it was all over, it took her a while to be her old self. She just wasn't the same for a long time."

"How is she now?"

"Oh, she's great. She's coming home for Christmas vacation next week. You can talk to her. She's very open about it, and she's talked my ear off about birth control. I've heard so much about the pill and condoms, I'm sick of it. And I'm still a virgin!" Kathy laughed. "She'd kill me if I ever got pregnant."

"I wish I had an older sister, someone who had already gone through all this and could tell me what to do," said Lisa. "I'd like to talk to her."

"Okay. Next week, as soon as vacation starts. God, I've known Jeff for so long, I just can't believe he could be a father."

Lisa sighed. "In a way I like the idea of Jeff being a dad—you know, living with him, being married, having a baby. But I also know it's crazy. I mean, there's no way we could support ourselves and take care of a baby. We couldn't begin to even pay for the hospital."

"Some people get money from the government—you know, welfare."

"That's not how I want to start out my life. I want to go to college and get a good job. Jeff does too. He's worried and he's trying to be involved, but he's kind of distant. He still hasn't told his parents. And it's hard for me to talk to him. I mean, something seems different between us. . . we're not as close, I guess."

"You're probably both scared."

"Yeah," Lisa said. "That's for sure."

○

The rest of the week crept by. It was very difficult to get up for school; Lisa woke up tired. Around ten each morning she felt sick to her stomach, but she only threw up once at school; it was awful being in the bare, scuzzy bathroom with her head in the toilet.

Her body was going in its own direction—her stomach in revolt and her breasts growing larger. Since Lisa had never been very big in the chest, she liked her increased size, but her breasts were also very tender. She felt exhausted all the time, and doing school work was impossible. Her junior year certainly was not turning out the way she had imagined.

O

The door was decorated with a giant wreath of holly and red bows. Lisa glanced around at the poinsettias and windows decorated with false snow. She had never had less Christmas spirit in her life; it all felt unimportant.

Kathy answered the door dressed in black sweat pants and a red sweatshirt that said "Ho, Ho, Ho." Her hair was all tangled

"Hi, Lisa," she mumbled. "What a mess I am. I just got up. How're you doing?"

"I've already thrown up twice this morning. I feel like shit, but I'm here."

"You want some tea?"

"That'd be great. Thanks."

"Come on in. I'll get Barbara."

Lisa waited in the kitchen listening to the tea water begin to boil. The sink was filled with cereal bowls and glasses, and she could hear cartoon sounds coming from the TV in the other room. She'd forgotten that Kathy had a younger brother.

Barbara appeared also dressed in sweats, but her hair was pulled back in a pony tail and she had a big smile. "Hi, Lisa, I'm Barbara. I hear you're not feeling so hot these days."

"Boy, that's the truth. But, up to now, I haven't felt too bad."

"How far along are you?"

Lisa felt embarrassed to be talking about it so openly. "A little over a month now," she said, looking around anxiously.

"Don't worry, no one's home except my brother Tyler, and he's only ten. Why don't you get your tea and come in my room. Well, it used to be my room, but now it's a kind of guest room. You leave for college and they take your room," Barbara said with a laugh. "At least it's near the bathroom if you need one."

Lisa looked over at Kathy. "You come too," she said.

"Ah, I don't think so. You two be alone. I've heard it all. I'll see you before you leave."

Barbara closed the door and plopped on the bed. Clothes were strewn all about. "Just toss that stuff off the chair, on the floor, anywhere. It doesn't matter." She turned on her side, her head supported by her hand, and looked sympathetically at Lisa. "It's hard, isn't it?"

Lisa nodded and felt the tears sting her eyes.

"Don't worry about crying. I cried plenty. I cried for days. I thought my life was over."

Lisa looked at Barbara's pretty face and easy manner. "But you look so good now. I'd never guess you'd had an abortion."

"Well, an abortion isn't something you can see. Thankfully, we don't walk around with an 'A' stamped on our forehead. In high school I only knew one girl who had an abaortion. Of course no one ever talked about it then, But in college there must be at least six girls in my dorm alone who've had one. And those are just the ones I know about."

Lisa was surprised. "I didn't know it happened that often," she said. "But how did you feel at the time? Weren't you scared? And didn't you feel that killing a baby was wrong?"

"Yeah, I was scared. But I went to the clinic and talked to the people there. They explained in detail what happens when you have an abortion. And, if you have one in the first three months, the process isn't so hard. Some women say it's not a big deal and some say it hurts a lot. Mine hurt, but the pain didn't last long.

"Now, about the killing part. That's really a tough one. There are so many points of view about whether it's right or wrong or whether it's really a 'killing.' I think it's something everyone has to make up her own mind about. Some people really think it's a sin and you'll be punished for it."

"But God, when I see a little baby there's no way I can imagine killing it," said Lisa.

"Me neither. No way. How I've come to feel is that I didn't kill a baby. I kept a life from happening. I killed the potential. It was the biggest decision I've ever made in my life—maybe I will ever make—and I know I don't want to have to deal with that again."

"Sometimes," said Lisa, "I think that having an abortion is just the chicken way out."

"Chicken-smicken. You just have to do what's right for you. And you have to think of the kind of life that the baby would have if it was born."

"So, are you sorry you had an abortion?"

Barbara was quiet for a moment. "I ask myself that question a lot. No, I'm not sorry. I'm grateful. I can go on with my life. I can go to college, have a chance to get a job, have some fun. I'm not ready to settle down and take care of a baby. To give up my life. I wouldn't be a good mother, not now. Someday I think I would be. I want to have children. But that's the key. I want to—when I can do it right and be married and both of us want to be parents."

"Can I ask you about the guy, the one you got pregnant with?"

Barbara paused. "His name is Dave. He tried to help; he came to the clinic with me. I still see him sometimes. We stayed together for a little while, but then we split up."

Lisa thought about Jeff. The idea of not being with him made her heart ache, but the truth was that he didn't occupy her thoughts now as he had before. This pregnancy had the dominant place in her mind; Jeff was a definite second.

When she thought of having an abortion, the future opened up. It seemed she could still have her life the way she'd imagined it: graduating from high school, going to college, getting a good job, and someday getting married. Having a baby now would wipe out all that future. Lisa felt herself relax with a big sigh.

"Somehow you've made abortion seem not so awful, not such a crime," she said to Barbara. "But, as soon as I feel okay about it, then I feel like I have this responsibility, like I have to pay for the fact that I'm pregnant. . . like I don't have a right to have the kind of life I hoped I could have."

"God, I know just where you are," Barbara said. "Everything you're going through now is exactly why I'm determined to never be in that position again." She pushed up her sleeve and pointed to the two small marks embedded in the flesh near her shoulder on the underside.

"What's that?"

"It's Norplant. I don't have to worry about getting pregnant—not for five years. It's a huge relief."

"Well, that sounds good, but. . . but do you have sex a lot then?"

Barbara laughed. "I haven't slept with a guy for six months, not since my boyfriend and I broke up. I don't have anyone in mind, but when I do find someone right for me, I won't have to even think about pregnancy; I'll just have to worry about STDs and AIDS—that's enough, I think. And, if I should ever get raped I wouldn't have to deal with a pregnancy. I know that sounds awful, but it does happen. I feel much more in control and that feels good."

"I guess it gives you a lot of freedom," Lisa said.

"It does. Of course you still have to use condoms. There's a girl in my dorm who is HIV positive. She's not showing any symptoms yet, but it's so sad when you think that eight or ten years from now she'll probably be dead—unless they find a cure."

"God," Lisa said." Sometimes I hate sex. It causes so many problems."

"I think all women must have felt that way at some time in their life. It's so weird. . . . .how can something that's so wonderful, something that can create a beautiful human being, be so complicated and cause people so much unhappiness?"

"Do you think every female has this many problems with an unwanted pregnancy?" Lisa asked.

Barbara laughed. "Oh no. Some women don't think twice about abortion. It's not a big deal for them. And others would never even consider having an abortion; it's just not an option for them. I was somewhere in the middle, and I never thought—or felt—so much about any decision in my life. I'll say this, any decisions I've made since that one have been a piece of cake in comparison."

Lisa was quiet. Was she any closer to knowing what she wanted to do? Maybe a little. Talking with Barbara somehow made the prospect of an abortion less frightening, less horrible. But damn! It made her so angry that one little slip up, one incident of sex that probably didn't even last one minute, could completely mess her up her life.

"What's the matter?" Barbara asked.

"This whole thing just makes me so mad. I never thought I'd do something so stupid."

"I know, I know. It's hard not to be as smart as we thought we were."

"And I get mad at Jeff too. Why wasn't he more careful? He was more experienced than I was. He knew better."

"I've learned since that most guys aren't able to think very clearly when it comes to sex. I think they should, but they don't. It's sad, but we can't rely on boys to take care of us; they're not thinking much about babies when they have a hard on."

Lisa sighed. She felt so tired. Her stomach was queasy, and she hoped she wasn't going to throw up.

"At least your parents aren't coming unglued and forcing you to decide one way or another. You're lucky," Barbara said.

"I know. The only thing they've said is they'll support my decision, but they won't raise the baby. I wouldn't want that, anyway."

There was a long silence.

"Well, thanks a lot for talking to me. I really appreciate it," Lisa said getting up. "I'm really tired. I think I'll go home and take a nap."

Barbara gave her a big hug. "Just remember," she said, "it won't always be this awful. It will all change. Take care."

"Yeah. Tell Kathy goodbye for me, okay? Thanks again."

O

The next few days were tumultuous. Lisa didn't sleep well, and everywhere she went she was bombarded by the issue of abortion: the nightly news was filled with footage of anti-abortion protesters being hauled away by police; women were pictured holding signs saying "Pregnancy is a Woman's Decision" or "I am Pro-Family and Pro-Choice." Other signs said "Abortion is murder." A doctor in Florida who performed abortions was shot and killed by an anti-abortion activist; the Pope, visiting in Colorado, spoke about the sin of abortion; abortion was discussed in U.S. History as a classic example of the American struggle of states' rights vs. the rights guaranteed in the Constitution.

Lisa felt exhausted and ready to crumble. She cried frequently, stayed home as much as possible, and felt sick to her stomach every day. Finally, on Thursday around noon her mother came home from work and knocked on her door.

"Lisa, honey? Are you sleeping?"

"Not really. Come in."

Her mother was dressed in a turquoise knit top and beige skirt; she'd had her hair cut short.

"You look great, Mom. Is that a new top?" Lisa felt old and tired lying in bed. Her hair was stringy and there were dark circles under her eyes.

"Yes, I bought it yesterday. Lisa, how are you feeling?"

"Awful."

"You're missing so much school. How far behind are you?"

Lisa turned and looked at the wall. She felt tears sting her eyes. "Way behind in just about everything. I don't care about school."

"Well, are you still passing?"

"Yeah, barely."

"Honey, you need to make some decisions. You can't just do nothing. If you do that, the decision will be made for you, and that's no way to have a baby. You need to figure out if you're going to go ahead and remain pregnant or if you're not."

"Oh Mom, I know. I just don't want to decide. I want this whole thing to go away. I want it to not be. I want you to decide. Tell me what to do."

Her mother was quiet for a moment, then said, "Lisa, I'd like to decide for you, but it would be a problem between us for the rest of our lives. I don't want to hurt our relationship. You're a woman now, and this is something you have to decide for yourself. Your dad and I will support whatever you decide, you know that. But," she said putting her arms around her, "I am so sorry that you even have to make this decision. Somehow you have to find a way to take something positive from this experience; at the very least, make sure that you never find yourself in this position again."

Lisa nodded her head. "Do you think abortion is a sin?"

Her mother glanced up at the ceiling and took a deep breath. "I think the decision to have a baby or not is one that a man and woman should make together if possible. Some churches believe it's a sin, and others don't. But I don't think in those terms." She paused, looking down at her fingernails and then went on. "I do believe it's a decision that no one ever feels good about making. It's a horrible decision and no adult—let alone a teenager—makes it easily. Anyway, sin or not, it has nothing to do with our loving you. You know, no matter what, we'll always love you."

She hugged Lisa tightly, lightly stroking her arm. Lisa leaned against her mother inhaling the warmth and the light smell of her perfume. It was familiar, one she'd smelled off and on for years. For a brief moment Lisa felt loved and secure, as though everything in the world was all right.

"I think," Lisa said, her chin quivering a little as she held tightly to the edge of her light green blanket, "I think I'm going to have an abortion. I just don't want to tear my life apart now. I want to still be a teenager. I want to graduate with my class." Great tears were rolling down her cheeks, and she was wiping them away with her hands. "I want to go to college and I want someday to get a good job and marry someone, and someday I want to have a family. I'm not ready, Mom; I just can't be a mother now."

Her mother was quietly crying too. "I know," she said. "I know. It will be okay. You will be okay. If this is your decision, then we'll find out where to go. Thank goodness it's legal now, so you'll be safe. We couldn't bear it if any harm came to you."

They sat together on the bed, mother and daughter, closer than they had been for a long time.

O

The next day Lisa called the same women's clinic she had been to before, but this time she noted that it advertised abortion services. Her mother had offered to call, but Lisa said she wanted to do it herself.

The receptionist listened to Lisa's request, then said there were several questions she needed to ask. Lisa leaned back against the pillow on her bed. It was hard to believe this was actually happening. She gave her name, address, phone number, and date of birth.

"Is it all right for our clinic to leave a message for you if necessary?"

"What do you mean?" Lisa asked.

"Well, some of our clients want to preserve their confidentiality and don't want anyone to know that they've contacted our clinic."

"You mean like parents?"

"Well, yes, in some cases. Other clients prefer not to tell their husbands or friends."

"No, it's okay. My parents know." Lisa expected the woman to comment on this, but she simply went on calmly.

"Have you ever been a client here before?"

"Yes, I came in once for birth control pills and later for a pregnancy test."

"Well, that makes it easier. Just a minute, I'll pull your file and be right back."

Lisa looked around her room while she waited. Her heart was beating rapidly.

"It looks here like it's been nearly seven weeks since your last period," the lady said. "Does that seem right?"

Lisa had gone over and over the date in her mind; she knew it by heart. She had circled it on her calendar. "Yes."

The lady went on. "In order for you to get an abortion at our clinic, it must be at least six weeks since the first day of your last period and less than 12; so you fall into the right category. And you've had one pregnancy test. That's good. We require positive results on at least two tests before we perform an abortion. Once in a while a test is inaccurate."

"I also took one of those home pregnancy tests," Lisa said.

"And that was positive too?"

"Yes."

"Well, those tests are very accurate if you follow the directions. Still, when you come in for your appointment the afternoon before the abortion, we'll give you another pregnancy test, check your blood pressure, and any signs of anemia. A nurse will give you a pelvic exam, which will help us better determine the exact date of your pregnancy. We also will screen you for gonorrhea and chlamydia."

Lisa's mind was still stuck on "the afternoon before the abortion," and she couldn't quite grasp everything the woman was saying. "What. . . what do you mean the afternoon before?"

"Oh? Sorry, I didn't explain. We ask you to come in the afternoon before for approximately two and a half to three hours. At that time we'll perform these various exams and you'll also be in a small counseling group where you can talk with other women who are pregnant and considering abortion. In addition, you'll have a private counseling session with a counselor to talk over any fears or feelings you might have."

"You mean I could still change my mind?"

"Oh yes. Sometimes women come in here Thursday night all set to get an abortion, but they decide they want to go through with the pregnancy."

"They do?"

"Yes. Well, ending a pregnancy is a big decision, and we believe a woman should know all her options and have as much information as possible before she decides."

"So, that's the purpose for coming in the day before?"

"That and, should you decide to go ahead with the abortion, we insert the laminaria that night. Then you come in the next day, about 15 hours later, for the actual procedure."

"What's laminaria?"

"It's a sterilized seaweed that's rolled up very small and placed into your cervical opening. It expands to as big around as a pencil and about two inches long. Then we put in some gauze and sulfur cream."

"Does it hurt?"

"It's like having cramps, and we give you a Motrin first and one to take home with you and another to take before you come in the next day."

"I guess I could stand that. Could someone come in with me when I . . . .when it's going on?"

"You may have another person of your choice, but we urge you to pick someone who will be a help to you, not someone you'll have to worry about. Of course, you can also have someone in the waiting room."

"Am I awake during the whole time?"

"Oh yes. You'll be aware of everything. We'll give you three injections of Lidocaine in your cervix so you won't feel anthing. In addition, if you want, we'll give you something to help you relax."

"What about that new pill, the one you take the morning after. Do you have that?" Lisa asked.

"You must mean RU-486. I'm sorry we aren't allowed to offer that just yet; it's still being tested." [1]

"Well," Lisa took a deep breath—how much will it cost?

"Including the pre-visit, the abortion, and a follow-up session plus any counseling or medication you may need, it will cost between $290, and $390 on a sliding scale. We do accept Medi-Cal and private insurance."

[1]In 1994, RU-486 was not available; however, it was approved by the FDA in 1996 and may now be obtained from a physician. This pill induces a miscarriage and may be taken very early in the pregnancy.

"Wow, $300," Lisa said. "Couldn't I get one for less?"

"You can if you qualify for Medi-Cal. Perhaps your family has insurance that will pay for most of it."

"I'll find out."

"If you would call and let me know how you plan to pay, I'd appreciate it. Meanwhile, can you come in next Thursday afternoon about 3 p.m.?"

"Yes, I'll be there." She wondered if she should ask Jeff to come too, but she had a hard time imagining him sitting in the waiting room. Maybe her mother or Kathy would be a better choice.

"Do you have any more questions?"

"No, that's all, I think."

"Okay, then. See you Thursday afternoon."

Lisa hung up the phone and burst into tears. Feeling caught up in something much bigger, much more powerful than herself, she cried for a long time. After she quieted down, she lay almost in a stupor and thought of at least 20 more questions she could have asked. She had made a decision, and she felt a great relief, but she also felt a sadness that filled all her insides; it was going to take a lot of energy to finally get through it.

That night she was watching the news, and it showed President Clinton addressing a large group of teenagers. To the girls he said, "Make up your mind you're not going to have a baby until you're old enough to take care of it and until you're married." And looking to the boys he said, " Having sex and fathering children is not a sport, this is a solemn responsibility. Is it right or wrong if you're a boy to get some girl pregnant and then forget about it? I think it's wrong. . . .It's something you pay for the rest of your life. You carry that in the back of your head: Somewhere there's some child out there you didn't take care of. . . ."

Lisa sat quietly on the couch. She knew the President wasn't talking about abortion as an answer, but at least she wouldn't be guilty of not being a good mother. . . still, this wasn't how she had planned for her life to be.

O

It rained Thursday, and Lisa was a few minutes late arriving at the clinic. She leaned over and kissed Jeff before getting out of the car.

"I love you," he said and gave her a hug. "I hope it goes okay. Here, don't forget this. He handed her $100 to pay the difference between what the insurance would pay and what was owed to the clinic. They had talked it over, and he had been adamant that he pay the money. "Look, Lisa," he had said, "we both did this. It took two of us. Now you have to go through the awful physical part of it and the pain. It's the least I can do."

She hadn't argued with him. It felt right that Jeff be more involved in the abortion. After all, he really hadn't participated in anything except to occasionally listen to her. Still, when he said those words, Lisa felt a warm love

154

for him.

"I'll be here in two hours," he said.

"Well, it might take three."

"That's okay. I'll be here in two. Good luck, Lis'."

There were six women and two men in the waiting room. Four of the women had their heads bent down filling out forms while the others sat looking through magazines. Lisa guessed that they were older than she.

She went to the receptionist, told her name, and the lady gave her a big smile. "Oh yes, I talked to you on the phone. I have your papers right here." Looking through them, she said, "Have you decided how you want to pay for this procedure?"

The word "procedure" rang in Lisa's ears. This wasn't a "procedure." It was an abortion. Still, she said "Yes," and took her insurance card from her purse.

"Okay. Thank you," the receptionist said. "While I make a copy of this card, why don't you fill out these forms." She handed Lisa at least four sheets of paper in different colors.

Lisa took off her wet coat and self-consciously pulled down her long, baggy shirt. A woman with dark, curly hair glanced up, half smiled, and moved over on the couch, making a place. Lisa glanced over the forms and noticed some were written in Spanish on the reverse side. Many of the questions were the same ones she'd answered on the phone, but others were new:

Check any symptoms you are currently having:
     frequent urination ————————
     nausea or vomiting —————————
     swelling of abdomen ————————
     breast soreness or tenderness —————————
     tiredness ———————
     diarrhea ————

She checked all except diarrhea; apparently she had been spared something. Her eyes scanned the list, and one question jumped out at her: "Have you taken birth control pills in the last three months?" God, how she wished she had! She read further, and at the bottom of the paper it said: "Urine pregnancy tests are usually accurate ten days after conception but are not guaranteed. Aspirin, caffeine, or marijuana within the last 24 hours may cause inaccurate results."

A long chart followed where she was to check her family history. Lisa was amazed by the detailed information they wanted. Some questions she didn't know the answers to, questions that dealt with problems of thyroid, sickle cell, DES daughter, chlamydia, gonorrhea, pain with intercourse. She smiled almost bitterly at that last item; did having sex as a virgin qualify her to know whether or not she'd had painful intercourse?

One by one, the various women left the room and then returned. Lisa was the last one called. As she went through the door, her heart was pounding wildly.

The lady who greeted her took her hand as she introduced herself.

"Oh, your hands are cold," she said.

Lisa nodded her head and mumbled something unintelligible.

"Are you nervous?"

"Yes, I guess so."

"Well, I'm only going to go over your forms with you and then take your blood pressure and a urine sample. Don't worry. There's nothing major that's going to happen now. And, if you want, you can still change your mind."

Lisa nodded again. She didn't trust her voice to speak out loud.

The woman wrapped the blood pressure cuff around her arm and squeezed the rubber bulb several times. She looked at the gauge, saying, "Well, it's a little on the high side but still well within the normal range." Then she gave Lisa a small paper cup and showed her the way to the bathroom. "One final pregnancy check," she said, "just to make sure everything's completely accurate and we can go ahead."

Closing the bathroom door, Lisa hoped this was the last one of these she'd ever have to do until she *planned* to be pregnant.

About five minutes later the woman came back and said, "Well, your test is positive, so you're eligible to join the counseling group which is meeting in just a few minutes. A counselor will explain what the procedure is and what the risks are. Also, you'll have a chance to talk with other women and have some tea or juice."

Lisa felt a great sinking. That was the last of her hopes. Slowly, she got to her feet.

The room had about eight chairs arranged in a circle. Several women were already seated and were sipping from styrofoam cups. They gave each other a quick glance and nervously looked about.

Finally, seven of the chairs were filled, and another woman came in the room saying, "Hi, everyone. My name is Clarice and my job is to answer any questions you might have and also to help you talk about your feelings regarding the abortion you're each scheduled to have tomorrow."

Lisa looked at the rest of the group. One young black woman wearing a beautiful purple and gold sweater asked, "Will the abortion take very long and hurt much?"

Another woman answered, "This will be my second time. It's over before you know it. It takes only 5 or 10 minutes and the suction part takes less than a minute."

Lisa looked intently at this woman, who was wearing her long hair partly down, the rest held up with a gold clip. She had on stirrup pants and a long red cotton top. How could she be going to have another abortion?

Apparently someone else had the same question. "You've already had one?" The woman smiled a little self-consciously, glanced down, and looked back up at the one who had addressed her. "Well, I had an abortion when I was just 16." Her eyes flickered briefly over to Lisa. "I was so young and so naive. Now it's ten years later and it's a very sad decision for me. My partner wants to have children some day, but just not right now, and I know it would be tough if we had a baby to raise in the next two years. . . I'm just so sorry to have to do this now. . . .again. And I feel guilty because I always used my diaphragm and jelly. . . .you know, the whole thing. Except now I know that diaphragms aren't that effective."

The rest of the group was quiet. Lisa felt like crying. A heavy-set woman with short, straight hair spoke. "I know. My mother-in-law thinks I'm a total sinner. She screamed at me one night when we went over to get our daughter when they were baby-sitting. She said I was breaking God's rules. But our life is so difficult right now. My husband just lost his job. I don't know how we're going to come up with next month's rent money. We just feel we can't afford another baby." She stopped and reached for a tissue to blow her nose.

The group leader said, "Every woman has her own reasons for deciding to end a pregnancy; it's rarely easy or simple. For some, the decision is the difficult part, and for others it's getting the money or arranging for child care."

Another woman spoke up. "Well, I have a friend who was raped by her stepfather when she was 15. That abortion decision was an easy one. The bastard got out of jail last year, and after 10 years she's still trying to get her life together."

Lisa squirmed in her seat. All this talk seemed a long way from her own life, Galt High, and Jeff, but then it seemed equally unreal that she could be pregnant.

A woman wearing a 49er sweat shirt looked over at Lisa; her eyes were soft and sympathetic. "Do you mind if I ask how old you are?"

The group leader cut in. "We don't want to ask personal questions. It's important to respect each person's privacy."

"It's okay, "Lisa said. She almost felt relieved to open her mouth. "I'll be 17 in a few months."

"I think you're making a wise decision," the woman said. "If I had a daughter your age who was pregnant, I'd urge her to get an abortion too. You have your whole life ahead of you, your whole life to have to be responsible for another human being."

Lisa nodded her head but found she couldn't say anything more. Still, she was grateful that her mother hadn't urged her to do anything. She really had let it be Lisa's decision—Lisa felt very close to her right at this moment.

"Is there anyone who perhaps is having second thoughts about going through with the abortion?" the leader said.

The black woman ventured, "Well, I was up till a couple of days ago, but now I just want to get it over and done with."

The group grew quiet, and Clarice finally said, "If there's nothing else, then each of you will go individually to the next room to talk privately with one of our coaches, as we call them, and to have the laminaria inserted. But remember, it's still all right to change your mind. No one is going to pressure you."

They all stood up and the woman with the 49er shirt briefly put her hand on Lisa's shoulder. "Tomorrow at this time," she said, "your life will look a lot different. . . .a lot better."

Lisa looked at her. "Thanks," she said.

Her name was the third one called, and as she went in and shut the door, Lisa felt she was stepping into another world. The woman who greeted her was older, about 50 perhaps, with short gray hair and glasses. She held out her hand and said, "Hi Lisa, I'm Lilian. How are you feeling?"

"Okay, I guess. I'll be glad when this is all over."

"Can I answer any questions for you?"

"When are you going to put that stuff in?"

"You mean the laminaria? As soon as we finish talking and you sign the consent forms. Now, you don't have to have the laminaria. Some women choose not to and so simply go home now and come back tomorrow."

"Well, is it better to have it?"

"It's our experience that the laminaria makes the abortion more comfortable and safe. However, you could just come in tomorrow and we can open your cervix by using small plastic rods. It might take a little longer and possibly hurt more, but we can give you medication."

"I heard that the laminaria is seaweed. How weird."

Lilian laughed. "Yes, it does sound strange, but it's been used for centuries by women to facilitate their own abortions. It comes to us from Japan. Here, let me show you." She held up a very small cylinder-shaped object. It was rolled very tightly to the width of a pencil lead and about two inches long.

"That does it?" said Lisa.

"It doesn't perform the abortion, but as it's inside of you, it swells open and so causes your cervical canal to open also; the canal is between your cervix and your uterus. It takes about 8 to 10 hours. . . . Are you questioning that having an abortion is the right decision for you?" Lilian asked in a soft voice.

"Well. . . I hate to do this, but I feel it's the best thing for me." Lisa was quiet for a moment. "No, I want to go ahead with it."

"All right then, you need to read over this paper and, if you agree, sign it."

Lisa looked at the yellow form. It had 10 statements that she was to initial and was called "Consent for Laminaria Insertion prior to an Abortion." She carefully read it, but was having trouble registering the meaning of the words. Finally, she signed it.

"And then we have another form which has to do with your giving approval to go ahead with the abortion tomorrow."

"I'm not real sure about what happens tomorrow, and it says here I should ask if I don't understand something."

"Good. When you come in for your appointment tomorrow, you'll be given medication to help you relax. Then, in about half an hour, you'll be given a pelvic. If everything checks out all right, we'll give you three injections to numb the pain. Then a small suction tube will be inserted into your uterus and the contents will be sucked out. It takes about 30 seconds."

"That's it?"

"Yes. Then you'll need to take it easy and go home and rest. You'll probably have some cramping, and you may feel very emotional over the next few days."

"You use suction?"

"Yes, we've found it's the safest and quickest way."

Lisa visualized some large vacuum cleaner with a huge hose like the one they had at home, so she was very surprised when Lilian reached in a cupboard and produced a small machine with a very narrow tube about the size of a new pencil. She felt relieved.

"So, that's it? Then it's over?"

"Yes, that's it?" The woman hesitated. "Do you have a question?"

"Well, I just wondered, do you think that's killing?"

Lilian removed her glasses and rubbed her eyes. "I'm asked that all the time. I think everyone has to answer that question for herself. I can say, though, that if I thought this process was killing, I certainly wouldn't be participating in it."

There they were—back to the same issue again. Then she remembered Barbara's words: "The way I've come to feel is that I didn't kill a baby. I kept a life from happening. I killed the potential. And I got to go on with my life."

Lisa sighed. "Well, I guess I'm ready."

"Okay," Lilian said putting on her glasses. She reached behind her and took out a bottle of what looked like aspirin. "Here, this is Motrin. Take one now, one tonight, and one tomorrow before you come in. It'll help in case you feel cramping. Now, you need to slip off your pants, cover yourself with this paper gown, and lie down on the table, putting your feet in the stirrups. I'll be back in a few minutes. We need to let the medication take effect." Her eyes softened with encouragement.

Lisa followed the instructions and positioned herself on the table. She suddenly felt quite chilly, especially when the cold metal touched her bare feet. She stared at the ceiling and had to laugh when she read the new poster that had been tacked up: "Life looks different horizontally." Boy, that was the truth Lisa thought. Three months before she'd never even been horizontal for a pelvic exam and now she'd had two of them. After tomorrow it would be three.

Lilian came in holding a tray which she placed on the table. "Okay now you need to let your knees fall apart." She put on sterile gloves and picked up the metal speculum. I'm going to put this into your vagina to hold it open. You'll probably feel some pressure and discomfort, but no more than a regular pelvic exam."

Lisa stared at the ceiling, feeling a heavy tug at her insides, almost like a pinch. Lilian took a swab and smeared her cervix. "This is to check for gonorrhea and chlamydia," she said, placing the swab on a sterile gauze pad. Next she lightly washed off Lisa's cervix. "This is a disinfectant just to keep everything clean as possible. We're just about done here. One more step. This is the laminaria," she said holding up the small dark cylinder. "You'll probably have a cramp or two as I slide it in," and she deftly inserted the lamanaria into Lisa's cervix.

Lisa was holding her breath and felt a sharp twinge.

"Okay, you're done," Lilian said.

"That's it?"

"Yep. Now I'll just put some antibiotic cream here on your cervical opening and pack you with a little gauze just to keep things sterile, and don't worry if the gauze and the laminaria fall out tomorrow morning. Just tell the doctor what happened." She took Lisa's hand and helped her to sit up.

"Now be sure that you don't put anything into your vagina -no tampons, fingers, or penises. Also, no baths or hot tubs, but you can take a shower."

Lisa grimaced when Lilian said "penis." That's what had gotten her into this whole mess..

"How do you feel?" Lilian asked.

"I guess I feel a little amazed by all this. I kind of don't believe what's happening. Plus, it's so different from the stories I've heard about from the old days."

"You mean back room abortions?"

Lisa nodded.

"They were terrible ordeals. And there was so much infection and many women died in the process. Some of the doctors who performed those abortions were good souls, but too many of them were scoundrels who were out to make easy money and didn't care what happened to the women." She paused., "Anyway, that's not the case now. You take good care of yourself. Do you have a ride home?"

Lisa thought of Jeff and was glad he would be waiting outside.

"Yes."

"Okay, see you tomorrow then. I hope your night goes well."

"Thank you, thanks a lot, Lilian."

Lilian left and Lisa quickly pulled on her clothes. She glanced in the mirror and felt a lump in her throat.

"Well, I'm on my way," she said to her reflection.

○

It was still raining when Lisa left the clinic. She spotted Jeff's car and he came over and put his arms around her.

"Hi. How're you doing?"

Lisa felt a mixture of wanting to be brave and strong and also wanting to collapse against Jeff and cry her eyes out.

"I dunno. Okay, I guess," she said with her face muffled against the rough wool of his jacket. They got into the car and sat for a moment.

"So. . . .has it started?"

"The abortion?" She was always aware of how hard it was for Jeff to say the word, so she purposefully said it out loud. "Yes. They put this stuff in me and I go back and it should all be done by tomorrow afternoon."

"Do you hurt?"

"Just a little now. I'd love to go home and take a bath, but I can't."

160

"Why not?"

"Risk of infection. But I'll take a shower. Jeff,"—she turned and looked at him—"I don't know how to say this. I'm so glad you're here but. . ."

"Yeah? What?"

"I just feel something's changed between us."

He was quiet for a minute. "My mom said that might happen."

"What? What did she say?"

"She said that going through something like this usually changes things. She said even married people find that's what happens."

"She told you that?"

"Yeah. We talked last night. I haven't been able to say much to either of them, but last night my dad was gone and mom asked me how you were doing. She knew you were going in today. So I just told her. Then she said that she'd had an abortion once."

"She did? When?"

"I never knew about it. I guess she got pregnant between me and my older brother. Only they found out there was some big problem, something was wrong, so they decided to end it."

"The pregnancy?"

Jeff nodded. "She said that it was really hard on both of them, but mostly on her. She said my dad was understanding and all, but he just didn't get how awful it was for her. I guess they didn't get along too well for a couple of years, but then they had me, so that helped. She said that it was sad that sometimes crises pull people apart instead of bringing them closer together. . . .and she wants you to know that she'd be real happy to talk to you if you ever want to."

It felt good to hear this. Lisa had never been sure how much Jeff's mother liked her, but this definitely showed she cared.

"I'm so glad you told me," she said, leaning over and putting her head on his shoulder."

They sat quietly for several minutes watching the rain drops slither down the windshield. "I'm really tired," Lisa said. "I need to go home."

Her parents were both waiting in the living room when they walked in. Jeff had wanted to leave, but Lisa insisted he come in and at least say hello. There was an awkward moment before her dad acknowledged Jeff. Her mother protectively put her arm around Lisa.

"How did it go?" she asked.

"It was okay. I just want to go to bed."

Her father stood there folding his newspaper. He cleared his throat and said, "This is a very difficult time for all of us. I feel I have to say something."

"Dad, it's okay," Lisa said.

"No, let me go ahead." He looked at both Jeff and Lisa. "Your mother and I are very unhappy that you two ever got yourselves into this mess. I would have thought, Lisa, that you were smarter and you, too, Jeff."

Jeff shoved his hands into his pockets and stared at the floor.

"But we also know that people make mistakes; we all make mistakes, and it seems like you're both trying to be responsible right now. Lisa"—his eyes filled with tears—"you know we're sorry you're have to deal with this at your young age." He paused and drew in a deep breath. "The main thing is, I guess, that you go on from here and learn from this. Let this experience add to the quality of your life, let it make your life better somehow."

Lisa's mother put her hand on his shoulder and wiped her eyes with a tissue. "Jeff," she said, "we don't hold you solely responsible, you know. It takes two. . . .I hope you know that we've always liked you and that you'll still be welcome here."

"Thanks," Jeff said. "Thank you both. I know how hard this is. I wish I could change it all, but I can't." He turned to Lisa." I'll see you tomorrow. Take care." He touched her hand, and they walked to the door.

"Bye," she said.

He reached over, kissed her quickly, and left.

Lisa turned back to her parents. "Dad, I know that wasn't easy."

He put his arm about her shoulder and gave her a hug. "It wasn't, but it's easier than what you're going through, sweetie."

She smiled; he hadn't called her "sweetie" in a long time.

"Do you want any help?" her mother asked.

"I'm just going to take a shower and go to bed. "Come up and say goodnight, okay?"

"Sure," she answered.

O

Lisa toweled off and stood in front of the mirror. The only thing noticeably different about her was that her breasts were larger and her stomach stuck out just a bit. She felt that familiar aching feeling in her lower stomach and back like menstrual cramps and longed to lie down. Her mother came in as she was pulling up the covers.

"Hi, honey. Do you need anything?"

"No thanks. I just want to sleep, wake up, and have this be over."

"Do you hurt much?"

Lisa was touched by her mother's sweetness. "Mom," she said, "thanks for not being angry, for not making it harder."

"Oh Lisa, I just wish I could make it all go away. The hardest thing for any parent is to see their child suffer, go through something painful. I can't say I haven't been angry; I have. But right now I'd just like to help."

"You are, Mom," Lisa said reaching for her hand. "Is Dad okay?"

"He's very upset. He's gone out for a walk. You know, we just weren't ready for our daughter to enter this tough adult world, so we have some stretching to do. Don't worry about Dad or me; you have to take care of yourself now; we'll be all right." She paused for a few moments. "Would you like your back rubbed?"

"Yeah, that'd be great." She was growing sleepy and her mother's warm hands were very relaxing. She soon drifted off.

162

O

She slept late, till 11 o'clock. Her cramps were bothersome, but she'd experienced that before. She took a Motrin and looked again at the clock—only about three more hours to go.

The day dragged on. Lisa read, slept a little, watched TV, ate toast and drank tea. Her mother had taken the day off to be with her. Finally, at 1:45 they were about to leave for the clinic when the phone rang.

"Hi."

"Hi, Jeff." Her voice was quiet.

"How are you feeling?"

"Not great. I've got cramps. I'm nervous. We're leaving in five minutes." There was a long pause.

"I've been thinking about you all morning. You sure you don't want me there today?"

"Yeah, I'm sure. " She just couldn't imagine Jeff being in the room while she had the abortion, or even in the waiting room.

"Well, okay. I hope it goes all right. Look. . . I. . . I love you; don't forget it."

Even though she didn't feel much but numbness, it was nice to hear him say the words. "Thanks. Well, I gotta go. Tell Kathy 'hi' for me. Tell her to call me or come over tonight, okay?"

"Okay. I'll call too."

"Bye, Jeff."

"Bye."

Driving over in the car, Lisa's hands and feet were so cold that no matter what she did, she couldn't get them warm.

"Lisa, I'd like to be with you," her mother said.

" Well, I'll have this counselor with me, Mom."

"Would you like me too?"

Lisa was quiet for a moment. "I would in a way, Mom, but I also feel I should go through this by myself. I don't want to hurt your feelings." She was afraid she'd just collapse like a little girl if her mother was there next to her. "I hope you don't mind, Mom."

"I do, a little, but I understand too. I'll be in the waiting room. How long do you think you'll be?

"Altogether about two hours. I'll be in the waiting room with you for about half an hour while the Motrin takes effect. The abortion only takes about five to ten minutes, but they do these tests before and you have to rest after." Why was she talking about this like an old pro?

"Five minutes," her mother said. "What a short time for such a big event."

The receptionist remembered her name. "Hi, Lisa. Here, you need to take your medication and wait for a while until we're ready for you."

Lisa swallowed the pill and sat down next to her mother. They were both quiet until finally the receptionist called her name and said, "Come on in."

Lisa suddenly felt overcome with fear, and for a moment she couldn't speak. She turned to her mother. She wanted to run away. "Mom. . . .?"

Her mother took her hand. "I'll be right here, honey. It will be all right."

Lisa nodded her head. "See you in awhile then." She went through the office door.

Lilian, the counselor from the night before, greeted her. "Hi Lisa. How are you feeling? Any bad cramps?"

"Yeah, a few."

"It won't be long. We still need to do a few tests just to make sure everything is all right. First I'll take your blood pressure, and then a doctor will examine you for a final check."

Having completed the blood pressure check, Lilian left. Alone in the room, Lisa took off her sweat pants. She felt so cold that she decided to leave her socks on, and she climbed up on the table and waited. She could hear the phone ring in the office and people's voices. Soon the door opened, and a woman about 40 came in. She was part Asian with long black shiny hair held back in a clip.

"Lisa Howard?"

"Yes, that's me."

The doctor looked over her chart. "Hi, I'm Dr. Evans. Everything seems normal. I imagine you'd like to get this over with."

"I would," Lisa said in a low voice.

"Well, if you'll just lie back on the table and put your feet in the stirrups, I'll get you checked out. You're probably getting to know this routine pretty well by now. That's it, just let your knees fall apart. She shone a light between Lisa's thighs and the heat felt good. The doctor put on latex gloves and removed the gauze packing. Then she reached inside and took out the lamanaria.

"It seems to have done its job. Your cervix is dilated."

She placed a couple of fingers in Lisa's vagina and pressed on her belly with her other hand in order to feel the size of Lisa's uterus. She then bent her head down to examine the cervical opening.

"Everything looks good. It's a go." She touched Lisa's shoulder and said, "It's a very difficult time, I know, but soon you'll be able to get on with your life."

Her words brought tears to Lisa's eyes, and she quickly looked away. *Please God, help me get through this.*

The doctor returned along with Lilian, who immediately went to Lisa and reached for her hand.

"I promised your mother you'd be in good hands. We talked for a while in the waiting room. She's a very nice woman," Lilian said. "Now just relax. Let your mouth go slack and your arms and legs as well. Breathe nice slow breaths." She glanced down at Lisa's feet. "Don't curl your toes. Let them relax too. Just squeeze my hand if you need to, but try to keep the rest of your body nice and loose."

The doctor gave her three quick injections in her cervix and Lisa was aware of a growing numbness. When she couldn't feel anything the doctor told her what she was doing and held up a small plastic tube. "This is the suction, the vacuum. I put this inside and move it around the wall of your uterus. It will remove the fetus and the tissue surrounding it." She turned on the machine. There was a low, almost buzzing noise, and Lisa could feel a tugging inside of her. There were several sharp pains, and she glanced at Lilian.

"Come on, grab my hand tight. Easy breathing through your mouth. That's it. Blow out, one, two, three."

The small vacuum sucked, and the tissue disappeared through a connecting tube.

There it goes.

"It's okay to cry," Lilian said. "Just let go of the tears."

The doctor withdrew the tube; it had been close to half a minute. "It's all done, Lisa. I just have to make sure we got it all." She inserted a small utensil and gently scraped the uterus' wall. Lisa held her breath, and then remembered to release it.

"Are you finished?"

"That's it. It's over. Everything looks normal," the doctor said, looking into Lisa's eyes.

"Really? Oh God. I can't believe it!" She felt an enormous relief, like a weight had slipped off her and fallen to the office floor. "She's really done?" She looked at Lilian.

"Yep. Now you just lie here a few minutes and rest. Then when you get up you'll need to wear this sanitary napkin to catch any blood you may have. Some women have a lot and some don't. Then get dressed and go relax in our recovery room. Have something to drink and eat. Here's some Motrin to keep with you in case you feel pain, and here's a sheet of instructions which I'll go over with you. Be sure to follow them and take good care of yourself. You did real good, Lisa."

Lisa looked at the doctor and at Lilian. "Thank you," she said. "Thank you for helping me."

She took the paper. It told her to alert the doctor if she developed a temperature or had excessive bleeding. It also said not to put anything in her vagina for two weeks, and that included taking a bath and sexual intercourse. Most important, it said to come back in two weeks for a follow-up appointment and to be sure to get birth control.

Though her mind was a little hazy, Lisa couldn't even think about birth control—and the idea of sex seemed like it was from outer space!

Her mother's anxious face was the first thing she saw as she entered the room. They hugged each other for a long time. "I'm fine, Mom," she said.

They sat down, and her mother stared intently at her.

"Oh Lisa, I was so worried. Everything's okay? Do you hurt much?"

"I hurt some, but really I'm fine. I'm so glad it's over."

They drank their tea and sat quietly. Several times Lisa heard her mother sigh. Soon another woman entered the room, and then another. They greeted each other with a big smile and the laughter of relief.

The nurse called her name and, on closing the door, said, "We just need to check your vital signs and any excess bleeding. This is the last time."

Lisa returned after five minutes and said, "I'm ready to go. . . .Mom, I. . . thanks for coming with me. You'll see. Things will get better now."

"I know, honey, I know. The worst is over," she said, putting her arm around Lisa.

○

Lisa slept for several hours and awoke when she heard her name being called. Sleepily, she opened her eyes and saw purple and pink colors and Jeff holding a big bouquet.

"Hi, Lisa, how're you doing?" he said bending down to kiss her and place the flowers in her hands.

"Oh Jeff. Thanks. They're beautiful." Feeling suddenly self-conscious, Lisa sat up and smelled the flowers.

They were both quiet for a minute and then Jeff said, "Your mom said everything went okay, that it's all done, and you're fine."

Lisa nodded and felt the tears well up in her eyes. "It's weird, I mean I feel really relieved, but I also feel like I lost something. It would have been a baby, Jeff, our baby."

"Jesus," Jeff muttered. "Don't do that to yourself, Lisa. You did the right thing."

Lisa sighed and looked at Jeff. "Yeah, but I can't help wondering. . . " Her eyes shifted to the flowers. "So, tomorrow's Saturday night? You have a game, don't you?"

"Yeah. It's a big one, against Lake City. I wish you could come."

"I'm not up to it. . . .not yet. I'm kind of scared to go back to school. Does anyone know besides you and Kathy?"

Jeff shook his head.

"I've gotten so far behind and this year was so important. Sometimes I think I'll never get over it."

They both sat in silence for a moment. Then there was a knock on the door, and Stephanie poked her head in.

"Hi, Lisa. Can I come in?"

"Look, I gotta go," Jeff said as he stood up. He leaned over and kissed Lisa. "Take care. I'll call you tonight, okay?"

"Okay. Thanks for the flowers. I hope you play good tomorrow. Good luck."

Stephanie sat on Lisa's bed, and they both watched Jeff go out and close the door. "I didn't mean to make him leave. I just wanted to see you," she said.

"It's all right. I think he was relieved to get out of here. So. . . .did Mom tell you everything? What's Dad doing?"

"He's watching the news. I saw him crying when he and mom were talking. God, Lisa, I just can't believe you had an abortion."

"I know. It sounds awful, doesn't it?"

"Was it?

"Not really. I mean, the actual abortion only took a couple of minutes, but still, it was hard. Look, you've just got to make sure that you never go through it, okay? You've just gotta be smarter than I was. I'll help you. Come talk to me when you think you might want to have sex. And don't think it can't happen to you."

"Lisa, I'm only in seventh grade!"

"Stephanie, you'll be there before you know it. Come on, promise me you'll come talk to me. Promise."

"Okay, I promise," Stephanie said. "What are you gonna do now?"

Lisa looked around her room at her stuffed animals, the pictures from Eugene, and back at Stephanie. "I guess I'm just going to go on with my life, but I can't pretend that it didn't happen."

○

Back in school, Lisa felt awkward and withdrawn. She tried to keep her mind on studying and managed to bring her grades up to almost a 3.0, not what she'd hoped for, but better than a month ago. She and Jeff went out at least every week, but he came over less frequently. She still had all the birth control pills in her bureau drawer, the ones she'd bought last fall, but she just couldn't bring herself to use them yet. She and Jeff had made out plenty of times, but they stopped far short of having sex.

It was Jeff who had said, "Lisa, I guess I'm just not ready. It's just too much."

Lisa had hugged him tightly when he said it. "I know," she whispered, " and I'm glad that you're the one who's saying it."

○

One day while cleaning her room with the radio on, Lisa heard an old song from the 60's—"The Thrill Is Gone." She stood motionless while the music swept over her. It was true—whatever she and Jeff had felt between them was no longer; their relationship had changed into something else, and Lisa knew she had to talk about it.

As part of her follow up to the abortion Lisa went to see a counselor. Two months had passed since she'd seen Lilian, who had let her short, gray hair grow longer.

"Lisa, it's good to see you," she said giving her a hug. "Come on into my office. I've moved up in the world; I have my own place now. I looked at your chart, and it seems everything is okay physically. Are you having any problems?"

Lisa settled into the comfortable sofa. "No, really, I'm fine."

"Are your periods back to normal?"

"Yeah. I feel fine. It's just. . . " Lisa's voice faltered. "I don't know how to explain it. . . .boy, it's strange being back here again."

Lilian waited patiently. "A lot of women have a tough time adjusting to life after an abortion. Some seem to go right back to their old selves, but that's not true for everyone."

"But I feel different. . . and I don't seem to want to get involved in anything. I wish I could, but when I think of like. . . .oh, going out for drama or something, I just can't bring myself to do it."

"Lisa, it takes time. You've been through a major event in your life. Don't be hard on yourself."

"I just wonder if I'll ever feel excited about anything again," Lisa said. "I feel so separate. And my boyfriend and I aren't close anymore."

"When we've been through a transforming experience in our lives, an experience that changes us, it sometimes takes a while to return and re-integrate ourselves—you know, put ourselves back together. And sometimes it changes our relationships too. But I'm sure you'll feel that wonderful rush of anticipation and the fun of being alive again. You have many great years ahead of you. Just don't push yourself."

Lisa sat quietly. It felt good to be reassured. "I guess this is one of those growing experiences," she said with a small laugh.

"Growing experiences are usually difficult," Lilian said. "That's why we call them 'growing pains.' "

○

The prom was only a week away, and Lisa and Jeff were going together, but instead of going to the beach after the dance with a big group of kids, they had decided to go over to Kathy's to watch movies and fix breakfast.

It had been a great evening—dinner at a fancy restaurant and a good d.j. They danced till the girls kicked off their shoes and the boys shirts were plastered to their backs with sweat. Now, as Jeff and Lisa sat in Kathy's backyard dressed in their jackets and sweat pants, they watched the eastern sky lighten and they talked.

"It's been some year, hasn't it?" Jeff said.

Lisa leaned against him. "I guess it's been the most important year of my life. I sure don't feel like the same person I was last September."

"Me neither. I wonder what would have happened if you hadn't moved here."

Trying to be funny, Lisa said, "Oh, you probably would have gotten some other girl pregnant." As soon as the words were out of her mouth, she regretted them. "Oh Jeff, I'm sorry. That was mean of me."

Jeff was quiet for a long time. "Do you really feel like that? 'Cause I don't have good feelings about what happened, you know. Do you really think I don't care? Do you?"

"No, I know you're unhappy about it. I'm sorry. It was a stupid thing to say." Now it was Lisa's turn to be quiet. "Thanks for a really nice evening," she finally said.

"Yeah, it was good."

"You know, I feel like something's ending. You know what I mean? It's more than the school year ending. . . "

"Well," Jeff said, "we're gonna be apart all summer, and next year will be the last year of high school."

"It's that, but I think it's us too. You know things aren't the same anymore. . . not between us."

Jeff looked out at the pale pink sky and listened to her words.

"You've been so sweet to stay with me, Jeff. A lot of guys would have split during the abortion or right afterwards. But you stayed. . . I'll always love you for that." Lisa took his hand and held it, the tears clouding her eyes. "But I think. . . I think it's time to let each other go. . . go off and have a summer and maybe a new life."

Jeff let out an enormous sigh. "It'll be good to get away, I think." He looked over at Lisa. "How'd you get so wise?"

"I don't know about wise, but I sure do feel older. Promise me though that we'll always be friends. Okay? Always—even when I see you at a class reunion 25 years from now."

Jeff put his arm around Lisa. "Always."

O

Spring ended, and summer would begin the next day as soon as finals were completed. Lisa had a job as a camp counselor up in Oregon and couldn't wait to begin. She just had one more final to finish—her English final.

Mr. T.'s voice broke into her thoughts. He was passing out a paper. "Keep this face down until I give the word. Before you begin this final, I want to say that this has been an extraordinarily good year. I think you all have grown, not only in your ability to express yourselves, but in your development as human beings. I like what I see and I feel better about the future of our world knowing that there are going to be adults like you out there. I want to wish you all good luck next year, and I hope the future will be kind. In the words of the famous *Desiderata:* "For all its sham, drudgery and broken dreams, it is still a beautiful world. Be careful. Strive to be happy.""

There was a moment of silence, and Lisa and Kathy glanced over at each other. Someone coughed, and Jeff looked at her and winked.

"Okay, you have the full two hours to write your final essay. You will be graded on the content of your ideas, the organization and the presentation of those ideas, and, of course, the correctness of your grammar and punctuation. You may use a dictionary. Okay, begin."

There was a shuffling of paper as everyone turned the sheet of paper over and started reading. A few students sighed, one slammed down his pencil in disgust, and almost everyone shifted in their seats. Lisa read the final:

"Throughout the year, beginning with *Our Town*, we have discussed individual and cultural values as a yardstick for measuring the quality of life. It seems clear that without values, life loses its brilliancy and importance. As far as we know, our values separate us from other forms of living creatures.

"In a thoughtful and well organized essay discuss the values that you believe to be important in life and provide specific examples of these values as revealed in at least four of the literary works and presentations we have experienced this year; to refresh your memory, a list of these is posted on the board."

Lisa looked up and read the list:

The Scarlet Letter
Our Town
Huckleberry Finn
Walden
Poetry of Robert Frost, Maya Angelou, Langston Hughes, Gary Soto, Emily
 Dickinson, e.e. cummings
The Grapes of Wrath
The Declaration of Independence
Beloved
The Education of Little Tree
The Color Purple
Presentations from AIDS and Sexual Harassment Awareness Days

Lisa inhaled deeply. It would certainly take her the full two hours to put all her ideas together. She jotted down several things she thought were important. Then she thought of all the literary works posted on the board and was sure she could easily include four of them.

Her mind drifted back over the long past year and she thought of the abortion she'd had nearly five months ago now. What kind of a value had she taken from that so very difficult experience? Had she chosen herself over a fetus? The answer was "yes." What did that say about her values? Was she selfish? Was that wrong?

How many times she wrestled with that issue! How much energy it took in the long process before and after the abortion! It had never been a clear-cut, black-and-white problem as so many tried to portray it.

She had known she couldn't have given the baby a proper life and so she chose not to have it. Couldn't she have had the baby and given it up for adoption? The truth was, she couldn't; she simply couldn't bear the thought of being pregnant for nine months and then giving the baby to someone else to raise. In some ways, she wished she'd been able to. And that was the key—she'd had to be honest with herself; she had to be honest about what she felt and who she was.

Perhaps that was a value—self honesty, being true to who you were and what you felt no matter what others said or thought. And woven throughout all this turmoil was the freedom to make a decision and then to face the consequences of that decision.

She glanced up again at the list on the board. Yes, she could make a case for adding the values of "Self-honesty" and the "Freedom to Choose" to her paper.

She could also include "Learning from Your Mistakes" as an important value. Because more than any other feeling that came through from the whole abortion experience was the determination to never—ever—have to make that hard decision again.

And that meant that it was important to have compassion for others who have to make difficult decisions in their lives. And to have compassion for yourself as well. Life was a process. Life was experiencing, learning, going on, and not giving up.

Lisa took a deep breath and began to write her final essay: "Four values emerge through the course of American literature and my own life: Self-honesty, Compassion for Our Fellow Humans, the Freedom to Make Our Own Decisions, and Learning from Our Mistakes. . . "

This was going to be the essay of her life!

○

Jeff Branley graduated from college in the Midwest and went on to medical school. He recently married a woman he met while studying to be a doctor, and they hope one day to have several children.

Lisa Howard appeared in the school play her senior year. Several years later she graduated from college and now lives in Philadelphia with her husband and two children. She works part time as a social worker with adolescent girls.

Jeff and Lisa send each other yearly Christmas cards.

About the Author

Linda Ward has been a public high school teacher and a psychotherapist for over twenty years. Among her many challenges has been being a mom to five wonderful human beings. She currently lives in Santa Rosa, CA with her twin teenaged daughters.